Praise for The Darker Side of Pleasure

'Bradley's excellent prose and clear shifts in point of view
create well-rounded stories that are sure to satisfy . . .
This is a very enticing read'
Romantic Times

'Ms Bradley's writing is intelligent, insightful, and lays
you into a hotbed of complexities placing her on my
SUPREME LIST of favoured authors'
NightOwl Romance Reviews

'I found myself unable to put this book down . . .
Eden Bradley is one talented lady and I can't wait
to read future releases . . . Her ability to make me
react and feel and become enthralled in her
work is truly amazing'
Romance Junkies

Also by Eden Bradley:

The Dark Garden
Forbidden Fruit

The Darker Side of Pleasure

EDEN BRADLEY

BLACK
LACE

1 3 5 7 9 10 8 6 4 2

First published in the United States of America in 2007 by Bantam Dell
A Division of Random House, Inc.
Published in the UK in 2013 by Black Lace, an imprint of Ebury Publishing
A Random House Group Company

The Random House Group Limited Reg. No. 954009

Addresses for companies within the Random House Group can be found at:
www.randomhouse.co.uk

A CIP catalogue record for this book is available from the British Library

The Random House Group Limited supports The Forest Stewardship
Council (FSC®), the leading international forest certification organisation.
Our books carrying the FSC label are printed on FSC® certified paper.
FSC is the only forest certification scheme endorsed by the leading
environmental organisations, including Greenpeace.
Our paper procurement policy can be found at:
www.randomhouse.co.uk/environment

Printed in Great Britain by Clays Ltd, St Ives plc

ISBN 9780352347169

To buy books by your favourite authors and register for offers visit
www.blacklace.co.uk

In memory of my big brother David, whose song "Love & Discipline" inspired one of the stories in this book, and who I know would have been proud of me.

ACKNOWLEDGMENTS

To author Laura Bacchi, my first writing mentor, from whom I learned so much. To my brainstorming buddies Jax Cassidy, Gemma Halliday, Lacy Danes, Crystal Jordan, Emma Petersen, and Eva Gale. And to my dear friend Desiree Nauman, who is always full of wonderful and helpful ideas and really ought to be a writer.

To B, always, for his endless support and pride in my work. I wouldn't be here without you!

THE DARKER SIDE OF PLEASURE

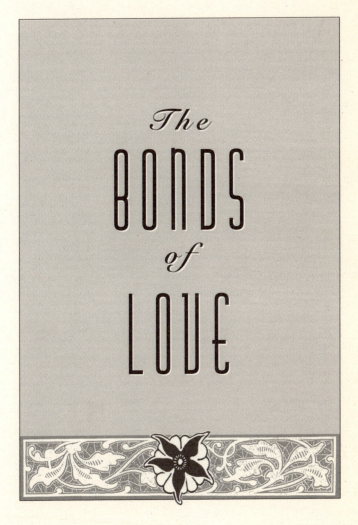

The
BONDS
of
LOVE

CHAPTER ONE

BONDAGE. THE WORD REVERBERATED THROUGH Jillian's head, through her body, making her muscles tense and quiver.

Her stomach clenched as she pulled her sporty BMW into the driveway after a long day at work. She peered up at the sleek, modern expanse of redwood and glass her husband had designed for them six years ago, right after they'd married and moved to Seattle.

She took a deep breath and forced her hands to stop gripping the steering wheel. Tonight was the night. The night she and Cameron were going to start trying to put their marriage back together.

She yanked a little too hard on the parking brake, then grabbed her purse and the pretty pink shopping bag that held the new lingerie she'd bought for the occasion. Cameron was right. It had been ages since she'd dressed up for him. Hell, she'd been sleeping in the guest room for months. Not that that was his fault. It was her. She knew that. She just couldn't stand to be so close to him, with so much distance between them. It hurt too much.

Her nerves jangled as much as her keys did when she opened the front door. "Cam? You home?"

No answer. She exhaled on a sigh of relief. She needed some time to make herself ready. Not just physically, but emotionally, too—even though they'd talked about this almost a week ago. Maybe she'd had too much time to think about it. She did have a tendency to overanalyze things. She let her purse fall to the hardwood floor, gripped the lingerie bag, and headed down the hall.

Stripping off her clothes in the half-dark bedroom felt like a ritual, somehow. The house was quiet. The soft glow of twilight filtered through the Japanese paper shades that covered the ceiling-high bedroom windows. There was the faint scent of him in the air, that sense of intimacy in the room where they'd slept up until she'd moved into the guest room a few months ago. But they hadn't made love for too long before that. And on those rare occasions when they had, she felt as though she weren't entirely present in her own body, as if she were watching it from the outside. But tonight was supposed to help change that. The idea made her stomach clench up again.

She stepped into the slate-tiled bathroom and blasted the hot water, wanting the sheer force and heat of it to wash her nerves away. This was her own husband, after all. She closed her eyes as she moved beneath the spray and let the water sluice over her, trying to steer her mind down a more positive path.

Cameron. He'd been so young when they'd first met,

only twenty-one. She was an old lady of twenty-five at the time. But he was so mature for his age, so somber and responsible. And there was always something of the darkness about him that made him seem older than he was. Perhaps it was the tattoo that circled his right biceps, a sinuous circle in a dark tribal design. Maori, he'd told her. She loved it. She'd loved his tall, lean, yet muscular body. God, he had the greatest abs she'd ever seen on a human being. And she loved the way his straight, coal black hair fell into his eyes, even the dark-framed glasses he wore for reading.

That's how Jillian had first seen him, in her English Lit class in college. He was bent over a book, and he glanced up as she passed a printed handout to him. And those smoky gray eyes peered up at her—eyes fringed in thick, sooty lashes any woman would envy. Those startling eyes and that serious expression on his angular features, yet his mouth was lush and sensual, a stark contrast.

He still wore those glasses. And even after all they'd been through, a small shiver of excitement would course through her whenever he put them on. If only he had come to bed early enough to read, while she was still awake, while she'd still been sleeping in their bed.

But no, she shouldn't think about that. Tonight was for new beginnings, not old pain.

She shut off the water, stepped out onto the cool tiles, and began to rub scented lotion into her skin. It was Cameron's favorite vanilla scent, the one he used to say made him want to run his tongue all over her body. Her sex gave a quick, involuntary squeeze, surprising her.

Drawing her pale green silk summer robe around her

shoulders, she went to pull her purchases out of the bag. The bra was black and lacy, with demi-cups that barely covered her breasts. The matching thong was a whisper of lace. It made her feel sexy, she had to admit, admiring her reflection in the big full-length mirror in her walk-in closet. Despite her breasts and thighs, which weren't as firm at the age of thirty-three as they'd been when she and Cam had met eight years ago.

No, don't think about that now.

She pulled her long honey blond hair up with her hands, considering, then decided to leave it down. Cam liked it better that way.

When she drew the first black lace stocking over one leg, she began to get a real sense of ritual, of formal preparation. For some reason she didn't understand it sent a small thrill through her, raising gooseflesh on the back of her neck. And when she slid her feet into the impossibly high black pumps Cam had insisted she buy, the feeling was complete. She understood suddenly that she was doing this for him, but that it also fulfilled some need in her. To please in order to feel whole.

This was a new concept for her. She'd been inside her own head for so long, immersed in her grief, that she'd forgotten to look outside. To look at her husband.

When Cam had first suggested they try to find their way back to each other through sex, she'd balked. In fact, that was putting it lightly. She'd flat out refused, thought he was being selfish and ridiculous. But then he'd reminded her that sex was intimacy, and that bondage was the purest form of mutual trust. It took her a while to absorb that, but she eventually came to realize he had a valid point. And they needed to try something, anything, before the gap between them grew any wider. Tonight was to be a true test.

She drew the stockings up her legs, her hand brushing the honey-colored curls at the apex of her thighs. Blood rushed to the area so fast, she had to cup her mound with her hand and press there. Strange! Why was she so hypersensitive, when she'd been completely shut down for almost a year?

The loud rumbling of her husband's prized Harley pulling into the driveway brought her head and her hand up fast. Cam!

She took one last, desperate look in the mirror, added a little lip gloss with a shaking hand. She was ready for him.

She thought she was. She shivered in fear and anticipation as his steps drew nearer. The door opened with a graceful swing, and there he was. Her husband. He looked so damn good standing there, she had to smile.

He smiled back. "Almost like the old Jillian. I love it when you smile like that. Like you mean it."

"I do." She dropped her head, suddenly shy.

He crossed the room, slid his hands around her waist, ran them up her sides, traced the curve of her breasts. "God, you're beautiful."

His words warmed her, but it was still hard for her to look at him. He tipped her chin up with his fingers. She thought he'd want to talk more, but he just leaned in and kissed her. That lush, kissable mouth of his covered hers, and when he parted his lips she could taste mint, and underneath it the faint sweetness of Scotch. So he'd been nervous, too. She suddenly wanted to cry. This was why she'd been avoiding him, why she hadn't been able to sleep in the bed next to his big, warm body.

He pulled away and said simply, "Are you ready?"

Her stomach grabbed again, but she nodded. "Yes. But what are you . . . I mean, how is this all going to happen?"

"We talked about it, remember? If this is going to work, you have to trust me enough to turn yourself over to me. That's what tonight is all about. We have to learn to trust each other again. Do you remember your safe words?"

"Yes. Yellow for slow down, red for stop."

"Good."

He stepped back and his eyes roamed over her. She knew she looked better than usual in this outfit, so she didn't mind. And she could see his eyes glittering as he looked at her, his pupils widening with lust. He placed his hands on his hips, licked his lips. He gestured toward the bed with his chin.

"Sit down."

She just looked at him for a moment. She wasn't used to this simple, commanding tone from him. He didn't sound mean, but it was clear she shouldn't try to argue with him. A chill of pleasure ran up her spine.

"Now."

Another command; this time his tone was low and demanding. Her sex exploded with heat. She sat.

Cam paced the room slowly, looking at her from all angles, before he said, "Get rid of the bra."

She unhooked it immediately, her full breasts springing from the lacy confines. They felt plump and tender and wanted to be touched, something she hadn't felt in a long time. The fact that she could have this sort of reaction to nothing more than a certain tone of voice was almost shocking. She was trying hard not to analyze it.

Cam walked up to her and touched her breasts with his fingertips, just lazily brushed them over the curved underside, traced them around the edge of the areolas. Her nipples sprang up, hard and ready. But he didn't touch them.

When she looked up at his face he was smiling, just one corner of his mouth quirked up. Rakish, sexy.

He stepped back again and unbuttoned his shirt. She had always loved him without a shirt. He had one of those long, lean, cut torsos, with just the right amount of silky black hair in a line down the center of his well-defined abs. He was built like a pro basketball player: well over six feet tall, with broad shoulders and those lanky, beautifully defined muscles. His black work slacks hung low on his narrow hips and she could see that he was hard already, the outline of his large erection shadowed against the fine wool.

She squirmed on the edge of the bed, her lace thong growing damp.

"I'm going to ask you to do things for me tonight you've never done before. Are you ready to do that, Jillian?"

She swallowed, hard. Was she? Her natural mental response was to fight against the whole idea. She was normally someone who was strong, in control. But her body was rebelling already. Still, how could it be this simple? She knew that Cam's angle had been that bondage was all about trust, that there had to be complete trust in order to make it work. He saw it as a way to get back to each other. It made a sort of weird sense, but she still had her doubts.

Cam repeated, "Are you ready?"

His voice seemed so different tonight; his whole persona was different. Confident. Commanding. But it was still Cam. She could do this. She would do it for him. For them. And, judging from the unexpected way her body was responding already, for herself.

"Yes. I'm ready."

He turned then and moved to the tall dresser, pulled a CD from the top drawer and popped it into the CD player. She recognized the trancelike tones of Enigma immediately. She watched him as he lit a pair of tall pillar candles. The scent of amber wafted into the air, and the warm candlelight was soft and sultry, aided by the glow of sunset outside the windows.

He bent and opened a bottom drawer and took out a long coiled length of black rope. She hadn't known it was in there, didn't know where he'd found it. She didn't really care right now. All she could think of was that he was going to use it on her. Nerves and pleasure washed through her in an exciting, confusing tide.

Cam came to stand before her while the music played, and he rested his hands on her shoulders. After a moment, he swept them up her neck in gentle strokes, then back down, over her arms to her wrists. Gently, he gathered them into one of his big hands and pulled her arms up over her head. She shivered again, feeling unsure, vulnerable.

"Cam?"

"It's okay."

His soft voice was reassuring, but he didn't release her wrists. With his free hand he began to stroke her breasts again, and despite her hammering pulse her body responded to his touch. Her breasts filled, her nipples aching as he teased her skin with the lightest touch. When he finally brushed one hard nipple with his fingertip her whole body arched toward him.

"Patience, Jillian." He sounded amused.

She moaned softly. He rewarded her by tweaking one nipple, rather hard, but she liked it. Somehow it was just what she needed. Her sex began to pound and she squeezed her legs together.

"Lie back on the bed," Cam said.

"Why? What are you going to—"

"Shh. No questions. You're mine tonight. Turn yourself over to me, Jillian."

Yes. She wanted this. And not just because she was following the plan. Now that they'd started she knew she was going to like it, even if it scared her a little. Or maybe the fear was part of what drew her?

She lay down on the bed.

When Cam came to stand over her with the ropes in his hands, her body gave a convulsive shudder. Of need. Of lust. She had never felt anything like it. Gazing up at his tall silhouette in the dim light, she suddenly knew she'd never wanted anything so much in her life. To give herself over. To let herself go. This was exactly what she needed. Yet at the same time, she struggled with the notion. How could this be what she needed? Wasn't it proof of her own weakness?

Cam bent over her and kissed her gently on the lips, then took her lower lip between his strong, white teeth and bit down. It hurt a little.

"You're mine, Jillian. Say it."

The chill that ran through her was part lust, part awe. And she knew that after tonight, she would never be the same again.

"Yes, Cam. I'm yours."

He smiled at her. "Very good. I want you to lie perfectly still now. I'm going to play with you a bit before I tie you up."

Tie you up. Oh, my. He really was going to tie her up. A thrill ran through her, bringing goose bumps to her skin once more, but this time they ran the entire length of her body.

But she didn't have long to think about it. Cam's hands were on her, stroking her stomach, running up her thighs. They seemed to be everywhere at once. She watched him, a look of intense concentration on his face. Finally his hands came back to her breasts, covering both of them, massaging, kneading. Her nipples were hard, hot nubs against his palms.

He looked up at her face, his gray eyes watching her as he took both nipples between his fingers and thumbs and began to roll them. Fire shot from her nipples straight to her already aching sex. She tried hard not to squirm. But when he pinched, hard, she shot up off the bed.

"No, Jillian." He pressed her back down onto the mattress. "Lie still."

She tried. She drew in a deep, shuddering breath, and then he began again, pulling at her nipples, twisting, pinching. They were so hard and engorged she thought they would burst. And her sex was full and throbbing. She wanted his hands there. But she knew she had to wait. To trust him.

Cam kept working her nipples, and she wondered for the first time in her life if it was possible to come just from that. She didn't know how long it went on, an impossibly long period of time in which she was finally able to shut her brain down, to stop thinking, analyzing. Her nipples were sore, but she didn't care. She bit down on her lip to keep from crying out, to keep from moving, but her thighs spread open of their own accord. God, she needed him to touch her there. To use his hands, his mouth. She didn't care. But she didn't want him to stop torturing her breasts.

Finally, he bent his head and flicked his hot, wet tongue at one rigid tip. She groaned. He moved his head and flicked at the other one. Then, using both hands, he pushed the full mounds of her breasts together and moved his head back and forth, his tongue a damp spike of heat as it flickered over her stiffened nipples. His hands felt so good on her, so firm on her flesh, and his tongue was driving her crazy. She almost begged him to take her into his mouth. And then, as if reading her mind, he did.

He drew one nipple in and sucked. He was almost too gentle. She could hardly stand it. She gathered and bunched the bedspread in her hands, trying to hold still, to keep from crying out, from begging him to suck harder. Her sex was absolutely drenched by now. Her whole body quivered.

And suddenly, he pulled back.

"Cam?" Her own voice sounded loud and breathless in her ears.

He straightened up, half turned away from her, and ran a hand through his dark hair.

"Cam, what is it?"

She heard his long, slow exhalation. Waited for him to turn back around, to talk to her. Her thighs clenched around the damp, swollen folds of flesh between them.

"Maybe we need to talk about this some more."

"What?" A startled laugh escaped her lips. "Now? When I'm just beginning to . . ." She couldn't finish the sentence, couldn't say out loud that her body was responding in a way it hadn't for months. Couldn't tell him how desperately she craved his touch. Why couldn't she say it?

When his eyes met hers she saw the confusion there, saw that his breath was coming in short, sharp pants.

"This is . . . already more intense than I expected."

"Yes." It was all she could manage to get out.

He came and sat on the bed next to her. His warm hand fell on her shoulder. "I need to know this is what you want. Not just with your body, but in your head. What is this making you think? Making you feel?"

How could she explain? "Like . . . like maybe I can let go, finally. But it's a little scary at the same time. And physically, it's . . . almost a shock. Do you know what I mean?"

He nodded, his gaze on hers. "It's like you're coming alive under my hands." He reached out and stroked a finger across her hot cheek. "But when you shiver, I don't know if it's because you like it, or because I'm making you afraid."

"Maybe a little of both."

His eyes swept her face. They were filled with concern and burning lust at the same time. "Jillian. Honey. I don't ever want to scare you."

She shook her head, her hair sweeping across her cheek. "It's not you that's scaring me. It's me."

"I'm right here with you. Okay?"

"Yes."

"This is for us. And if it doesn't work, we'll try something else. But I want to do this. And the more I touch you, the more I want this."

"Yes. Me, too. Maybe that's what scares me the most."

Cam leaned in and brushed his lips over hers. Again came that hint of mint and liquor. His hand curled around the back of her head, firm, possessive, as he parted her lips with his hot, wet tongue. Her mouth opened beneath his, letting him in. Her tongue met his, curled and tasted. Her shoulders relaxed as the heat of his mouth flowed through her and came to rest somewhere deep in her belly.

Then he was pushing her down onto the bed, holding her there. She had a quick moment of panic when she realized how firmly he held her, but she was too turned on to let the panic take hold.

Don't think, Jillian.

Again he grasped her wrists and drew her arms over her head, making her feel vulnerable, exposed. Her eyes fluttered open so she could see his face above her. And again she saw that expression of concentrated lust in his gray eyes. He was so focused, so intense. And still his mouth was that lush slash of deep pink that made her want to kiss him.

"Stay right there." His voice was low, a little rough around the edges.

It was hard to hold still all by herself, without him holding her there, while he moved about the room. She tried to concentrate on the music still playing in the background while he knelt beside the bed and wrapped some rope around the bed frame. She could sense what he was doing more than she could see it, but the idea sent a ripple of hot anticipation through her.

Cam moved to the other side of the bed, securing the ropes. If she turned her head a bit, she could see the muscles of his back and shoulders move beneath his golden skin as he worked. He was so beautiful.

He stood, towering over her. When he bent to part her legs with his big hands she tensed. But then he stroked the tender skin on the insides of her thighs, warming her flesh, making her sex fill with a quick rush of lustful heat again, and she opened for him.

He took her right hand in his, stroked her palm open with his fingertips, and leaned in to lay a kiss there, sending a shiver of heat up her arm. Her nipples immediately went hard once more.

Cam moved his mouth over her hand, kissing her fingers, her wrist. It took her a moment to realize that he followed the trail of kisses with a length of soft, darkly colored rope, winding a loop of it around her wrist. Her eyes flew to his face, and a small, reassuring smile played at the corners of his mouth.

"Breathe, Jillian."

Yes. She took in a lungful of the amber-scented air, let it calm her racing pulse. When he pulled the rope so that it had a firm hold, he dropped one last kiss on her hand, then moved to the end of the bed and took hold of her right foot. He massaged it for a moment, stroking with his fingers, then laid a soft kiss on her instep.

She couldn't remember him ever paying much attention to her feet. She couldn't remember ever thinking about it. But somehow that one brief kiss set her body on fire, a trail of flame burning its way up her calf, over her thigh, and straight to her sex, which was hot and needy already. She was soaking wet in an instant.

Cam glanced up, as though he sensed her reaction. He smiled, then kissed her foot once more. Again her sex throbbed with a sudden lance of need. She moaned softly.

"Amazing what we can learn after all this time together." His voice was barely above a whisper.

She couldn't respond. He was already wrapping the rope around her ankle, pulling it tight. Then he moved to her other foot, pulling it to the side, so that her sex was wide open and exposed, except for the scrap of damp lace that still covered it.

He ran his hand up the inside of her leg, brushing the top of her thigh. Her sex clenched in anticipation. But he moved away, back to her foot, stroking the skin of her arch, the undersides of her toes. When he bent his head and began a slow stroking with his lips, she thought she'd go mad with need. Her hips arched up off the bed. He held her ankle more firmly in his hands.

"Hold still, Jillian."

She loved the commanding tone of his voice every bit as much as she loved his mouth on her skin. But in a moment the rope was there again, wrapping firmly around her ankle. She pulled against it once, and found she couldn't move more than a millimeter.

Cam bent over her left side, taking her free hand in his. Once more the blazing trail of kisses, hot on her flesh.

Her whole body was on fire, her sex aching and wet. But when Cam pulled the rope around her wrist, she froze.

"Cam, wait!"

He paused, looked into her face. His was calm, but his eyes sparkled darkly. "Breathe, honey."

She tried, but the air seemed to catch in her throat. Somehow this last rope meant that she would be truly bound, unable to move. Completely under his command. As exciting as it was, it was also frightening on some deep level. She wanted to let go, wanted to trust him, but how could she when she didn't even trust herself?

"Jillian." His tone was low but firm. "I want you to listen very carefully. I am going to bind your wrist and you will not be able to move. You need to give yourself over to me. You need to let it all go. You will be in my hands. *My* hands. I love you, Jillian; you know that. This is your last chance to turn back before we really begin. Tell me yes or no."

She couldn't seem to think. Her body strained against the ropes already binding her feet and her other hand. Was this what she truly wanted? Could she do this?

Her mind was a whirl of chaos edged in panic. She took a deep breath, trying to calm down.

Cam put a hand on her chest, warming her skin. She closed her eyes, let the firm reassurance of his palm absorb the pounding of her heart. Her breasts tingled, her nipples came to peak, and she focused on the scorching heat funneling through her system. Despite her confusion, her body screamed one word at her. And finally she was able to let that word escape her lips.

"Yes!"

CHAPTER TWO

CAM SMILED. HE COULD READ THE YIELDING IN Jillian's beautiful face as she spoke the word he needed to hear. The way she was responding to him physically was amazing. Even in their earliest days together she hadn't been like this. But he could see the fear and confusion in her wide brown eyes.

Still, he knew this was the right thing to do, the right way to do it, to reestablish intimacy between them. The idea of bondage had been in the back of his mind for a long time. It was something that had always fascinated him. Bondage and maybe a little sensation play. BDSM. He'd had fantasies since he was a teenager about spanking a woman. The feel of a firm, feminine bottom beneath his hand, the sound as his palm landed hard on naked flesh. The idea of doing it to his wife was an incredible turn-on. He'd had a hard-on pretty much all week just thinking about tonight, ever since they'd talked about it.

He'd never thought Jillian would go for it. When they'd reached the point where he was willing to try anything to tear down the wall that had sat so stubbornly between them for the last year, he was surprised to hear her agree. He was glad she had, because he needed this chance to fix their marriage, to make it right. They'd tried couples counseling early on, but it had been a disaster. The therapist had spent every session blaming him for Jillian's pain. The woman had acted as though he was some insensitive bastard. He'd ended up walking out. Jillian had wanted to try going to someone else, but he'd had enough. Jillian had continued to see another therapist. It had helped some, but there was a level she'd never been able to break through. It wasn't her fault; he knew she'd tried. So it was up to him now. This had to work.

And now, watching her breath catch and her nipples swell, he was pretty sure she was as into it as he was. He was hard already, just from touching her, from tying her up. From thinking about what he was going to do to her.

Her full, rounded breasts rose and fell with her ragged breathing. Her nipples were tight and rosy pink. His groin tightened just looking at her. She was so damn beautiful, spread out on the bed for him, her little pink tongue darting out to moisten her lips.

He could feel her nerves, still, could feel his own heart thunder in his chest. But it was pure lust hammering away at his composure. He took a lungful of air and commanded himself to rein it in, to stay in control. That was his job here. And he needed to be in control now as much as Jillian needed him to be.

He reached out and stroked her smooth skin with his fingertips, ran them over her rib cage, around the edge of her breast, down her side. She shivered, and he felt the urgency of her need as a physical sensation. Suddenly, he couldn't resist. He dipped his hand down into the velvet folds between her thighs and stroked at the edges of her wet cleft. God, she was soaked! His cock filled and jerked against his slacks. He pulled his hand back.

Slow down.

A quick glance at her face and he saw her eyes screwed tightly shut. He smiled to himself at the sense of raw power that suffused him, as it began to dawn on him just how much power he had over this woman he loved. She was his now in a way she'd never been before. He wanted to take her right here, right now. His cock was throbbing, begging for release. But that's not what he was here for.

Instead, he took another deep, steadying breath, and concentrated on Jillian.

He ran a hand over the length of her body, tracing the line of her hip, her thigh, her leg, and back down to her sensitive foot. Her skin was as warm and soft as living silk. He'd never thought of himself as having a foot fetish, but the way she had responded earlier made him rethink the whole idea. As he stroked her toes she trembled and curled them. But there were even more interesting things to do, and her entire body to explore.

Jillian had had a hard time coming in the last year. She didn't seem to feel comfortable enough in her own body anymore, couldn't shut her thoughts down. He intended to change that tonight. He would make her come. Over and over again. He would make her beg. Make her scream. And when he finally took her, when his cock was buried deep inside her body, she would belong to him completely.

His rock-hard cock gave another jerk, but he focused on the sight of his wife spread out on the bed, open and vulnerable. He would fuck her, and fuck her hard, but that would have to wait. For now, she was his to feast on, to please. For now, it was all about Jillian.

※

Jillian opened her eyes, peering up at Cam. Why was he just standing there, when she needed so badly for him to touch her? God, when he'd shoved his fingers into her she'd almost screamed. And now she was pulsing and so drenching wet it was trickling down onto the silk and linen bedspread beneath her.

Please, touch me again.

But she couldn't say the words out loud. She watched him as his eyes swept over her body, her nipples stiffening even more as though it were his hands on her, rather than his intense gray gaze.

Finally, he bent over her and placed a series of quick, hot kisses over her stomach, then moved to her breasts. His mouth was everywhere and all thought left her head as he kissed and nibbled his way over her skin. When he reached her breasts she arched up to meet him. And when he took one nipple into his hot mouth, she went rigid all over, pleasure sweeping through her in a powerful tide. Her mind stopped entirely when he began to suck.

He drew her nipple into his mouth, pulling on it until it almost hurt. She didn't care. It felt too good. With his free hand, he caressed her other breast. Her nipples felt like they were going to explode, her sex was thrumming with heat, and it was almost as though his mouth were there between her legs.

Yes. Use your mouth there.

But it was too good, his tongue swirling over her hard nipple as he sucked with his mouth, while his other hand tugged and twisted and began to pinch.

Jesus.

She'd never felt anything so good. Her arms wanted to twine around his neck, to pull him closer, but the rope held her tight, heightening the desire burning through her body.

Cam pulled away and she let out a groan.

"Easy, honey. We've got all night. And I intend to make good use of it."

"Wh-what are you going to do?"

"Do you really want to know?" His sexy mouth pulled into a wicked grin she'd never seen on him before, and it made her tremble with anticipation.

"Tell me."

"I'm going to touch you everywhere. With my hands. With my mouth. I'm going to stroke you gently, I'm going to pinch you in all the right places. I'm going to lick every inch of your gorgeous skin. I'm going to play with you in a way I never have before, with my hands and mouth, and maybe a few other things."

He paused and Jillian's sex clenched and tingled. She wished she could press her thighs together to ease the ache there, but she was spread wide open. All she could think of was Cam putting his mouth there as he had said he would. His hot, damp tongue stroking her, his fingers pushing inside her. *Oh, God.*

He continued, his voice low and smoky. "I'm going to make you come, Jillian. I'm going to make you come so hard, with pleasure and maybe a little pain. What do you think of that?"

Think? She could hardly think. All she could do was feel. But Cam was demanding an answer from her.

"I'm waiting, Jillian."

"I . . ." Her voice was nothing more than a raw whisper. "I want that. Yes. Please, Cam."

"Good girl."

The term made her go warm and soft all over. She didn't know why.

He began to stroke her breasts again, tracing the full outline, avoiding her nipples. She shivered.

"And after you've come for me, I'm going to fuck you, Jillian. I'm going to bury my cock inside you and fuck you forever. Tell me you want that."

"I . . ."

He took one nipple between his fingers and pinched, hard. She rose up off the bed, the pain shooting through her and somehow transforming into a deep pleasure that lanced straight to her core.

"I want . . . I want you to fuck me, Cam." Yes, she could hardly think of anything else but his enormous, beautiful cock, golden-skinned as the rest of him was.

"That's my good girl."

Again that warm wash of pleasure at his words.

And then he was on her, with his mouth, with his hands, roaming over her body. He licked her skin, and stopped to kiss and suck here and there. Everywhere he touched her it was like a tiny electric shock, sending bolts of pleasure coursing through her system.

"Does this feel good, baby?"

"Yes . . ." It came out on a soft hiss.

"How about this?" His fingers squeezed her nipples, then were replaced with his mouth. His hands moved over her hips, gripped her thighs for a moment, then his fingers plunged into her dark, waiting heat.

She moaned aloud, the walls of her sex grabbing around his fingers as he moved them inside her. It was almost too much, all this sensation. And when he pressed his thumb over her clit, she thought she'd scream with pleasure.

"Oh, God, oh, God," she murmured, already on the edge of orgasm.

Cam pulled back.

She squirmed on the bed, pulling against the ropes that held her so firmly, that held her spread apart. Cam moved around the room, but she couldn't seem to care what he was doing. The only thing she knew was that he wasn't touching her anymore.

In a moment he returned to the bed, a pair of scissors in his hand. She gasped and tried to sit up. Of course she couldn't.

He smiled down on her, his eyes literally glowing. "I just need a little help getting rid of these pretty panties you wore for me."

With a quick snip they were gone.

His hands were on her again as he knelt on the bed, stroking her thighs, encouraging the muscles there to relax. When he brushed his fingers back and forth across her clit, the fire there roared to a full blaze once more. And then he did something he'd never done before. It began with a gentle tapping of his fingers, but soon moved on to a rhythmic slapping against her mound. She was surprised at how good it felt, teasing her clit into a rock-hard nub. By the time the slapping became a little painful, she was too hot to care. The pain felt good, intensifying the pleasure, until it all melted together and became one sensation.

Her sex throbbed, pounded beneath Cam's hand, until she was right on the edge of coming. And then he reached a hand up and pinched her nipple, hard. And at the same time he pinched her clit between his strong fingers, and the pain and the pleasure shot through her at a hundred miles an hour.

"Come for me, honey." He pinched harder.

Her body ignited, her sex went into a clenching, grabbing spasm and her mind emptied completely. Her orgasm rocketed through her, making her thighs tremble. The trembling turned into a shaking that spread through her body and she called out his name as she gasped for breath.

"Cam!"

As the wave subsided, she ended on a quiet sob. And suddenly her bonds were being released and her husband's strong arms were around her. He kissed her face, whispering her name.

"Jillian, honey, I'm right here."

"Oh, God, Cam . . ."

"Shh. It's alright now. You're fine. You're good."

And for the first time in a long time, she suspected he was right.

⟋

Cam held Jillian tight, rocking her as he would a small child. Not that he thought of her as childlike, not at all. She was more a woman to him at this moment than she'd ever been before. But infinitely precious in a way that was new for him.

He could feel the ripples of emotion coursing through her body as he held her, just as earlier he'd felt her waves of response. He had some idea of what she was experiencing. At least, he was trying to understand. It had been such a long time since she'd been able to reach orgasm, and she had never had one like this! Was he really doing anything that different? He was trying harder, but not in the usual goal-oriented way, that much he knew. He'd made a mission of it, of just pleasing her. His own body was still hard and humming with her pleasure as much as his own need. And it gave him a profound sense of accomplishment to have brought her to this point.

He wanted to do it again. And again.

He sensed when Jillian began to calm. The tears stopped, her limbs relaxed, and she lay soft and pliant against him. He still wanted her; his raging erection was a testament to that. But right now it felt good just to hold on to her, to know what he'd given her, and to feel close again.

They sat for a long time before she stirred, tilting her face up to his. He kissed her pink mouth, savoring the familiar sweetness of her mixed with a few salty tears. His heart pounded in his chest. This was what they'd been missing—maybe more than they'd ever had to begin with. He felt his limbs loosen with the realization that he really had a good shot at making it all better. He had to, damn it. He was not going to allow things to fall apart. He couldn't allow it. It was up to him to keep it together. To keep them together. And he would, no matter what it took.

"Cam." Her voice was a husky whisper.

"Right here, baby."

"That was . . ."

"Yeah. How do you feel?"

"I feel . . . good. Lighter. Does that make sense?"

"Yeah, it does." He smiled down at her, pushed her tangle of honeyed hair away from her face. God, he loved her mane of hair. So soft and sexy, especially the way it was now, all tousled around her flushed face.

She smiled back at him. Then, after a quiet moment, "I want more."

"So do I. And I want it now. Are you ready? Because I don't think I can wait one more minute to be inside you."

"Yes, Cam!"

It was all he needed to hear. Picking her up in his arms, he shifted her until she was laid out on the bed again. Quickly, he stripped off his slacks and his boxers. He lay on top of her, careful not to crush her. He needed to feel her silken skin against his. Her plush breasts pushed against his chest. He could feel the hard points of her nipples already. He wanted them in his mouth again, but first, he needed to kiss his wife.

Her lips were plump and warm beneath his. Her

mouth was hot and wet when he opened her lips and drove inside. It made him think about her tight, wet pussy. He knew how good it would feel around his shaft. He lowered his hand between their bodies, between her thighs. Found her slick opening and stroked. She moaned against his mouth. With his fingers, he played with the soft folds, pulling and pinching a little before dipping inside.

She contracted around his finger, hot and tight and wet. He added another finger, then another while she gasped. God, she felt so damn good, he had to be inside her. But not yet.

He pulled his fingers out and stroked her mound, finding her hard little nub and tugging at it, rolling it between his fingers and thumb. Her hips were moving against him, her pelvis rubbing hard against his straining cock, and he thought for a moment he was going to lose it. To come all over her stomach like a high-school kid.

Hang on.

He raised his hips. Using his hand to spread the lips of her sex wide, he carefully guided the head of his cock into her opening. Careful because he knew he was big and he didn't want to hurt her. Not that way, at least. He paused there, meaning to catch his breath, but Jillian wrapped her smooth legs around him, and all he could do was plunge inside. Into that dark, moist heat, into that tight, pulsing tunnel. He pulled out, thrust again, all the way to the hilt. He was buried deep inside her, exactly where he needed to be, and it felt damn good.

"Yes, honey, that's it. You can take it all," he ground out.

Jillian met each thrust with her own, driving him on.

He grabbed her firm ass cheeks in his hands, pulled her hips up higher, knowing at that angle he could grind against her clit with each thrust.

She was gasping rhythmically now, bucking beneath him. His cock was heavy with blood and lust, burning with the need to come, but he held back, waiting for her. Her clenching pussy was driving him wild. Each plunge drove him higher, sent shards of pleasure lancing through him. He couldn't hold on much longer.

"I need to fuck you hard, baby."

"Do it, Cam!"

"I need to fuck you, baby . . ."

He thrust into her, into her hot, waiting sheath. She wrapped her legs around his back, pulling him in tighter. Her arms were around his neck, her face buried in his shoulder, biting, sucking. He loved it. His hands dug into the soft flesh of her ass as he sped up, pounding into her like a freight train now. In and out, harder, faster. His cock was ready to explode.

Jillian let out a guttural cry and her velvet pussy convulsed around him, setting him off. He came hard and fast, like a rocket going off in his cock, reverberating through his belly, his whole body. He yelled something, he didn't know what. Didn't matter. Just keep coming. Coming so damn hard he couldn't think of anything else. Just feel. Just feel this ripping-hard orgasm and Jillian shaking beneath him.

He kissed her face all over, couldn't seem to stop kissing her. God, she was fucking beautiful.

"Love you, honey."

"Love you, too."

When was the last time he'd felt this good? When was the last time he'd felt so close to her? This is what they'd needed. This would fix them. Maybe not all at once. But eventually. Meanwhile, even if the practice killed him, what a way to go!

Jillian lay beneath the warmth of her husband's big body. She felt wonderful. Her whole system was still buzzing with the aftershocks of two of the most powerful orgasms of her life. Her husband, the man she loved, was pressed against her still. And for the first time in far too long, she felt a hint of the happiness she'd been missing.

Cam had been right, she thought. This was going to help them. It was going to help her. While she'd been in his arms, while he'd been tormenting her with pleasure, she hadn't thought once about losing the baby.

Damn!

There it was, the memory that had kept her mind tied up in grief for almost a year. She squeezed her eyes shut.

Not now.

But it was too late. She pushed Cam off her, rolled onto her side.

"Honey, what's wrong?"

He sounded truly confused. Well, he was a man. She couldn't expect him to be psychic, especially only moments after sex.

The tears started. She couldn't help it. Maybe it was the powerful orgasms, or just the hour of closeness, but she felt all opened up inside. Cam's hand slid over her shoulder, but she flinched away. Despite the closeness they'd just shared, she couldn't stand his touch. She was too raw. It would send her over the edge, and she might never come back.

"Jillian. Please." He bent over her side, kissing her shoulder, trying to pull her against his body, but she couldn't let him.

She sat up, intending to flee to the bathroom, but he wouldn't allow her to. He held her tight in his arms, pressing her into the warmth of his big, solid body. A sob escaped her.

"I can't do this, Cam."

"Yes, you can. And it's about time. You have to share this part of yourself with me, too. Don't you get it? If you don't, it'll always be there between us."

"It's too hard!"

"You have to do this. It's the only way you'll come back to me."

Was that a note of desperation in his voice? Cam, who was always so strong, who could handle anything? Her heart melted a little at the thought. She was hurting him. She'd known it before, in a distant kind of way. Now she began to understand that losing the baby had been hard on him, too.

"Jillian, talk to me. I can't lose you again, after just beginning to get you back. Come on, honey. We've lost too much already. Too much time, too much of each other."

"I know." She sniffled, and Cam grabbed a tissue from the nightstand and put it into her hand. "I'm trying. And this was . . . wonderful. It was the first time in so long I've felt even vaguely good. Maybe it was too good."

"Too good?" She could hear the hurt in his voice.

"I mean that it's such a contrast to the way I've been feeling for so long, it's a shock. To feel good. To feel close to you again."

The room was almost entirely dark now. The sun had set and the only light came from the candles burning on the dresser. She felt dark inside, too, yet the darkness of the room was welcoming, womblike. She couldn't have faced Cam now, in the stark light of day.

He was stroking her hair, kissing the top of her head, and she allowed herself to relax into his embrace. To feel the safety of him. This was her own fault, she knew. It was her body that hadn't been able to hang on to their baby, and her selfish grief that had driven a wedge between them. It was time to try to make it all right. And she would try. She wasn't as sure of her strength as Cam seemed to be. But she knew she could lean on him, on his strength. He was always there for her. She needed to appreciate that more. She was so damn lucky.

"I love you, Cam. So much!"

He paused, as though he was surprised at her words.

"I love you, too, honey. You know I do. Come on. Lie down with me. Rest. I'll be right here."

She snuggled into his strong arms. She wanted to learn to trust him again, to learn to trust herself. She didn't know how long it would take. She only knew it would be hard. But here she was, with her wonderful husband: a man who loved her in a way she didn't truly deserve. She tried to remember why, but her mind began to drift, and soon, she was fast asleep.

Sometime in the night Jillian awoke. Cam's arms were still wrapped around her as he spooned her from behind. His cock was hard again. His deep, even breathing told her that he slept. She tried to relax back into sleep, too, but she couldn't. Her body was too aware of him. She pressed her buttocks back, pushing and rubbing against his thick erection. She wasn't even sure he was awake when his hand snaked down between her aching thighs and he began to play gently with her. She moved her thighs apart to grant him better access. His hips thrust against her, his big cock seeking entrance. Moving her buttocks higher and her leg up, she arched against his hips until she could guide his cock into her already wet and ready sex. He pushed into her slowly. The pleasure was exquisite, yet it was all softer and sweeter than it had been earlier.

Cam gave her a sleepy kiss on the top of her head as he began to move. His cock was thick and heavy inside her. His fingers glided over her swollen clit, sliding in the damp heat. Her whole body was filled with sensation. Sharp, electric. The dual sensations were incredible, taking her quickly toward the peak. She pushed back into him, onto his hot and throbbing shaft. His hand followed her movement, rubbing, rubbing on her tight, hard nub as he thrust harder into her.

She felt his sharp intake of breath just as the first wave of orgasm hit her. He pounded into her, filling her to bursting, while his fingers pressed hard into her clit, and she came with a blast of fireworks going off in her head. She felt the hot spurt of his seed inside her as she spasmed around him, as they came together in a glorious burst of sensation.

They were both breathing hard. His cock softened inside her, but he didn't pull out. Even soft, Cam was always big. She didn't want to think about anything else right now. He felt too good to her, her big husband with the wonderful cock and magical hands. Why hadn't she remembered this about him? She was going to try very hard never to forget again.

But for now, she was so tired. Once again, she slept.

CHAPTER THREE

THE NEXT DAY AT WORK PASSED IN A DREAMLIKE haze for Jillian. Sensual dreams that distracted her, making it hard to concentrate on anything. Her limbs were sore from straining against the ropes, yet she reveled in the sensation. Her skin was sensitive to the tiniest breeze, to the scant friction of her silk blouse when she moved.

She sat at the enormous glass expanse of her desk at the F. D. Leighton Gallery, where she was the director. Images flashed through her mind: the intensity of Cam's expression as he held himself over her, thrusting into her body. The sensation of the ropes twining her wrists and ankles. Imagining what else he might do to her.

The ring of the phone startled her out of her reverie.

"F. D. Leighton Gallery, Jillian Ross speaking."

"Jillian, it's Briana. How's it going there without me?"

Briana Douglas was her assistant at the gallery, her right hand, and her best friend. She was currently at home recovering from a broken leg, the result of a skiing accident.

"It's fine . . . not the same without you here, Bri."

"Of course not." There was laughter in her voice. "So, what's happening? How's the Madonna and Child installation going?"

"Oh . . . it's going fine."

"Jillian? Wanna tell me what's wrong with you?"

"Wrong? Nothing's wrong. I'm fine. Really good, in fact. Yeah, really good." She smiled, remembering the previous night. Had Cam ever played her body so expertly before?

"Well, you seem pretty spaced out. What is *up* with you?"

Jillian grinned to herself, and tapped her coffee mug with a pen. "Um . . ."

How much to tell? Briana was her best friend, but she still couldn't tell her she was as sexually sated as she'd ever been in her life because her husband had tied her up last night.

"Things are really good with Cam and me right now, that's all."

"You got laid, didn't you?"

Jillian was surprised to find herself blushing. "I, uh . . . yeah."

"Sounds like it was fabulous, too. With that gorgeous husband of yours! So, was it awesome? Please tell me it was. I haven't been laid in weeks. It's just been me and my little electronic toys since I broke my leg. I need to live vicariously through others."

"Too much information, Bri."

"Sorry. But, you see what bad shape I'm in?"

Jillian felt a sudden need to change the subject, before her lust-dazed mind caused her to blurt out too much. "So, when are you coming back to work?"

"My doctor says I can come back on Monday. That's what I called about."

"That's great news. We'll try to make sure you don't overdo it."

"So, I'll see you Monday. Maybe your brain will be working again by then."

Jillian laughed. "And maybe not, if I'm lucky."

They hung up and Jillian went back to her earlier musings. Briana was right: Cam was gorgeous. And great in bed. How had she forgotten that for all those months? The things he could do with his hands and his mouth, not to mention that big, beautiful cock of his.

Her sex began to heat up just thinking about him, and she suddenly wished she had one of Briana's toys at work with her.

Lord, she was never going to get any work done this way! She gave herself a stern mental shake, and opened the folder on her desk. Inside were photographs of paintings by a new artist, a woman who painted nudes in the neoclassical style. Normally it was not something a progressive gallery like Leighton's would consider, but the subject matter in each piece set the series apart.

In the first one, a woman sat on the edge of a bathtub, her auburn hair coiled high on her head, the line of her slender neck and shoulders lovely to look at. In her hands she held a small phallus. The colors were lush, yet subtle at the same time, the overall chiaroscuro giving it a hazy, dreamlike quality that was apparent in all of the paintings.

Jillian stared at the dildo in the picture. It was lifelike in style and done in great detail. Wonderfully done, though this was not what she needed to cool her blood. But she couldn't stop looking.

She forced herself to turn the page. The next painting was of a man with a long, lean body like Cam's. He leaned against a roughly textured stucco wall, his head back, his eyes closed, while he stroked his erection with his hand. Wrapped around his wrist was a small piece of barbed wire. Jillian realized she was getting wet just looking at it.

She'd seen some of these paintings in person at the artist's studio. They hadn't had this effect on her then. But her response now was entirely different. What had changed?

It wasn't the paintings. It was her. Her experience with Cam had awakened her body, her sex drive. Not just awakened it, but blasted it wide open. Now it was a force to be reckoned with, and something she wanted to explore.

She moved on to the next one. A woman again, this time bound to a tree with what looked to be vines. They wrapped sinuously around her arms and legs, with one piece sliding between her thighs.

Jillian squeezed her own thighs together beneath her desk. Her sex had begun to throb with need. She got up and went to lock the door of her office.

The ring of her phone startled her, making her blush as though the caller could see her, knew what she was thinking, feeling. She took a deep breath before she picked it up.

"F. D. Leighton Gallery. Jillian Ross."

"Hey, honey. How's your day going?" Cam's deep voice was sexy enough to make her heat up all over again.

"It's fine . . . um, it's going fine."

"You okay? You sound a little out of breath. Sorry if I caught you in the middle of something."

You have no idea. "No, just reviewing some pictures."

"What kind of pictures?" Cam asked, making her wonder if he really could see through the phone somehow.

"Uh . . ." She bit her lip. "They're just . . . well, they're pretty hot, actually."

"Tell me about them."

"Cam, I don't think—"

"That wasn't a request, Jillian."

"Oh." She was taken a bit by surprise, but his commanding tone had gone straight to her already heated sex.

"You're alone?"

"Yes."

"Good. Lock your office door."

"I, uh, I already have."

"Good girl. Are you sitting down?"

That now-familiar shiver ran through her. "Yes."

"Hike your skirt up and spread your thighs. Then tell me what you see."

She slid her skirt up around her waist and eased her thighs open. She could hardly catch her breath. "It's a painting, beautifully done. Very realistic, but sort of soft all over." She paused to lick her lips. "It's a large piece of a nude couple entangled. Very sensuous, pretty even. But the man is scratching the woman's back with a thorny rose. Long, pink grooves are on her buttocks and the back of her thighs."

"Does it make you hot, Jillian?" His tone was low and smoky.

She could barely get the word out. "Yes."

"Good. Look at it. And touch yourself for me, just a little."

Jillian glanced at her office door, then slipped her hand between her legs. Pushing her panties aside, she drew her fingers across her damp slit and shivered.

"I can hear your breathing change. I can hear how turned on you are. Do you know what that does to me? I'm getting hard just listening to you breathe."

God, the sound of his voice! It was making her crazy. That and the way he was in total command, even now over the phone. And the pictures were making it even hotter.

"What's next?" Cam asked.

She turned the page. This one was even better. She pressed her whole hand against her mound. "It's a woman bent over a bench of some sort. She's naked except for a collar of twining twigs and leaves around her neck. There's a naked man behind her." She had to pause to take a breath. She couldn't believe how it made her feel to talk about it. Her hand was still pressed to her sex, putting pressure on her pounding clit.

"The man is . . . holding his cock in one hand while he sweeps a flogger over her ass."

"I'm holding my cock, too," Cam murmured. "Holding it and stroking it. I'm imagining it's your hot little mouth on me. I'm so hard. I want to touch you, to fuck you. I want you to move your hand for me. Massage your clit the way I know you like it."

Jillian pressed into her mound, grinding against the throbbing heat. The image Cam had created was almost too much for her. Cam with his big, beautiful cock in his hand. Moving his tightened fist up and down the length of his shaft. The head of his cock would be big and flushed with blood, fully engorged. Her mouth watered and her body flamed with desire. She focused on the swollen cock in the picture, on the sight of the flogger against the woman's porcelain and innocent-looking skin.

"Tell me more," Cam said.

"They're both very beautiful. And the skin on her ass is red and welted."

"Yours will be, too, someday. I want to flog you, baby. Would you like that?"

"Yes, Cam!"

"Keep looking. Imagine that it's me with that flogger, with my cock in my hand." His voice was rough with lust. "And I want you to spread for me, honey. Spread your legs and put your fingers inside yourself. Do it."

She leaned back in her chair and spread her legs, then moved her hand down to press two fingers into her wet folds, still rubbing her clit with the heel of her hand.

She was only marginally aware of her short, panting breaths as she worked herself. Her hand moved faster and faster, and her orgasm began to bear down on her like an approaching freight train.

"Come on, honey. Push them in deeper, faster. I want you to come. I can tell you're close. And I'm so damn hard for you. I'm going to come soon. I want to fuck you, and I will, later. But now, come for me."

"Jillian?" Her secretary Marie's voice came loud and clear through the door, followed by several sharp raps.

"Oh, my God," Jillian breathed into the phone. "Somebody's at my door. It must be important to disturb me." She was already pushing her skirt back down over her thighs.

"Damn." Cam gave a short laugh.

"I know!" Her whole body was still buzzing.

"Jillian?" Marie again. "There's a client here to see you. I tried to buzz you but you didn't pick up."

"Be right there!" She got out of her chair, smoothed her hair. "Sorry, Cam. I really have to go."

"We'll have to make it up to each other later. Meet me at Fiorello's after work for dinner." It was their favorite Italian restaurant, the best in Seattle. "I'll meet you there at six-thirty. Be ready to celebrate."

"Celebrate?"

"We have something to celebrate, don't you think?"

Jillian smiled. "Yes. Yes, I do."

They were getting their marriage back, if last night and today were any indication. And perhaps even more important, and crucial to the marriage, as well, she was getting herself back.

❧

The restaurant was dimly lit, the glow of the candles burning on each small, round table accented by light sconces on the walls. The décor was classically Italian, with heavy red curtains draping the windows, the walls accented by Roman-style pillars. Everything was accented here and there in gold: the light sconces, the framed pictures on the walls, the large vases of flowers.

The scent of garlic and freshly baked bread was in the air. The food here was wonderful, but tonight Jillian wasn't thinking about the food.

She found Cam already seated. He stood as soon as he saw her, ever the gentleman. He was handsome in his black slacks, crisp white shirt, and dark, narrow tie. When he leaned over to kiss her cheek, she caught the faint scent of good Scotch. It reminded her of the night before, and her limbs went warm and loose. She drifted into the booth. Cam slid over to sit beside her.

"How was your day, baby?"

"It was good, actually. Not terribly productive, but good. How was yours?"

"The best I've had in a while."

He smiled, his gray eyes sparkling in the candlelight, and she was sure she detected a wicked glint there. She was feeling pretty wicked herself. Her near-orgasm earlier had done nothing to quench the need thrumming through her body since last night. If anything, she wanted Cam even more, had been thinking about him all day, desperate for his touch.

They ordered their favorite pasta and a good bottle of Chianti. Jillian couldn't wait to get home, already.

Their wine came first and while they sipped at it Cam covered her hand with his.

"We should talk about last night."

"Yes, I suppose so." She rubbed her fingers over the fine, dark hair on the back of his hand, traced the heavy band of white gold encircling his ring finger.

"Are you still okay with all of it?"

Was she? She didn't want to spend too much time analyzing it. There was something nagging at the back of her mind. Something about the idea of yielding to another person, even her own husband. She'd always been strong, completely in command, whether at work or in her personal life. Well, until she'd lost the baby. Then she'd sort of crumbled. She'd been trying ever since to put herself back together again. And something about submitting to Cam, even in bed, spoke to her of the intrinsic weakness she'd felt lingering in her system for months.

But no, she didn't want to think about that. She didn't want to think about the enormous burden of guilt she carried. Because last night had brought her and Cam miles closer than they'd been since before the miscarriage. And it had felt damn good.

"Yes, I'm okay with it. There's still some mental stuff to process. Just give me some time with that. But the rest . . . yes, I think so."

She looked into his beautiful gray eyes, saw the corners of his sexy mouth turn up, the lust etched on his face. She loved that she could do that to him. Maybe there was something of power for her in this situation, even with Cam calling the shots in bed.

"Come here."

Cam pulled her closer to him in the leather booth, took her hand, and guided it to the zippered fly of his slacks. He had a huge erection.

"This is what you do to me, Jillian," he whispered into her ear.

She squirmed in her seat, her sex coming alive. Yes, maybe she did have some power here.

"Spread your thighs for me," Cam said in a low voice.

"What? Here?"

"Yes. Now."

She was surprised that she simply did it, with no more

argument. When his hand slipped beneath the hem of her skirt, under the band of her panties, and found her already slick folds, she tensed momentarily.

He told her quietly, "Nobody can see us under the tablecloth. Spread a little wider for me."

She did as she was told. His fingertips teased at the edges of her sex, stroking the full, tender lips. Brushing across the tender, engorged nub there.

"Take a sip of your wine."

She lifted her glass with a shaky hand and held it to her lips, swallowed. She almost choked on it when he slipped a finger inside her.

"Cam."

"Yes?" He sounded amused.

"I can't do this."

"You can. And you will. For me."

Yes. For him. Her hips moved of their own accord against his hand. As his thumb pressed onto her clit and began to rub in lazy circles, she thought, for me, too.

She still gripped her wineglass in her hand. The darkness around them made her feel hidden, yet at the same time she was marginally aware of the other diners around them, the waiters moving through the room laden with trays.

Oh, God, what if their dinner came now? What if she did?

Cam was rubbing her harder now. She glanced up and her eyes came to rest on a couple at another table. They were arguing. The woman was beautiful, dressed all in dark red. A long strand of pearls hung from her neck. Her face was flushed with emotion. Cam pushed another finger into her, and she squeezed around them. God, so close!

The man at the other table was handsome. Big, like Cam, but built more like a football player. Jillian would bet he had a big cock, like her husband's. His eyes glittered in the candlelight, his expression intense. He had big hands, like Cam, like the hand that was playing with her so expertly beneath the table.

"Come for me, honey," Cam whispered into her ear.

Her fingers squeezed the stem of the wineglass. The walls of her sex squeezed his fingers. And she came for him, into his hand, biting her lip hard. She closed her eyes as pleasure washed through her. Her breath came in sharp pants, which she tried to hide by burying her face in Cam's neck. Her sex throbbed with heat and she tried hard not to squirm.

So good. Yes!

"Good girl." Cam withdrew his fingers from her, tugged her skirt down. He was smiling. He calmly took a sip of his wine. "I want to fuck you right here on the table, Jillian."

She almost groaned out loud. The waiter arrived with their salads. "How is your wine?" he asked.

Cam smiled at her, sexy and wicked. "How is it, Jillian?"

"It's good. Very good." Could the waiter hear how breathless she was?

"Excellent. Is there anything else you need right now?" the waiter asked.

"Do you need anything, Jillian?" The grin on Cam's face was frankly amused.

"No." She turned to the waiter. "Thank you."

Dinner passed in a blur. All she knew was that Cam

kept one hand possessively on her thigh, and she couldn't wait to get home so he'd slip that hand between her thighs again. His hand, his mouth, his cock. She didn't care. As long as he kept on touching her.

Was she becoming obsessed with sex, suddenly?

Doesn't matter.

As long as she was with Cam, really *with* him now, nothing else mattered. The way he was making her feel was pretty mind-blowing. And she was safe with him. She could trust him. Maybe trusting herself would come later.

The house was dark when they got home. Jillian jumped out of her BMW, waited while Cam pulled his briefcase and portfolio case from the leather saddlebags on his big, pearl black Harley-Davidson. His job as an architect seemed to require that he carry an armload of work with him everywhere he went. Luckily, his prized motorcycle could accommodate not only Cam's size, but all of his job-related accoutrements, as well.

Once inside, he set his things down and pulled her close. She could feel the heat of his big body radiating from him when he bent to kiss her lips.

"Go get ready for me, Jillian."

Oh, she was ready. But she knew what he meant.

Upstairs, she stripped her clothes off, clipped her hair up, and stepped into the shower. The hot water felt good running over her skin. Since last night her body was alive, sensitive to every sensation. She had a feeling it was only going to get better.

She eyed the loofah sponge hanging from a hook, and

imagined the rough surface of it running over her skin, her nipples. Her body gave an involuntary shudder. Everything was a potential new sensation, everything wore an aura of sensuality. She wanted to be touched in every way, to experience texture in all its endless variety. This adventure with her husband had awakened her in such an unexpected way, but she was open to it, wanted it.

But right now she wanted him. She turned the water off, not wanting to keep Cam waiting no matter how good the shower felt. No matter how enticing the needle-sharp spray of the showerhead, how interesting the idea of the loofah sponge, the bristles of the long-handled back brush. He would feel even better.

Dried and lotioned, she slid her silky robe over her shoulders and stepped out into the bedroom. Cam was there, his hair wet and a little spiky. He must have rinsed off in the bathroom down the hall. He wore a pair of black boxers and nothing else. He had turned the lights off and lit the amber-scented candles again. And once more music played in the background, low and moody.

The candlelight glinted off the ripple of muscle across his shoulders, the tight six-pack of abs.

Cam came over to her, circled around until he stood behind her. His hands came up, briefly cupped her breasts beneath the silk of the robe. Her nipples sprang up hard immediately. He slid his hands over her shoulders and bent to kiss the back of her neck. His mouth was hot, sending shivers down her spine.

"Time to get naked." He drew her robe down her arms and it fell to the floor.

Cam's hands were back at her breasts again. He

tweaked her nipples, making them harden even more. She held still, waiting to see what else he would do while her sex contracted in expectation. Her mind was emptying already as he led her to the bed. The ropes were still there from last night, tied to the corners of the bed frame.

"Lie facedown, Jillian." There was that same commanding tone again, the one that made her wet with need.

She obeyed.

He tucked a pillow under her hips, so that her ass was raised into the air. She felt extra naked, somehow. Exposed. Vulnerable. But she liked the feeling.

Cam was fastening the ropes. First one wrist, then her ankles, then the other hand, just like last night. But this time she couldn't see what was going on. It was a little unnerving.

The first thing she felt was his smooth palm sliding over her skin. Down her spine, her buttocks, her thighs. He just touched her like that for a while, until she was loose and relaxed. Then he began a gentle tapping on her buttocks. Just a small slapping with his fingertips. It didn't really hurt, but almost. Yet it felt wonderful at the same time, if her dampening sex was any indication.

He began to slap a little harder, so that it stung a bit. The stinging seemed to go straight to her sex, making it fill and swell.

Cam bent over her and whispered, "Good?"

"Yes!"

He slapped harder, using more of his palm now, and the stinging increased. So did the lust running hot in her blood. She moved her hips into the pillows.

"Ah, none of that, Jillian. Hold still." He gave her a good, hard slap.

She yelped. But why did it feel so good? She wanted him to do it again.

Cam seemed to read her mind. His spanking—for she realized now that was what he was doing—became gradually harder. A slow, rhythmic buildup. His hand coming down hard on her ass, inflaming the skin as the blood rushed to the surface to meet the punishing little slaps. And she was as turned on as if he had his hand between her thighs.

He was spanking her hard now, and then he slipped a few fingers into her tight, waiting hole, and she lost all ability to reason.

All she knew was his hand coming down hard, the sting turning to thud, then back again, as he created some wicked cadence that changed and flowed. And his fingers inside her, moving in and out in rhythm with his slaps. She arched, moving her ass higher into the air. And Cam, knowing immediately what she needed, as always, slid his fingers out of her and used them to stroke her clit.

He was still spanking her hard. Her buttocks burned with heat. She pushed against his fingers, her clit hard and aching for release. And when he shoved his thumb into her and pressed up onto her g-spot, she came in a long, powerful shudder. His hard, slapping hand on her ass drove her on. His thumb buried deep inside her, his fingers rubbing over her swollen mound. It was almost too much, she was coming too hard.

From somewhere far away, she heard herself scream. In pleasure. In pain. It didn't matter.

When the waves subsided she thought Cam would stop, but although he took his hand away from her drenching wet and still-spasming sex, he continued the spanking.

Postorgasm, her skin was even more sensitive than before, but still it felt good. His hand landed one hard smack after another, stinging, throbbing against her raw flesh. She wondered why he didn't stop, then understood when she heard him cry out, felt the spurt of his hot come all over her ass.

The spanking stopped. She realized she was panting. So was Cam. He used his fingers to rub his semen into her skin. It felt good on her fire-hot flesh.

She waited. The ropes holding her tight felt good to her. Safe. Her flesh burned. Her mind was numb. Her body was relaxed, lambent.

She heard Cam walk into the bathroom. When he came back a moment later, he used a warm washcloth to wipe his sticky seed from her. Then he bent over her and trailed soft kisses up and down her spine, bringing goose-flesh to her skin.

She was still burning with need. Still wanted him to fuck her, but she knew he'd need some time to recover. Meanwhile, she was happy enough just to lie there, safe and snug in the ropes, with Cam kissing her like this.

What was it about being tied up that made her feel so safe? She didn't understand. She wasn't sure she cared right now, except that when she stopped to think about it, it seemed so strange. It was as though nothing was her fault right now, her responsibility. Nothing could be while she lay here, bound and helpless. It was a huge relief.

Cam rubbed her arms and shoulders with his big hands, massaged even her fingers. He was so loving, so gentle. It was a stark contrast to the spanking he'd just given her, but that made it all even better.

After a while he laid his body over hers. She felt the hard planes of his chest pressed against her back. She'd always loved that he was such a big man, loved the sheer size of him. And she loved his big cock. The first time they'd had sex, she wasn't even sure she could take it all, but over time her body had become accustomed to his size. And now all she could think about was having it shoved deep inside her.

She squirmed her hips, and realized he was growing hard against her. His cock was filling, lengthening, until it lay heavy and engorged between her buttocks.

Cam growled into her ear, "I'm going to fuck you now, baby. And you're going to love it. And you're going to come for me again."

"Yes," she whispered as he slid the tip of his cock between her spread thighs and into her opening.

She tried to push against it, to take more of it. But he wouldn't let her.

"You're not the one in control here, Jillian. Are you?"

She took a deep breath. "No, Cam."

"That's better."

He slid in another half inch. Her sex contracted, grew wet again. He slid out, until just the tip remained. She felt his hands on her ass. He spread her ass cheeks apart, slid his thumbs down, and spread the lips of her sex wide. She'd never felt so exposed, with her ass in the air, her sex wide open. And the idea of it made her even wetter. She wanted to squirm, could barely hold still. But she would do whatever Cam told her to do.

"You have the most beautiful pussy in the world, honey. It's so fucking hot. So wet and pink. Makes me want to put my mouth there. To lick you until you come again. But right now I need to fuck you hard."

With that he slid home. Shoving the length of his cock inside her, he filled her almost to bursting. And then he began to move. He thrust into her, his hips pistoning in and out. There was no mercy. He fucked her hard, just as he said he would.

Her inner walls gripped his engorged cock with each thrust. She shoved her hips back against him, taking him all in. It hurt. It felt good.

She pulled against her restraints, but they held her tightly in the safety of the rope's embrace. And all the time Cam was fucking her, fucking her, until she thought she was going to come apart. And when she came, it was an explosion that ripped through her, singeing her sex, her entire body, with the heat of it.

And then Cam was coming, too. His body went rigid all over. He yelled her name. And went limp against her.

CHAPTER FOUR

SUNDAY MORNING. SUNLIGHT STREAMED THROUGH the tall windows, casting a warm golden gleam across the hardwood floors. Jillian could smell the rich, acrid scent of coffee drifting up from downstairs.

She stretched out on the big bed, wishing Cam were still there with her. Glancing at the clock, she was surprised to see it was almost eleven. She never slept this late. She supposed the fact that Cam had kept her in bed all weekend might have something to do with it.

Her sex was raw and aching, her arms and legs a bit stiff. Her ass was sore as hell. But she'd never felt better in her life. Well-used. Well-loved.

Why was it that Cam spanking her, hurting her, made her feel his love for her in a way she never had before? Why did it help her to comprehend the depth of her own feelings for him? She didn't understand it.

"Morning, sleepyhead."

She smiled as her incredibly sexy husband came into the room with a pair of coffee mugs clenched in one big fist. He was wearing only a pair of striped pajama bottoms and a half-cocked smile. Her eyes roved over his tight, defined abs, his broad shoulders, the tattoo circling the bulge of his biceps. God, he was something. She never tired of looking at him. Well, except for that year of numbness she was just coming out of. He sat on the bed and handed her a cup: plenty of cream and sugar, exactly the way she liked it.

"Just in time," she told him. "I was beginning to miss you."

He leaned over and brushed a coffee-scented kiss across her lips. Then he sat back and grinned. "I've created a monster."

"Yes, you have."

"My little nymphomaniac is going to have to wait."

"Have I worn you out already?"

"Never. But I got a call from Tom this morning. I have to fly to Chicago to oversee a job there."

"There's no one else who can go?"

"Sorry, honey, but I headed up this project. It has to be me."

Jillian sighed. She'd counted on having the rest of the weekend. "How soon do you have to leave?"

"I just booked a three o'clock flight."

"You already took a shower," she stated, taking in his wet hair, the fresh, soapy scent of him.

"Yes, but I still have to pack."

"I'll help you. We can have you out the door in half an hour."

"I don't need to leave for an hour."

She set her coffee down on the nightstand, took his and did the same. "Then hurry up and come here."

Cam grinned. "Getting a little bossy, my girl?"

But he leaned over and drew the sheet from her body, kissed the tip of one breast, then sucked her nipple into his mouth. She arched against him. The heat of his wet, sucking mouth shot straight to her sex.

"I learned it from you."

He chuckled against her skin, dipped his head lower, trailing hot, wet kisses down her stomach. Spreading her thighs with his strong hands, he moved lower still. He gave her clit one long, slow lick, bringing it to life. "I guess I'm not in that much of a hurry."

❧

Jillian balanced the box of sushi on one arm and knocked on the door of Briana's condo with the other. She heard scuffling from inside, then Briana called out.

"Come in! It's open!"

She swung the door open and was greeted by Briana's cat, Van Gogh, an enormous long-haired tabby with most of one ear missing. He must have smelled the sushi, Jillian thought, grinning down at the old tom.

Briana sat on the overstuffed dark red velvet couch with her bad leg on a pillow. "You went by Sushi to Dai For! You are my best friend!"

"I thought I already was your best friend." Jillian set the box on the heavy Indonesian wood coffee table, then went to the small kitchen in search of plates, which she found easily. Briana's place had been her home-away-from-home since the two had met, especially whenever Cam was out of town.

She returned to the living room laden with plates, napkins, and two pairs of black-lacquered chopsticks. She moved Van Gogh's furry bulk off the couch and sat down to prepare their plates.

"I got some yellowtail for you. And some California rolls."

"Mmm, my favorites!" Briana flipped her long, dark braid over her shoulder and grabbed for her plate.

They chatted through dinner about work, mostly. After the meal they sat on the sofa, sipping the Chardonnay Jillian had found in Briana's fridge.

"So," her friend started, "when are you going to tell me about this supernatural glow of yours?"

Jillian laughed. "What?"

"Oh, come on, Jillie. You're lit up like a firefly, yet you sat here eating and gossiping about the gallery like everything was perfectly normal. Fess up, girl."

Jillian's cheeks went warm. Was it really that obvious? She tried for a casual tone. "Like I said on the phone, things have been really great with Cam."

"It's clearly not as simple as that, and I know you're dying to tell. You're a girl. We can't go through anything, good or bad, without wanting to share it with our girlfriends. It's genetic."

"This is . . . really personal."

"Ooh, even better!"

"Have I ever told you you're incorrigible?"

"All the time. Now spill."

"Bri, I don't know if I can talk about this."

"Okay, sorry. I'll stop kidding around. I can see it's more than that you guys have started having sex again."

"It's a lot more. I don't even know where to begin." Jillian took a sip of her wine, letting it cool her suddenly dry throat. "You're right, though. I do need to talk about it. And you're definitely the only person, other than Cam, I can trust with this."

"You go ahead, honey. I'll shut up and just listen." Briana's big hazel eyes sobered.

Jillian chewed on her lip. "Well, have you ever done anything . . . a little kinky?"

"Please. This is me. But, how kinky are we talking?"

"Um . . . how about bondage?"

"Really." Briana's generous mouth spread into a slow grin and her brows arched.

Jillian's cheeks fired. "Bri. Please."

"You just took me by surprise. But no, I've never tried bondage. Not that it hasn't crossed my mind a time or two. But I think you need to do that with someone you really trust."

"Exactly. That's what it's all about for us. Rebuilding our trust."

"And how's it going?"

"Good, I think. I just feel so . . . so different. Like we've discovered each other again. We're so much closer already. I feel like I can really count on Cam. Not that there was ever a time when I couldn't. But things were really rough after . . . after the baby."

Briana reached out and put a hand on her arm. "I know, honey."

"The last year has been kind of a blur for me. I mean, I

go to work every day, function pretty well, do my thing. I come home at night. I cook dinner. We watch a little television. But it's all felt so empty. Even when we were sitting right next to each other, there was no cuddling. No hand-holding. And that was my fault. I pushed him away." Tears stung her eyes, but it was good to talk about it, to get it out of her system.

"Poor Cam. He's been so patient with me. I thought he was nuts when he suggested this. But therapy was a disaster, and it got to the point where I knew we had to do something, or our marriage was going to be over. And I really love him, Bri. I couldn't let that happen."

Briana made a comforting cooing sound.

"So . . . there we were the other night. I was scared but excited, too. And when it all began, I panicked a little, but I got through it. It felt too good from the start. And it's been this . . . I don't know. Like a journey. And I'm figuring things out as I go. Does that make sense?"

"Absolutely. I think we can learn a lot about ourselves when we operate from that sort of primal place."

"Exactly. And the sex is nothing short of amazing."

"I could see that much on your face." Briana was grinning again.

"God, am I walking around with a sign on my forehead, or what?"

"Yeah, kind of. But don't sweat it. It sounds like what's happening with you guys is more important than everyone around you wondering what you've been up to. Let them wonder."

Jillian leaned in to hug her friend. "You're good for me."

"You know I love you, Jillie. And I'm so glad to see you feeling better." Briana released her and settled back onto the pillows. "So, what did you bring for dessert?"

❧

"Did you get everything on the list I gave you?" Cam's deep voice came over the phone.

"Yes." Her body surged with lust remembering her trip to a local sex toy shop earlier that day.

"Good girl."

As always, those words sent a shiver of pleasure through her system.

"First, put me on speaker phone. I want both of your hands free. Then I want you to strip. I want you completely naked. Then go sit on the chair in front of your big vanity mirror. And take everything I asked you to buy and set it on the vanity."

It only took her a minute to get undressed and sit, as Cam had instructed her.

"I'm ready, Cam."

Already an odd calmness was seeping through her body, a lambent, sexual buzzing that made her feel excited, yet serene at the same time.

"Spread your legs open so you can see yourself in the mirror. I want you to be able to see your pussy. The mirror is low enough. Can you see?"

"Yes." She was surprised that the sight of her own sex was exciting to her, but it was.

"Now spread your lips open with your fingers. And tell me what you see. What you feel."

God, could she do this? If she stopped to think about it, maybe not. But she was on fire already, just from the sound of Cam's disembodied voice in their bedroom.

"I can see . . . the pink folds." She took in a deep breath.

"Go on, Jillian."

"And . . . and my clit is swelling up already."

"Are you wet, Jillian?"

"Yes!" Her voice was a quiet hiss in her ears.

"Good. I could tell you were, just by the sound of your voice. Do you know how exciting it is to hear you all out of breath like that? I love to know you're turned on. But I want you more turned on. I'm going to make you come for me. And you're going to do it. You're going to do everything I ask. And you're going to love it."

Her sex contracted at his words. At the idea of what might be happening next. Her fingers were wet with her own juices already.

"Now pick up the vibrator and turn it on. Just touch the tip of your clit with it."

She did as he asked. Holding the folds of her sex open with one hand, she used the other to grab the vibrator, turned the dial, and touched it to the hard, throbbing nub there. A bolt of pleasure shot through her.

"Oh!"

"Feel good, honey? I knew it would. Now hold it there. Let it vibrate against your clit. How does it feel?"

"Oh, God," was all she could get out as the vibration rocked her, drove deep into the core of her sex.

"How good? Are you about to come?"

"Yes!"

"Then stop."

Stop? He had to be kidding. But nothing in his firm tone allowed her to think she should do anything other than obey. She pulled the vibrator away, leaving her breathless and shaking at the edge of orgasm.

"Take out the clamps."

With trembling hands she set the vibrator down on the vanity and picked up the small metal clamps. They were attached by a short chain running between them.

"Put them on."

She pinched her right nipple between her fingers and tugged. It felt so good. Her whole body was burning with lust. And suddenly she craved more than anything to have those wicked little clamps pinching her nipples.

She applied the clamp and gasped as it bit into her rigid flesh. That sharp pinch dove straight for her sex. She was soaking wet now and barely able to hold still in the chair.

"Sounds like you've got it on. Now adjust the screws. Tighten it as much as you can. How does it feel?"

She twisted the screw a bit. "It hurts. Oh, God. It hurts, but it feels good."

"I knew you'd love it, baby. Now do the other one."

She obeyed. The clamps in place and tightened, her nipples burned with pain, and a sharp, stabbing pleasure she'd never felt before. Her entire body felt hot and shaky. And her nipples were absolutely screaming with sensation.

"Okay, baby?"

"Yes . . . yes, I think so."

"Just breathe into the pain. Long, deep breaths."

She pulled in a lungful of air, then another. It helped to steady her.

"Now I want you to use the vibrator again. I want you to cover the tip of it in lube. And I want you to rub some lube over your pussy."

With shaking hands she managed to coat the pink phallus in lube, then she smoothed some over her fingers. She touched her sex with her lubed fingers, rubbed over her whole mound. It felt incredible. She could hardly wait to use the vibrator.

"Now, Cam?"

"Now."

She turned the vibe on, let it hover over her waiting sex for a moment, teasing herself. Then she touched it to her swollen lips, lightly. The buzzing rocked through her body, making her more aware of the clamps on her tits. They ached with heat and pain. She wanted more.

"Move the vibrator over your pussy, baby," Cam told her. "Tease yourself a little for me. Run it over your pussy lips, your clit. But don't let yourself come yet."

She followed Cam's directions, watching herself in the mirror as she slid the vibrator over her outer lips, spread them apart to tease her inner lips, then back up to touch the hard and swollen nub peeking out. She thought she'd die of pleasure. It was almost too much. Her burning nipples, the vibe between her thighs, and the sight of her sex spread wide open, almost dripping with her own damp heat. She wanted to watch as she slipped the vibrator inside herself, into that small pink opening.

"Now sit back in the chair and spread your legs wide. And push the vibe inside."

Yes!

She leaned into the back of the chair, lifted one leg and rested her foot on the edge of the vanity, opening herself up wider. And then she watched in the mirror as she slid the vibrator into her wet hole, one slow inch at a time.

She'd never felt anything like it before. Her body was quivering from deep inside. And she loved seeing the vibrator buried inside her. Again, she trembled on the edge of orgasm.

"I don't think I can wait, Cam!" she gasped.

"Then come for me, honey."

"Yes!"

She angled the vibrator so that it hit her g-spot. And her orgasm swept over her in a swift tide of pleasure, while her nipples screamed in pain, making it even better. She used her free hand to rub her clit hard, heightening the orgasmic waves thundering through her. She moved the vibrator in and out, thrusting deep into her sex while it convulsed around the rigid shaft.

She came and came; it seemed to go on forever, the vibrator and her hand driving her climax on mercilessly. And when it was over, she slipped the vibrator out and collapsed in the chair, breathing hard.

"Good girl."

Even now those words, his deep, sexy voice, caused a shiver of pleasure to run down her spine.

"That was good, wasn't it, baby?"

"Oh, God, yes!"

"And it'll be even better in a few days when I get home. Now take the clamps off. Be careful and do it slowly. You'll get a rush of pain as you take them off. Give yourself a minute to catch your breath after the first one. Your nipples will be sore for a while. Then get into bed and sleep."

"I love you, Cam."

"I love you, too, honey. You know I do. Now go to sleep. And dream about me, Jillian. Dream about all the things I'm going to do to you when I get home."

They hung up.

Removing the clamps hurt worse than putting them on had, making her suck in a sharp breath, but still she reveled in the pain. It was all too good.

She went to bed and slept, dreaming about what Cam would do to her with their new toys, about the pleasure he would bring her. About the oddly lovely pain. Just as she had been instructed.

❧

Cam's return home was delayed an extra day. Jillian missed him, but more than that, it gave her too much time to think. While he'd kept her in a state of intense arousal, she'd been able to turn her brain off. But now she was home from work, with nothing to do. She sat in the living room with a glass of white wine in her hand, staring through the tall windows into the night.

Cam had designed this house himself, and Jillian had always loved it. It was more glass than it was solid walls, letting the outside in. There were fireplaces everywhere: The living-room hearth was two-sided, with the other side opening into the dining room; there was one in the master bedroom, another small one in the master bath.

The house was sleek modernity at its best, with hardwood floors that warmed up the bold architectural lines. They had decorated together, choosing simple, contemporary furnishings and neutral tones with splashes of bold colors here and there, giving the place a Zen feel.

It had always felt peaceful to her, serene. But tonight it just felt lonely. Too big. And all that glass made her feel that the world could too easily intrude.

She leaned into the dozens of Moroccan-inspired throw pillows on the long, L-shaped, tan suede sofa and pulled a handwoven blanket over her. The skylight overhead showed the faint twinkle of stars through the thin sheen of fog in the sky. Seattle was almost always fogged in, often making her wonder why Cam had bothered to build the skylights here, as well as in the dining room and their bedroom. But it was part of his idea of letting everything in, of building with as few boundaries between the inside and the outside as possible.

Boundaries. She was having some trouble with that tonight. Now that she had a span of time when she wasn't being stimulated, when her sex drive wasn't in control, she had some time to think things through. For a while it had been fine just to go along with what was happening. After all, she and Cam were much closer than they'd been in a very long time, and that was good. But she had to stop, finally, and question what they were doing.

The whole power play thing was pretty intense. Potent. And all-consuming while it was happening. It shut out the outside world just as effectively as Cam's glass house let it in. But was that really for the best? She had certainly needed a break from all her thinking, from the guilt that ate away at her insides day in and day out. From her whole head trip that had caused such a rift between her and her husband.

A shard of guilt stabbed through her. She knew it was all her fault. Cam didn't deserve what he'd had to put up with this last year. She'd been so distant—physically, emotionally, sexually. Even when they'd had sex, she was always at a distance in her head, and she knew he could feel that she wasn't really there with him.

The BDSM stuff had certainly changed that. And she was glad for Cam. Glad for herself. But was it really going to fix them? Was it really going to fix her? She wasn't even sure she was fixable.

She was learning to trust her body again, the body that had betrayed her so deeply when it had let go of their baby. God, it was all a tangle in her mind. Her body, her grief.

Her culpability.

Tears stung at the back of her eyes and she took a big sip of her wine to ease the constriction in her throat.

No, too much to think about now.

But when was she going to think about it? Every time she started, she got to this point and had to stop. It was too much. Too much to think about and far too much to feel. That whole line of thought reeked of the horrendous self-pity she had sunk into right after she'd lost their baby.

Too much, too much. Stop.

She bit down on her lip, hard. She had to try to make this new beginning with Cam. They had to make this work. It was time to get her act together and begin to live again. For Cam. For herself.

She wasn't as certain about how to move beyond her doubts and fears when it came to the whole dominant/submissive thing. She couldn't push the questions about whether or not this was normal out of her mind. She wasn't ready to quit, necessarily. She just needed help getting her head around it.

She fell asleep on the sofa, her eyes on the stars glimmering through the skylight, her thoughts a tangled mess of old despair and new hope.

CHAPTER FIVE

THE ALVINA KRAMER SHOWING AT JILLIAN'S gallery had consumed every moment of her attention for weeks. Alvina was a new artist, but she was already internationally known. The only reason the Leighton Gallery had even been able to get her was because she lived in Seattle. Her fame had gone to her head, unfortunately, and "La Kramer," as the gallery folk had taken to calling her, was behaving in classic prima donna manner. She'd been driving Jillian and her staff crazy for over a month already.

Finally the day arrived and Jillian was looking forward to having it over with. She spent the morning checking in with the caterers, having her staff make adjustments to the lighting. She wanted every detail to be perfect. Briana stuck by her side all afternoon, seeing that Jillian's instructions were carried out by the staff. Finally, an hour before the opening, it was just the two of them in Jillian's loft office. Jillian stood by her desk, running her gaze down the list on her clipboard.

"I think everything is ready to go. Why don't you take a breather before you change, Jillie?"

"What? I'm fine. I want to get ready and do some last minute spot-checking."

"Everything is done. I've already checked everything myself. Maybe you should have a glass of wine."

Jillian looked up from the pile of notes on her desk. "Why? You know I never drink at these things."

"You just seem a little more . . . tense than usual."

Jillian sat back in her chair and exhaled a long breath. "Sorry, Bri. I've just had so much on my mind."

"I know this artist has been a real pain in the ass—"

"No, it's not that. I mean, that hasn't been helping, believe me. I'm ready to throttle that woman. It's just . . . me."

Briana sat down in the chair across from her. "What do you mean? What's up? I thought things were great with you and Cam."

Jillian pushed her hair away from her face. "God, I don't know, Bri. Everything was good, but suddenly I'm questioning it. I'm questioning everything. I mean, is what we're doing really right?"

"Why not? You're two consenting adults. Nobody's getting hurt. I don't see the problem."

"It's a lot more complicated than that."

"Then why don't you tell me?"

"I'm not sure I can." She paused, trying to gather the thoughts that seemed to be whirling through her brain at a million miles an hour. "It's like, life was good, you know? Everything was fine, and then I got pregnant." She made herself stop there for a moment, not wanting to reveal the one secret she'd never admitted to anybody. She took a deep breath and tried again.

"Then I lost the baby. And at five months I was showing and everyone knew. When I came back to work, everyone wanted to know what had happened, but nobody came up to me and asked. They just stared at me. Like they expected me to fall apart at any moment. What they didn't know was that I was falling apart all the time on the inside. I lived like that, in a constant state of falling apart."

"I know, honey. I tried to buffer you here at work as much as I could."

"I know you did. But the thing was, no matter what anyone else did, I still had to deal with what had happened. And it drove such a wedge between Cam and me. I couldn't seem to stop it. And now things seem to be getting better, but I don't know how real it all is."

"If it seems to be getting better, than it just *is*, Jillie."

"No, I don't think so. I mean, maybe. But maybe it's all on the surface."

"Let me ask you something. You don't have to answer if it makes you uncomfortable, okay?"

Jillian nodded for Briana to continue.

"When you two are having sex, do you ever have one of those moments when you look into his eyes and feel totally and utterly connected?"

"Yes. It's been happening a lot lately."

"Well, I don't think you can fake that. I don't mean fake as in pretending. But that just does not happen unless it's real."

"I know you're right. I think I know it. Maybe I just

worry too much. And this last week has been out of control with Alvina always on my back. Maybe after tonight I'll feel better."

"I know I will. Lord, that woman is a nightmare!"

"She is." Jillian had to smile. It was always so much better to suffer with a friend, and poor Briana had been putting up with "La Kramer's" crap as much as she had.

Briana grinned and grabbed the clipboard out of Jillian's hand. "Okay, chicks, let's get this party started. You brought that hot little red dress with you, didn't you?"

⊘

The lighting was flawless. The crowd was beautiful. The music was muted, filtering over the hushed conversation as people walked around looking at the enormous bronze sculptures set throughout the gallery.

"La Kramer" was dressed in a flowing golden robe, like ancient royalty, her long flaming red curls a sharp contrast against her pale and overly made-up face. She held court in one corner, alternately laughing and glowering at the crowd of admirers surrounding her.

It seemed to be going well. Only an hour into the show and the small red "Sold" stickers were already posted on almost half of the pieces. The artist would be pleased.

By the time Cam arrived she was able to relax a little, knowing the show was a success. He stood just inside the doors of the gallery, looking around. For her, probably. God, he looked good, she thought as she made her way across the crowded room toward him. In his black pants, black shirt, and black leather jacket, he was all dark, mysterious male beauty. Always a little bit of the bad boy about him, which she loved. Finally he spotted her, and his killer smile made her go warm all over.

She swung into his arms and kissed him. His lips were cool from being outside in the chilly evening air.

"Hi."

"Hi, baby."

She leaned in and whispered into his ear, "I'm sorry if I've been a little tense lately with this show coming up."

"That's okay. I'll make you pay for it later."

When she pulled her head back he had a perfectly wicked smile on his face, and she had no doubt he meant it. A small thrill went through her.

"Come on. Let's get you a glass of champagne and come say hi to Briana."

For the next couple of hours Jillian was kept busy playing hostess, flitting from group to group, occasionally checking on her artist. The evening was a huge success and even "La Kramer" couldn't find anything to complain about.

Finally Gianni, one of her assistants, sidled up next to Jillian and whispered, "The last piece just sold. It's all socializing for the rest of the night."

"Thanks, Gianni. That's wonderful."

Jillian grabbed her first glass of champagne from a passing waiter. She could relax now. Her staff was good; they'd make sure everyone was kept happy and had whatever they needed.

She looked around the room for Cam. Now that her duties were over, she could spend some time with her husband. She spotted him at one end of the room, talking to a group of people. As though he felt her stare, he looked up, caught her eye. She motioned with her head and smiled, and he left his group and came to her.

"How's it going, honey? Good turnout, it looks like."

"A great turnout. We sold everything."

"Ah, hence the celebratory glass in your hand."

Jillian smiled and took a sip. "Yes. Plus, it's the only thing that'll kill the pain of these shoes. I've been in heels all night and my feet are killing me."

Cam moved closer and brushed his fingertips over her cheek. "Poor baby. I have just the cure for that."

"A good foot rub?"

"Hmmm, maybe," he growled in her ear. "But I had something else in mind."

"Since we're standing in the middle of the gallery in a large group of people, I think your cure is going to have to wait."

He moved his hand over her back. The plunging lines of her dark red cocktail dress left her back bare all the way down to the base of her spine. His hand was warm as it slid over her skin, leaving a trail of sensual tingling in its wake.

His head moved back to her ear again, and she could feel the warmth of his breath there. "Come up to your office with me."

"I can't." But something about the way he was touching her, his breath in her ear, was making her hot all over.

"Come on, honey. They don't need you here anymore. And I do need you."

"Cam—"

"I've never fucked you on your desk before, have I? I'd really like to bend you over and spank you as I fuck you from behind."

A warm shiver started deep inside her. Her legs went a little weak. She couldn't speak.

"Don't think about it. Just do it. Follow me."

Cam took her by the arm, and she kept a small smile plastered on her face as she let him lead her through the room and up the stairs. She couldn't get the image he'd created out of her mind. Bent over her desk, just as he'd said. Her dress hiked up around her waist. Cam behind her with his big cock ready to thrust into her.

Yes.

In her office Cam turned one small lamp on and locked the door. He held her arm and guided her to the front of her wide glass desk.

"Bend over it, Jillian. Do it."

God, she loved that commanding tone. She bent over, settling her elbows on the desk, knowing her short, red dress would pull taut over her ass, and her high heels made her legs look great.

Cam came up behind her and hitched her dress up around her waist, just as she'd imagined he would. She felt the cool air hit her bare thighs and buttocks. She was wearing a G-string, which didn't cover much.

"Beautiful, baby," Cam crooned, sliding his hands over her ass.

She was excited even before the first small slap landed. But at that first stinging contact her sex convulsed and she was instantly soaking wet.

Cam smacked her again, harder this time, and she absorbed the sharp thrum of it. She wanted him to do it harder.

He began a series of slaps, playing them over first one cheek, and then the other. The blood rushed to the surface of her skin, which grew hot and tingling. He sped up his rhythm, spanking harder, and she squirmed her hips as pleasure poured through her. She pressed her breasts into the cool glass surface of her desk, needing to rub her full, aching nipples against something. And still, Cam's blows landed on her smarting ass, one after another.

When she thought she couldn't stand not to be touched anymore, he pulled the small scrap of her G-string aside and pushed a few fingers into her. God, it felt good! She moved back against him, trying to take more inside.

And still he kept working on her ass and down the back of her thighs, the slaps coming harder and harder, his fingers thrusting inside her. And then he stopped.

"Cam," she breathed.

"Wait," he commanded.

She spent one long, panting moment while she heard him unzip his pants. Then the head of his engorged cock was rubbing up against her swollen lips.

"Spread your legs apart for me."

She did as he asked. And then his cock slipped inside, and with one hard thrust, he shoved it all the way to the hilt.

She had to bite her lip to keep from crying out. He was so damn big and it hurt. But it also felt so damn good. She moved against him, wanting more, no matter how hard it was to take.

Cam moved inside her, sliding in and out. The walls of her sex clenched around the heavy length of him. She could feel every ridge of his shaft, every delicious detail of him. And each thrust brought an exquisite pang of painful pleasure.

Cam threaded a hand in her hair and gripped hard, kept on spanking her with the other. She loved the feel of his hand in her hair. Loved the way he held her head so tightly, so possessively. And all the while his enormous cock filling her to the brim, pushing and pulling at her insides. At this angle, the head of his cock had full access to her g-spot, rubbing right against it. That and his hard, fast slaps were creating an incredible combination of sensations. Her ass burned, her sex burned. The two sensations joined together, fused, set her body on fire.

The first tremors of orgasm shook her system. And when Cam started plunging into her wildly, then sunk his teeth into the back of her neck, it sent her right over the edge. Her sex exploded with searing heat, the shockwaves roaring through her body. She cried out. Cam growled in her ear, and she felt the hot spurt of his come inside her.

His big body collapsed on top of her, and only the desk supported her quaking legs.

"God, that was fucking fantastic, baby." Cam's breath was coming in short pants.

"Mmm." Her mind was still numb and her body hummed with the aftermath of pleasure.

Cam levered himself off her, helped her over to the sofa. They lounged there, with her draped across his lap, catching their breath.

"So, honey," Cam said after several minutes.

"Hmmm, what?"

"I had a thought."

"About what?"

"I found this place on the Internet. It's a place where people go to play. A dungeon."

Jillian laughed. "A dungeon? They really call it that?"

"Yeah."

"So they have rooms with what . . . racks and chains and stuff?"

"Yeah, sort of. From what I could see, it's just one big room."

"You mean there's no privacy?" Jillian didn't think she liked the sound of this.

"There are different areas where people play. And other people watch. I'd really like to go. For us both to go."

"I don't know, Cam. It all sounds pretty serious to me."

"It might be interesting. To watch what other people do, you know?"

"I don't need to see other people having sex." She wasn't liking this at all.

"It's not sex. They don't do that there. It's just bondage, BDSM play."

Well, that was a little better. Maybe. But she still didn't like the idea of taking it that far. BDSM was just something they were playing around with, wasn't it?

"I still don't know, Cam."

"Just think about it, okay? For me?"

She sighed. "I'll think about it."

"Good girl."

For once, those words did nothing to warm her.

A busy week passed quickly, but when Friday night came, Cam brought up the dungeon again while they were finishing a late dinner at the small table in the kitchen.

"There's a discussion group tomorrow night I'd like to go to," he said nonchalantly, draining his wineglass.

"What kind of discussion group?"

"It's at that dungeon I told you about."

Jillian's stomach tightened. "Oh." She paused. "Cam, I don't think we're ready for this."

"I'm ready for it. Look, it's just a discussion group. Nobody will be playing or anything. Come on, baby. I really want to do this."

Obviously he did. But why was he pushing so hard? Was he beginning to become obsessed with this BDSM thing? Sure, she'd been enjoying it, but why did they have to get so extreme about it? She wasn't sure she liked where Cam seemed to be going with this.

She played with her fork, pushing the remains of her meal around on her plate. "I don't know . . ."

"Just give it a try. If you're really uncomfortable, we'll leave. Okay?"

He sounded so reasonable, and he wasn't leaving her much room for argument. As long as she had an out, she supposed it wouldn't hurt to just go and listen.

"Okay."

Cam leaned over and gave her cheek a quick kiss. "You're the best. I love you, Jillian."

She groaned. What in the world had she just agreed to?

The place was called The Underground. True to its name, it was in the basement of an industrial building down-town. They parked, and Cam directed her to a dark purple door set into a long concrete wall. There was no sign say-ing what was behind that door. Just the door and a huge bouncer type of guy standing out front. Cam handed him an invitation he'd printed from the dungeon's Web site, and the bouncer let them in. Not a word had been ex-changed.

"That was a little creepy," Jillian whispered to Cam as he led her down an interior flight of concrete stairs.

He gave her arm a reassuring squeeze. They ap-proached another pair of purple doors. Cam pulled a door open and music flooded out, the same light trance tones of Enigma she and Cam listened to while playing. Inside, the place was lit with dim red and purple lights. It took a few moments for her eyes to adjust. She was surprised to see that they were standing in front of a normal-looking re-ception desk. A plump woman in a red leather corset sat behind it. Jillian guessed her to be in her forties. She looked like she could be anybody. A teacher, a banker. Somebody's mother.

"Hi, there," the woman said in a perky tone. "You must be here for the discussion group. Just go to the chairs at the back of the room and take a seat. Enjoy." She smiled warmly.

They passed behind the table and Jillian tried not to goggle at what she saw.

The place was mostly empty, with just three men in black leather vests who seemed to be cleaning and testing equipment. Everywhere Jillian looked were giant wooden crosses, a pair of big, boxy wooden frames with eye hooks set into the tops and sides that she imagined were for some sort of bondage. There were several metal cages on the floor in various shapes and sizes. Long lengths of chain hung from the ceiling here and there, some with leather cuffs dangling from the ends. In different corners were benches and tables covered in what looked to be leather, or maybe vinyl. There were several items she couldn't identify.

The floor was covered in a dark red carpet and the walls were painted black. As Cam led her across the center of the dungeon, Jillian felt incredibly vulnerable in this strange place.

At the back of the room was a half-circle of folding chairs surrounding a low stage. Several people already sat there. One heavily carved wooden chair with a plush red velvet seat sat empty directly in front of the stage.

"What do you think?" Cam asked her once they were seated.

"It's a little overwhelming."

"I think it's awesome."

Obviously Cam wasn't nervous about this at all. He was excited. She wished he wasn't so into this. Just being here was making her feel shaky inside, an odd combination of nerves and what she could only identify as sexual excitement. She didn't like that it excited her, but she couldn't help it.

More people filed in and filled up the remaining

chairs. After a few minutes a couple stepped onto the stage and the music stopped. The sudden silence was a small shock in itself, leaving Jillian's ear's buzzing.

The couple looked to be about her age. The man was tall and thin, with a dark, close-shaved goatee. The woman was tiny beside him. Her dark skin glowed beneath the stage lights. They were both dressed in black, with the man in dark jeans and a leather vest. The woman was dressed much as Jillian was, in a short black skirt and a lace top. But she wore a thick leather collar around her neck, set with metal rings, and boots that buckled all the way up to her knees, with such impossibly high heels Jillian wondered why she didn't just topple over.

The man came to the center of the stage and said in a deep, booming voice, "Welcome to our play space. Our learning space. Our place to explore ecstasy unknown in any other walk of life. Welcome to The Underground."

CHAPTER SIX

CAM FELT JILLIAN SHIVER BESIDE HIM AS THE man onstage began to talk. He slid an arm around her shoulder and focused on the speaker.

"I'm Vincent. This is my girl, my submissive, my slave, Nya." The petite raven-haired beauty with the smooth coffee-colored skin nodded and smiled.

Vincent stepped off the stage, then helped Nya to do the same. He settled into the big wooden chair. Nya knelt at his feet and he laid a hand on the back of her neck. It was a proprietary gesture, yet tender at the same time. It was something Cam understood very well, that feeling of treasuring his woman.

Cam glanced at Jillian, but she sat quietly staring straight ahead, her face an unreadable mask. He turned back to tune in on the discussion.

"Here at The Underground, we feel that submission is a gift given willingly and with love. It should be accepted as such. Our slaves and bottoms are to be played with, tortured, titillated, beaten, but always with love, and with their safety and well-being in mind."

Vincent spoke for a few minutes about the dungeon's play party rules. All Cam could think about was getting started. Without being too obvious about it, he glimpsed some of the play equipment from the corners of his eyes. He could imagine strapping Jillian down to one of the leather-clad tables, cuffing her wrists and ankles to the corners.

They didn't allow sex at the club, so playing here would only be a prelude. Not a problem. He could control himself; he had no doubt of that. The self-control was part of it, and something he wanted to explore further. Since they'd always played in private so far, he'd never had to think about it much. This would be good for him, make him stronger.

Vincent was still talking. "As a top, it is your responsibility to see to it that your sub is well cared for. Not only physically, but emotionally."

Cam liked that theory. Ever since Jillian had begun to submit to him sexually, he'd felt even more protective of her. She seemed somehow more precious to him than she had before. He was liking the whole idea better and better, and he hoped Jillian would learn to like it, too.

Cam slipped an arm around Jillian's slender waist and asked her quietly, "What do you think?"

"Well, I'm not sure. I mean, they sound very organized."

He nodded. "That was one of the things I liked about what I saw on the Web site. They seem to keep everything under control. I think that's important. But I was talking more about the idea of playing here."

Jillian bit her lip. "I don't know. It's all so . . . strange to me."

"Yeah, me too, but that's part of the attraction, I've got to admit."

Even during this quiet discussion, a sense of hushed expectancy filled the air. And the vibe was distinctly sexual. His pulse raced in his veins, his heart thudded in his chest. He loved it already.

How the hell had Cam talked her into going to this? Jillian sucked in a long breath. Just being in the place made her feel shaky, but she had to admit it was a surge of sexual excitement as much as it was nerves.

She scanned the faces of the other people there. She was surprised at how normal everyone looked. Some were dressed in black leather gear, but most were wearing casual street clothes, with the occasional collar around someone's neck.

She focused again on Vincent's voice.

"Tonight we're going to talk about the psychology of BDSM. That's right, the psychology. Because this lifestyle is about a lot more than just what we do physically. Most of it, in fact, is about what goes on in our heads.

"A lot of people have trouble in the beginning accepting this side of themselves. Some of you are probably wondering how you can actually like pain, like having your power taken away from you. But the pain *is* pleasure, and as a bottom you don't give anything without your consent. Therein lies your power. It's the power to say yes or no. To give only what you want to give, and because you *do* give, it's not taken away. There is power in the act of submission itself."

Jillian liked that idea. It was a conclusion she'd come to on her own, if not in such a formal manner.

"Some of you may be wondering how you can possibly enjoy hurting anybody. But it's fun." His eyes twinkled and he grinned as most of the group laughed.

"Again, the pain is pleasure. And it's more than that, isn't it?" He paused while a few people nodded in agreement. "It's about the exchange of energy. We feed off it. It's endorphins for the bottoms and adrenaline for the tops. It's chemical. But it's also largely mental. Let's talk about that. Who wants to start?"

A woman with long red hair raised her hand and Vincent nodded at her.

"For me, a big part of it is the preparation. Bathing, making myself pretty. It puts me into that head space. And I can't play without the head space. But the one thing that really puts me there is the collar. All a top has to do is put that collar around my neck and I start to go down. Down into sub space."

God, Jillian knew that feeling, understood exactly what she was talking about! Her body grew warm all over.

The redhead went on. "It's all about symbols for me. And there's something about the formality of it that I love. The collar, the low lights, a commanding tone of voice. It feels . . . ancient, somehow. I get this feeling of participating in something very primal. Very deep. Does that make sense?"

Jillian's limbs went liquid and weak as several people nodded and murmured their agreement with the woman. Yes, she knew exactly what she meant. Maybe part of what frightened her about this was the sensation of falling into that head space, of being helpless against it. It didn't feel safe to be that vulnerable in a public forum like The Underground. But maybe that was part of it, allowing herself to feel vulnerable.

She spoke before she realized what she was doing. "But doesn't that scare you?"

Cam's head whipped around to look at her, his dark eyebrows raised in surprise.

"Maybe. Yes." The redheaded woman shrugged. "But overcoming fear is part of what this is about. For me, anyway."

Overcoming fear. Lord knew that was one thing Jillian needed to work on. Fear about her marriage, about her own body, about her capability to operate as the strong woman she'd always thought herself to be, and now spent so much time doubting.

It had started when she lost the baby. After that, the whole world seemed unsafe. But she was beginning to re-gain a sense of safety. And it was through the BDSM play, because the only time she felt truly safe was in Cam's arms, and even more so when she was bound in the ropes and at his command. When the responsibility for the world, for her own actions, was taken away from her. It was then that she could just *be*. It was then she could allow herself to feel, to be in the moment, without worrying she was going to break down. And even if she did, in those moments, Cam was totally in command, responsible for her. And she felt so utterly treasured by him, she knew he'd take care of her. Not that he hadn't before. But within the BDSM play that surety came through in a way which was defined by the very roles they played. Maybe this was more than a temporary fix, after all?

Her shoulders dropped. She hadn't even realized how tightly she'd been holding them. She reached over and found Cam's hand, wrapped her fingers around it. He smiled at her, that lush, beautiful mouth curving sweetly.

The rest of the discussion passed in a sort of blur. She had so much to think about already. But she was feeling better, calmer. Yet excited at the same time. Even without anything more than discussion going on, a certain air of expectancy lingered in this place. Her gaze drifted to the play equipment set about the room.

Maybe someday . . .

Suddenly, she couldn't wait to get her husband home. Her sex grew damp and she pressed her thighs together.

She didn't want to think anymore. She just wanted to *do*. She wanted Cam to touch her, to tie her up, to spank her, to put the evil little clamps on her nipples, which were springing to attention just thinking about it.

And someday, maybe, she wanted him to do those things to her here.

Oh, God.

Her panties were soaked. She had to leave, had to be alone with him.

"Cam," she whispered to her husband, "I need to go."

He looked at her, his smile fading. "Now?"

"Yes, now." How to communicate her need to him?

She slid her hand from his grasp and brushed it across the front of his slacks. His eyebrows shot up but she'd felt his erection. He leaned in to whisper in her ear. "Are you trying to tell me what I think you are?"

She kept her voice low. "Yes. Now. Please?"

"No problem."

The talk was over, anyway. They stood and quietly made their way to the door while everyone else was still chatting.

They hurried along the dark street to Jillian's car. Cam handed her into the passenger side, then went around the car and got behind the wheel.

"Are you sure about this, honey?"

"I'm sure."

He put the key in and revved the engine. "I guess going to the talk tonight was a good idea."

She nodded, smiling at him.

She watched him shift as he pulled into the street, the way his big hand caressed the stick shift. She wanted that hand on her body, on her breasts, between her legs. She wanted that hand to spank her, pinch her. She could hardly wait. Her pulse hammered in her veins all the way home.

They didn't speak. She figured Cam probably didn't want to risk blowing the mood. She didn't, either. She didn't want to talk about it. She just wanted to do it.

They arrived home and Cam led her into the living room. The amber glass sconce mounted on the wall in the foyer cast a dim glow. Cam took her hand, and when they were in front of the big sofa, he pulled her sweater over her head. He covered her breasts with his hands. She could feel the heat of his palms even through her black satin bra. He squeezed a little, as though testing the fullness of her breasts and she arched into his touch.

"Not yet," he said firmly. He leaned in and kissed her, slipping his hot tongue into her mouth.

He pinched one nipple as he slid his hands away and Jillian could swear she felt it in her sex, as though he'd pinched her there. She shifted, rubbing her thighs together.

"Hold still, Jillian. I'll be right back. I don't want you to move."

That soft, commanding tone again. She loved it. And she did her best to hold still, even with Cam out of the room. It was a strange sensation. Strange in that she found some deep satisfaction in doing exactly as she was told. He came back in a few minutes, his hands full. He emptied the items onto the coffee table, taking a moment to line everything up: a coil of rope, a pair of leather handcuffs she hadn't seen before, the clamps, a small crop. A deep shiver went through her.

Quietly, Cam undressed her, took everything off, until she was standing there naked. The air was cool, but not uncomfortable. She could hear the chirping of crickets outside. There was no other sound but her own heartbeat thundering in her ears.

"Lie facedown on the couch, Jillian."

There was not a single part of her that thought about discussing the issue. She obeyed.

Her mind was going still already. All worries and doubts drifted away as she focused on her body.

The suede of the sofa was soft against her skin. She pushed her breasts into it, savoring the sensation against her erect nipples. But then Cam's hands were on her and that was all she could think about.

He ran his palms over her skin: her back, her buttocks, her thighs. She could feel the heat of his hands on her, the intensity of his energy. Then he slipped a hand between her legs, brushed it across her aching mound.

"You're wet already, baby. You are so fucking hot I can't stand it."

He withdrew his hand, gave her ass a small slap. She arched into it, raising her ass in the air, needing more.

"Ah, in a hurry are you? Don't worry, you'll get exactly what you need." He chuckled softly.

He pulled her arms behind her back, and she felt the strange sensation of the leather cuffs being buckled around her wrists. She could smell the earthy scent of new leather. It made her shiver. The bonds gave her that feeling of safety she so loved. And something else, something about the leather itself, and the fact that these were handcuffs—actual handcuffs. The idea of it was a huge turn-on.

She waited, her whole body buzzing.

The slap came hard, taking her by surprise. And she realized immediately it wasn't his hand, but the crop. She loved the feel of the leather on her skin instantly. Realized she had been craving it since the moment she'd laid eyes on it.

He smacked her again. It stung deliciously. She wanted more.

And Cam gave her more. He began with a few light smacks of the crop, working it in a pattern over her buttocks. She could feel her skin heating up, growing more tender. Yet at the same time each slap of the leather felt better than the last, sending shock waves of pleasure through her system.

The smacks came faster and harder. And with each one her sex filled and ached, even though he hadn't touched her there.

"Do you like it, Jillian?" His voice was a little ragged, husky with lust.

"Yes, Cam."

"Do you want more?"

"Yes!"

"Say please, Jillian."

"Please, Cam. I want more. I need it."

She felt his lips on her as he trailed soft kisses over her heated skin. It was such a lovely contrast to the bite of the crop.

When he pulled his mouth away and the crop came down hard, the sting was incredible. She almost cried out at the pain. But the pain immediately converted to a pleasure that swept her body.

"Tell me what you want." Another hard, loud smack.

"I want more. Please, Cam!"

The leather singed her flesh as he started a volley of hard slaps. She writhed on the couch, pressing her hips into the cushions, her body begging for relief. And still it went on, smack after smack, and nothing but her own rough breathing in her ears. Her mind was going to some far-off place, yet at the same time she was more present in her body, and in the moment, than she'd ever been.

She groaned aloud when he stopped.

Cam grabbed her around the waist, lifted her, and suddenly he was sitting on the sofa and she was draped facedown across his lap. She could feel the hard ridge of his cock pressing into her hip. Her sex gave a convulsive shudder.

He ran his hand over the hot flesh of her buttocks, tracing the welts left by the crop. He said softly, "I'm going to give you the spanking of your life, Jillian."

And then it began. First it was a tapping of his fingertips

against her skin. The gentleness of it was excruciating to her and she squirmed.

"Hold still, Jillian."

But she couldn't; she didn't want to. She wanted more.

He gave her ass a good, hard slap, and she smiled.

When he smacked her again the sting reverberated through her system, making her sex throb and her hips dance. She pushed her buttocks higher into the air, giving Cam access to every inch of her, craving the touch of his big hands. On her ass, on her wet sex.

Cam rubbed his palms over her skin for a moment, and then began again, only this time he didn't stop, didn't pause to let her take a breath. The volley of slaps grew in intensity and speed, and she really started to lose it. Only the awareness of her hot, aching sex kept her anchored in her body. The pain and the pleasure were a sweet mixture that made her whole being thrum with need. She writhed in his lap, wanting, wanting. It was never enough, no matter how much it hurt.

The sting turned to a heavy thud and still he went on, his hands coming down on her, feeling as though they were almost abrading her skin. The sensation was unbelievable, the pain at a point where she almost couldn't bear it, and yet she still loved it, still needed more.

She was dimly aware that her breath had turned to ragged pants, that she was moaning aloud in between. And still the spanking went on.

When she thought she'd die if she couldn't come, just from the pain and the pleasure, Cam reached down with one hand and rolled her clit between his strong fingers. And he didn't stop smacking her with the other hand. The slapping and his fingers working her were too good. The pain from the spanking was sending shock waves through her, straight to her core. Then he gave her swollen clit a good, hard pinch and she went right over the edge, into the most earth-shattering orgasm she'd ever felt in her life. Her sex spasmed, her legs shook, and she screamed something entirely incoherent. Cam kept spanking, kept pinching her, and the waves pounded over her. The harder he pinched, the harder she came, and she didn't ever want it to stop.

Finally, it did. But still he was spanking her, and she found through the lovely postorgasm haze that she wanted him to. Now that she'd come, she focused in on the sharp sting of his hand on her flesh. Over and over his palm smacked her. The pain was exquisite. Hard and beautiful.

She felt light, yet the pain kept her in her body. It was as though she could truly feel in a way she never had before. But it was too good to really think about it.

"God, I love you, baby," Cam said through gritted teeth while he smacked her ass, over and over.

And she felt it, felt his love pouring into her. Tears she didn't understand stung her eyes. And soon she was crying, then sobbing. Cam stopped what he was doing and pulled her upright into his lap, cradling her.

"Baby, baby. Shh," he crooned.

But the tears wouldn't stop. She felt so good all over. Felt *more*, somehow. Physically, emotionally. And it all seemed like too much. The sensations and emotions overwhelmed her and she couldn't stop the tears.

Cam held her tight while she shook in his arms, the sobs wrenching her whole body. All of the pain she'd held inside for far too long came pouring out, and the sobbing turned into hard, wrenching howls until she thought she might choke.

Cam smoothed her hair, whispered to her, but she didn't know what he said. All she knew was the white-hot pain of grief and loss stabbing through her. She couldn't bear it; it was far too awful. It flowed through her limbs, thundered like a hammer in her chest.

She didn't know how long Cam held her shuddering body, how long the tears were wrenched from her. When it was over, she ached everywhere. She felt empty, wrung out, exhausted.

Cam seemed to know she couldn't talk about it. He picked her up, carried her upstairs, put her into their big bed. He lay down beside her, kept his arms around her, held her close. Almost instantly, it seemed, she slept.

❧

Cam woke in the dark to an empty bed. He knew immediately something was very wrong. He felt the stillness in the house even before he went outside to find Jillian's car gone.

No. He would not lose her like this.

It was early, barely six A.M., but he knew where she would be. The sky lit with the pale blush of impending dawn as he drove the route to Briana's place. The streets were silent, lonely, laced with wisps of fog.

Why had he pushed her so hard? He'd thought he was doing it for her own good, for the good of their marriage. But how much of it had been purely for his own desires? And now he'd pushed her away.

He knew she'd had some sort of emotional break-through last night at the end of their play session. He'd read about that happening, and he'd thought he had handled it the right way. But maybe it was simply too much for her. He loved what they'd been doing together. But not more than he loved her. He needed to tell her that.

When he pulled up in front of Briana's, Jillian's car was parked out front.

Briana opened the door at his knock. She was wearing sweats and her hair was mussed, but she didn't look angry. That was a good start, he guessed.

"I need to talk to my wife."

Briana looked away, then swung her gaze back to his. "She asked me not to let you in. But I think she needs you."

He started to move past her, into the house, but she put a hand on his arm. "Cam, she's very fragile right now. Very raw."

He nodded. "I know."

"Okay. She's in my room."

He found her in Briana's bed, wrapped in a white down quilt. A cup of tea sat on the nightstand beside her. He could smell the chamomile and the sweet tang of honey.

Jillian turned her head away from him as he sat down beside her. "I can't talk to you now, Cam."

He could hear the weight of grief in her voice and his heart ached for her.

"I think we need to talk. Right now."

"Please, Cam—"

"No, Jillian. You can't run away from it anymore. That's what this is all about. Don't you see that?"

"All I see is that it hurts too much."

"I know. But it's time to stop hurting. It's time to stop blaming yourself."

Her head whipped around. Her eyes were huge, her lashes damp with tears. "How did you know?"

"It wasn't your fault."

"No. It was my fault. You don't understand why, but it was. And I can't stand to lie to you anymore. I can't stand to be with you and feel everything I'm feeling, finally. I love you too much, and you deserve better." The tears spilled over onto her pale cheeks. She said in a whisper, "I lost the baby because I didn't want it."

The admission was almost too much to bear. The words tore through her chest, into her heart, but she had to say it. Had to say the whole thing out loud.

She looked into Cameron's eyes. They were dark with strain, his brows furrowed. "It was my fault, Cam, because I didn't want the baby."

"What? What do you mean?"

She went on, the words tearing like shards of broken glass as they left her mouth. "I didn't want it. Not at first. We weren't prepared. We hadn't planned on ever having children. After the first three months, when the morning sickness was gone and I'd had some time to accept how much our lives were going to change, I started to really love the baby. But it was too late." Her voice broke on a sob and she pressed a hand to her mouth.

"Oh, my God, Jillian. You have to know that's not true. You've been carrying this around with you this whole time? Jesus." His voice was thick with emotion. "You have to let this go."

She shook her head. "It hurts too much, Cam. Especially now."

"Why now?"

"After . . . after last night. It was as if my whole being just opened up. And everything came pouring out. Good stuff, but the bad stuff, too. It's like I've been split wide open. It was too much, realizing how much I'd hurt you. How much damage I've done. I feel . . . irredeemable."

"Is that why you came here? Why you felt you had to get away?"

The pain in her chest was fierce, burning. "I don't think I can do this anymore, Cam. I don't think I can be with you and feel like this." She began to shake all over.

"No, honey. Don't say that." Cam tried to take her in his arms, but she shook him off. She couldn't stand it if he touched her now.

"Don't pull away. I can't lose you, Jillian. I won't."

He reached for her again, and again she tried to fight, but in a moment his arms were around her and she couldn't get away. She struggled in his grasp, but the tears were starting again, making her weak. It hurt so much! She couldn't bear to feel so much at once. Cam's embrace was too warm. There was too much love there. She couldn't stand what she was doing to him.

He held her tight. "Baby, baby, no. Come on, let me hold you. I love you, Jillian."

She went still in his arms, too tired now to fight. But the tears poured down her face, her mind a mass of confusion.

"We can get through this, honey. You don't have to do this alone anymore. Not if you let me be there with you."

She sniffed, wiped her face with a corner of the quilt. "How can you not hate me?"

"It wasn't your fault. I love you. I love you more than

anything in this world. You didn't lose the baby because you wished it away. You lost it because that was the way it was meant to be. And if it's just the two of us for the rest of our lives, then that's okay. As long as I have you, I have everything."

"You deserve more, Cam. You deserve better."

"I don't want anything but you. If I haven't made you feel that, then that's my fault, not yours." He held her face in his strong, warm hands. "Be with me, Jillian. You're all I want."

She heard the sincerity in his voice. Saw it in his eyes. And something about it made her heart open up, but this time it felt good. She let her body relax and leaned into him. Relief washed over her in a warm tide as his words hit home.

"I thought I had to let you go, Cam."

"Never. We'll never lose each other again. I promise you that."

His gray gaze was more intense than it had ever been, and she saw the pure emotion there. And suddenly she understood.

"You've been carrying some guilt, too."

He looked surprised for a moment, then said simply, "Yes."

"Why?"

"Because I couldn't fix it for you."

"Oh, Cam." She slid a hand around the back of his neck. His skin was warm there. "Nobody else could fix this."

"I know that. But still, it was my responsibility. And I failed."

She could see how hard it was for him to say that, and she knew why. "You're not your father, Cam."

"I'm no better than he was if I let you down."

"But you never did." How was it possible that he thought he had? He'd always been there for her. She was the one who had turned her back on their marriage. And he was the one who kept fighting so hard to get it back. And they had, she realized. Why had she thought it was over?

"Cam, I love you so much."

His tight features softened. "Then come home with me. Let's keep trying. I need you with me, Jillian."

"I need you, too. I can't do this without you. I don't know why I ever thought I could."

He leaned in and kissed her with that lush mouth of his, and the warm safety of his love swept through her. They would get through this. Together. And for some reason, that knowledge made her feel stronger than she had in a long time. Stronger than ever before.

"Let's go home, Cam."

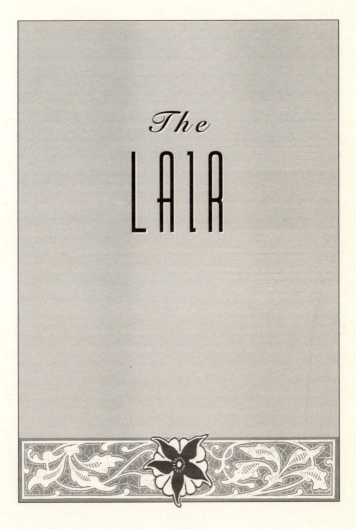

The

LAIR

CHAPTER ONE

THE SUN WAS JUST SETTING IN A BLAZE OF orange and pink flame as Cassandra drove along the Pacific Coast Highway. Her hands tight on the steering wheel, she scanned the street signs, looking for her turnoff into the Pacific Palisades area of the Malibu hills.

There it was, Pacific Crest Road. She made a right turn and wove her way up the narrow, twisting lane. Million-dollar homes up there, with million-dollar views of the ocean. But she wasn't thinking about any of that right now. She was thinking only of why she was there. Of what would happen to her on her first visit to Master Robert's home.

Training house, she corrected herself. Her sex gave an involuntary squeeze.

She flashed back to the first time she'd seen his ad on the Internet site she'd found.

"Experienced trainer looking for a female submissive. If you are new to the BDSM lifestyle and are in need of proper training,

please contact me. Inexperience is an asset, not a liability. References provided upon request. Serious inquiries only."

The ad read like a simple statement of every one of her darkest fantasies. Fantasies she had ever only dared to imagine until now.

The Internet. This was something she had shied away from, believing only perverts (but what, really, was she?) lurked there. But here was someone who understood the kind of deep yearning she so often felt. Someone who could see that inexplicable, aching void that was invisible to the people in her everyday life. She'd felt an immediate sense of community with this stranger whom she'd sensed instantly would know the emptiness inside her, that cavernous hole waiting to be filled up in a way "normal" people could never understand. Someone who accepted that dark place she had kept secret, tightly locked within herself for fear of what others might think.

She knew immediately this man was earnest. The wannabes all had ads saying things like *"Come to Daddy, you bad girl."* This man was the real thing. And exactly what she needed. To be trained; taught. He did not expect her to know anything. She'd felt a strange sense of relief reading his words as her body went warm and weak all over, even as the idea of serving him brought back that old need for perfection. But this time, it would be for him. She would serve him perfectly.

She downshifted and her car climbed as the street steepened. The scent of eucalyptus trees filtered in even through her closed windows.

She'd brought Master Robert's ad up on her computer screen over and over before she'd finally dared to answer.

His reply had been quick, terse. Following his instructions they had met at a small café in Santa Monica, where she lived and worked at a trendy clothing boutique. There they had talked over coffee about her desires, about what she could expect from him. It had all seemed ideal. And so odd to have that conversation in the middle of the busy café, among the casual crowd in their sweats and T-shirts. Master Robert had been dressed in what she supposed was his version of casual: a pair of Armani slacks and a black cashmere sweater that were an elegant contrast to his dark gray hair.

He was the most naturally dominant person she had ever met in her life.

Caught in her musings, she almost missed the house. A pair of iron gates were partially obscured behind tall hedges and eucalyptus trees. She rolled down her window to ring the buzzer on the security box, and the rich scent of the trees flowed in along with the sea-tainted air. Her damp fingers flexed on the steering wheel, her heart hammered in her chest. She waited.

It seemed as though several minutes passed before a female voice came over the system.

"Yes?"

"Cassandra Lowell to see Robert di Sante . . . to see Master Robert." Even the word "Master" rolling over her tongue seemed lovely to her. Dangerous. Exciting.

The gates rolled back as if by magic and she pulled her car through.

The house was gorgeous. Set into a wooded hillside, it was a majestic, two-story Mediterranean-style, with white stucco walls. Dark tiles were layered onto the multilevel roof, and high, arching windows were accented by a tastefully brief bit of ironwork. Despite the lack of spires, the structure reminded her of the churches she had seen when her parents took her on one of their missions to Mexico. But this seemed an almost holy place to her. And imposing enough to bring gooseflesh to her skin. She could only imagine what lay behind the heavy wood door.

Master Robert had told her during their conversation a week earlier what to expect. Weekends only for the first month, at his house, with the weekdays in between to go home, have a normal life, absorb whatever happened to her during her visits. At the end of that month, if she pleased him, he would ask her to stay on, to sign a slave contract in which she would hand herself over to him completely. If she accepted, her life would change utterly.

He had made her fill out a long questionnaire before meeting with him, to answer questions about her wants, her desires, her limits. Her limbs had gone warm and weak just reading the questions, saying them aloud to herself, searching for the answers. Did she have a desire to be bound? Did she fantasize about pain? Did she feel a need to be under another's command?

Yes, and yes, and yes!

Of course, her imagination had had a week to run wild since her meeting with Master Robert. What exactly would she be facing? A torture chamber with naked women chained to the walls, lashed until welts rose on thighs strained with pain and tension? A small shiver ran up her spine at the image.

She parked her car, grabbed the small bag holding her

toothbrush, hairbrush, some perfume and lotions, a clean pair of underwear. This was all she'd been told to bring.

The night was warm against her goose-bumped skin as she stood before the door, unsure as to whether she should knock. Surely they knew she was there, since someone had opened the gate for her? She waited a few moments more, then raised her hand to knock—and paused, still unsure, her imagination working at warp speed about what might lie ahead. Her fondest dreams were, perhaps, about to come true. And the sense that she was about to do something very wrong both nagged at her and titillated her.

She took in a deep breath, smelling the salt of the ocean, and a lovely humidity that soothed her lungs. Again she raised her hand. The door opened.

She was surprised, completely flustered. And there was Robert, or Master Robert as she was going to have to get used to calling him. He was cool and elegant in the same type of finely cut black slacks she'd seen him in before, and a white shirt, rolled up at the sleeves. He smiled warmly, his steel gray eyes crinkling at the corners, as though he were truly pleased to see her.

She felt a strange rush of relief and warmth all over, suddenly glad she had come despite her jangled nerves.

"Cassandra, welcome."

He reached out a hand and stroked her cheek, just a gentle caress, barely grazing the skin, but she was on fire immediately, as though his soft fingertips had touched between her legs rather than her face.

Then his hand moved to her shoulder and he exerted a gentle pressure. "On your knees."

His tone had changed. It was harder, yet not cruel in any way. And she stood there, hardly believing it would all start so soon, with her standing outside, still on the doorstep.

His hand snaked around to the back of her neck and he squeezed, not hard, just firmly, and he pressed down. "Now, Cassandra."

She dropped her overnight bag, wanting to comply, but feeling frightened at the suddenness of it all. Tears stung her eyes. She searched his face wildly.

He pressed a bit harder, locking his hard, gray gaze to hers. "I am not in the habit of having to repeat myself." Then, more firmly still, "Now."

Something in her snapped, gave way, and she went down. The hard flagstone scraped at her knees a bit, but all she really saw were his eyes. His gaze was command- ing, yet kind at the same time. He seemed pleased that she had acquiesced. Pleased but not at all smug. She didn't think he was the sort of man who needed to be.

Her head was emptying out at an alarming rate. The black lace panties she had bought especially for the occa- sion had grown damp the moment her knees hit the ground. She hadn't expected to react so strongly to such a simple thing. But she was too much in the moment to dis- sect it.

"Very good." He stroked her hair. "You will follow me into the house. Do not get up."

The idea was alarming, and under any other circum- stances she would have been mortified, but something in her trusted that this was simply how things were done here. And a part of her was secretly pleased that it felt a bit to her like praying, being on her knees on the hard floor.

He stooped to pick up her fallen bag, then gestured her into the hall while he closed the door behind her. Then he turned and made his way down the hallway.

She followed. There was no question that she would. He didn't even look back. She was so focused on following his feet, which were clad in very expensive-looking black loafers, she barely even noticed the smooth terra-cotta tiles of the floor she crawled on.

Down the hall, then off to a room on the left, where the tile gave way to a Persian rug, in deep shades of red, black, and amber. He brought her into the center of the room. She hadn't dared yet to look up.

She was fairly confused, yet savoring the moment. She was really there! Kneeling on the floor at the feet of the man who would be her trainer. Her head reeled with the thought. Finally, someone she sensed she could please. She wanted to cry. Then she felt his hand on the back of her neck again, his voice soft against her ear. "I'm going to blindfold you now."

She shuddered all over with a wave of desire at the idea of it. And when the soft, black blindfold came over her eyes, was pulled tight around her head, she melted into it. Every nerve ending in her body came alive, electric with anticipation.

He helped her to her feet and she swayed a bit, but he steadied her. His voice was still quiet, but strong. "Stand still, Cassandra. You will be undressed now."

Hands pulled at her clothes; feminine hands she

discovered as soon as they touched her bare flesh. Her blouse was unbuttoned and slipped from her shoulders, then came her skirt, and she realized there was more than one of them.

She had to take in a sharp little breath as her bra was removed. Her nipples immediately peaked, then peaked harder as a soft hand brushed them, by accident, she thought.

Her panties were whisked away and she stood there in nothing but her thigh-high black stockings and her high black pumps. For some reason the blindfold comforted her, made her feel less afraid.

A finger ran around the edge of one stocking, inserted itself beneath the elastic. "Very nice," Master Robert whispered against her cheek, his breath warm and fragrant. "I love that your hair here is a little darker shade than the hair on your head. Gorgeous against your pale skin. Did you know it's said that witches most commonly have red hair, just like yours; red and long and wild? You could bewitch anyone with this hair of yours. With those emerald eyes hiding beneath the blindfold. You're like some ancient Celtic beauty."

Her heart swelled, thrilled that he was pleased with her. Then there were hands on her again, feminine fingers running over her stomach, her collarbone, up her spine. She wasn't sure how many. Two? Three? More? Then lightly touching her breasts, which had begun to ache. She surged a bit into that touch, but the hand was immediately pulled back.

"No, Cassandra." His voice came, harder now. "You

must hold still when you are being examined, unless you are told otherwise. Is that clear?"

"Yes, Sir." She could hardly believe it was her own voice saying the words to him.

The "examination" continued. She was stroked, squeezed, pinched a bit here and there: her stomach, her thighs, buttocks, even her calves and arms. Then it was his hands parting her thighs, his voice ordering her to move her legs apart. His hand, larger than the women's hands and harder in texture, although still soft for a man's, brushed the hair between her thighs. The briefest touch, so brief that when he plunged a finger inside her, it came as a shock that reverberated through her body and she almost fell, on the edge of orgasm already.

He withdrew it almost immediately, but she was left shaking and gasping for breath.

"Take her away."

What? Away? Away from him? Where was she to be taken, and in this state of almost excruciating arousal?

The women's hands propelled her quickly, her heels clicking over a hard floor. One turn to the left, then one to the right, and into a room where she could feel the dense softness of carpet beneath her feet. Her hose and shoes were quickly stripped from her, and she was pushed again through a door.

She felt the change in temperature immediately. The air was warm, soft with moisture, and smelled faintly of lilacs.

"Wh-what now?" she asked, but a palm quickly covered her mouth and she understood she was not to speak.

Two pairs of hands helped her to lift her legs over what she instantly recognized as the rim of a bathtub, and she lowered her body into the steaming, scented water.

It felt glorious against her flushed skin, as did their soft hands, the soapy sponge they washed her with. All of her senses were heightened in a way they never had been before. With the blindfold on it was so easy to simply give herself over, to whoever these women were. All she needed to know was that Master Robert had given her to them.

She was beginning to understand the purpose of the blindfold already. It was a release from responsibility every bit as much as it was meant to make her tune in on her body, her senses. It worked like a charm.

They pushed her back so that her head rested on what felt like a rolled-up towel, and then a stream of water washed over her skin, rinsing the soap away. She imagined it was one of those handheld showerheads, shiny with chrome.

The water hit her chest in a gentle massage, played over her breasts. When it hit her sensitized nipples, she almost cried out, but they swiftly moved on to other areas.

She discovered quickly that she could feel the stream even under the surface of the bathwater. It rolled across the undersides of her breasts, down her stomach, then lower, to her thighs, relaxing the taut muscles there.

Then their hands again, urging her thighs apart so they could aim the sharp stream of warm water at her sex. She lost it almost immediately, coming so hard she had to cry out, her whole body jerking with the spasms. And right in the middle of that mind-bending orgasm, one of them pinched her nipples, hard, making her arch into those wicked hands as the pain lanced through her, driving her orgasm on, sharpening the edge of it until coming itself almost hurt.

When it was over a sob escaped her lips and she found herself murmuring, "Thank you."

Again the quick hand over her mouth, but she smiled beneath it. She felt wonderful, grateful. Grateful for the pleasure those female hands had brought her, but also for being made to feel as though she were a part of something, finally. At the same time, the old sense of guilt nagged at the back of her mind. But she knew that soon Master Robert would cleanse her of her sins in a way going to church, confessing, praying, never had.

She hadn't prayed since she was nine years old and her older brother, her idol, had run away, leaving her to take the brunt of her parents' constant moralizing, their need for absolute control. But here she could finally give that control over willingly, without it being forced from her, somehow taking her full circle in the most beautiful way.

They let her lie there in the water for a while. She heard them busying themselves in the room, but had no idea what they might be doing. She was too dazed to care. Then they lifted her from the tub, dried her carefully, rubbing her skin until she thought it might shine. When they rubbed her down with lotion it was almost too much for her, their slick little hands on her body. But when she let out a moan one of them pinched her hard on the back of her arm, a punishing little pinch that told her to behave as easily as any spoken order.

When they were done she was led out of the room, back onto the plush carpeting. They sat her down on the

edge of a bed, pushed her back onto a small mound of pillows.

When they snapped a cold metal cuff around one wrist
her first reaction was to struggle, but she fought it down.
This was what she was here for, after all. But when the
second cuff came around her other wrist she had a bad
moment of panic.

She could hear the sharp intake of her own breath. She
went hot all over and began to shake.

Their soft hands soothed her, rubbing her shoulders
and her arms. One of them whispered, "Shh. You are in
the Master's house. You are safe in his hands."

She calmed. Her mind was a whirl of confusion and
she felt oddly exhausted, as though she had taken in about
as much as she could in one evening. Cuffed to the bed,
she relaxed back into the pillows, and slept. She dreamed
of black leather boots, sinuous lengths of rope. And a face-
less man who would share her deepest, darkest desires.

CHAPTER TWO

WAKING WAS CONFUSING. HOW LONG HAD SHE slept? It took her several moments to remember where she was and that it was dark because she was still blind-folded. She wondered if this was done on purpose, this enforced sense of disorientation. She thought Master Robert wanted her to be a bit off balance, and she had to admit that this would probably make her more compliant. It already had.

She was calm lying there, thinking about how she had ended up in this place, in this situation. About the books she had read, the years of empty longing, the sense of iso-lation that had kept her from socializing with other people for so long. She had always felt different, alone in her dark yearnings. After only her first night in a place where those yearnings were understood, catered to, she was suffused with a sense of peace she'd never felt before.

She didn't know what would happen to her today, to-morrow. It almost didn't matter. What mattered was that she was here, and she knew already she would endure whatever Master Robert wished her to.

The faint squeak of a door being opened brought her more fully awake. Immediately the soft, feminine hands were on her, at least four of them, pinching her thighs and reaching beneath her to pinch her buttocks. The pinches weren't too hard at first, merely sensitizing her skin, but they quickly escalated into real pain, and came in a dazzling flurry of torturous fingers.

She began to squirm. She couldn't help it. Her breath came in sharp gasps. Their rough little fingers hurt, yet at the same time she was as wet as a cat in heat, and just as needy. Even as she wriggled to avoid their hands, her body arched upward, asking for more.

She had a brief, passion-induced, hazy moment where she wondered if it were possible to come just from this. She almost felt that she could. If only they would touch her breasts, put their punishing fingers between her thighs.

She was working into a real frenzy, panting and writhing in pain and pleasure, when they stopped.

She could hardly breathe. This is what she had wanted, waited for, searched for. Her blood surged hot through her veins and came to rest just beneath the surface of her raw, abused skin. She had never felt so alive, so sexual. So aroused.

And she knew this was only the beginning.

The cuffs were unhooked from the bed, although they still dangled from her wrists, and she was lifted roughly to her feet. Her hands were pulled behind her back and the cuffs snapped together.

She was left to stand alone for a few moments, and then they brushed her hair very thoroughly. Even that felt sensual to her. And then she was once again led away.

Down the hallway and through several turns, and she thought perhaps she was in that same room with the Persian rug she had crawled into when she'd arrived.

One of the women pushed down on the back of her neck as Master Robert had, and she knew this time to lower to her knees while one of them steadied her arm.

She smelled the clean, strong, masculine scent of him as he entered the room. And someone else, another scent, this one woodsy and dark. Lovely. Who else was there?

Then hands were on her again and she was pulled roughly over Master Robert's lap. She knew him by his scent, by his thighs solid beneath her. Her naked breasts were pushed into the wool of his slacks, and before she had a chance to appreciate being so close to him he said quite calmly, "I'm going to spank you now."

The blows started immediately, only stinging at first. But it was enough, along with the realization that this was her very first spanking with him, to have her trembling and so soaking wet she was afraid the moisture would drip down her thighs. And all the while she couldn't help but remember those other spankings, years ago, the wooden paddle wielded by the old priest who had run her school. She had secretly loved it even then, that pain rendered through the innocence of her white cotton panties.

Master Robert played her skin in an even tempo, which built up slowly. The pain increased, and all she was aware of besides the pain was the sound his palm made as it smacked her flesh, the insistent pull of wanting heat in her sex, and the feel of his hard thighs through the fabric of his slacks.

The wool scratched a bit at her nipples, which were rock-hard and throbbing. When he paused for a moment she thought he was done, but then his hand came down in a really hard wallop that brought tears to her eyes.

She cried out, and heard from him a soft, satisfied, "Yes."

And from the other man in the room a quiet laughter.

Then the spanking began in earnest. He slapped her already sore flesh harder and harder, the sting of contact turning to fire. The heat of it burned through her body in spearing lances that began on the surface of her skin and traveled quickly to every cell. When she squirmed he ordered her to be still, but how could she? Between the instinctive reaction to escape from the pain, and the seemingly irrational response to strain toward it, it was impossible.

The rain of blows came fast and furious over her buttocks and the back of her thighs, with no time between to recover or to catch her breath. She was dimly aware of her mind slipping away until she was nothing but sensation, until she could no longer differentiate between what hurt and what felt good. Her head reeled.

When he stopped she felt like crying. She didn't know why. Because it hurt—it still hurt. Because she was so grateful. Because she needed more!

He ran gentle hands over her heated flesh, whispering to her, "That was good, Cassandra, very good. I'm very pleased."

And then she did cry. She couldn't help it.

She had no idea what would come next. She couldn't think about much of anything. She was happy and exhausted and warm all over. And half in love with Master Robert's evil hands.

He moved her until she was kneeling on the rug, and then he gently pulled away the blindfold. She blinked in the light. And saw him.

The stranger was dark, so beautifully dark, sitting in a big leather chair, watching her carefully. His hair was black, his skin a light golden brown. He had one of those strong, angular jaws that she knew would be shaded with stubble even right after he shaved. A wide, lush mouth that made her want to touch it with her fingertips, to feel its softness, to kiss. Her sex tingled. She was too worked up for this man not to affect her. Did she dare look at his eyes?

When she did she found they were a deep shade of whiskey. His hair fell over one of them and he pushed it back with a large, capable hand. What would that hand feel like on her burning flesh?

Her heart was absolutely hammering in her chest.

Who was this man? Was he there simply to watch? She couldn't stand the idea that she might never feel his hands on her, might never see him again. He was too fascinatingly beautiful, his dark eyes mesmerizing.

The man leaned forward and surprised her by wiping away her forgotten tears with his fingertips, as though she were a frightened child. She felt like one. So completely vulnerable it scared her half to death.

But still needing him to touch her. She needed someone's hands on her, needed release. Especially now, looking into this man's calm gaze that seemed to see right through her. But she suspected it was not going to happen.

"You did well, Cassandra," Master Robert told her again, distracting her. "You're probably feeling a bit light-headed now. And wide open. Yes?"

She could only nod her head.

"This is perfectly normal. It's an aftereffect of all that adrenaline and then endorphins running through your body. You'll be very tired; I'll make sure you're rested, then given a good breakfast. Here, you feel cold."

He wrapped a soft blanket around her shoulders, then held a glass of water to her lips for her to sip. She felt utterly cared for. They sat quietly for a while, leaving her to wonder again through the dreamy haze of endorphins and burning lust what would happen next and who the other man was. No one seemed inclined to introduce her. And then the women came in, lined up in a row next to Master Robert's big leather wing chair, and she saw them for the first time.

They were all three lovely—and all three naked, except for the collars around their necks. Two blondes: one tall and willowy with large, beautiful breasts and long flaxen hair that gently waved halfway down her back; the other a petite woman, with a perfectly proportioned frame. Her pale, curly mop of hair and her pink baby mouth made her appear doll-like. Her sex was completely shaved, making it look all the more naked and vulnerable. If it weren't for her high, pointed breasts, her dark, rosy nipples pierced by fine silver hoops, she would almost look like a child.

The third woman was really stunning. She looked to

be Japanese, with a sheet of jet-black hair that fell to her waist. Every inch of her golden skin was flawless, unmarred by a single pore. Her body was decorated with a most unusual tattoo of a dragon done in classic Japanese style, all gold and black. The design started on her right hip, and wrapped around the small of her back; the long tail twined down her left leg, ending at her ankle, all of it done in exquisite detail.

Her face was masklike in its perfection. Her almond eyes were a deep, rich brown, fringed in thick lashes, and her perfectly bow-shaped lips matched the dusky shade of her small, pink nipples.

Cassandra was instantly fascinated with her, and wondered if she had been one of the women to attend her.

"Mika." Master Robert nodded to the tattooed woman. "See Cassandra back to her room." He didn't bother to introduce the other two, who stood silent with hands clasped behind their backs, heads bent, and eyes riveted to the floor.

Master Robert helped her to her feet and Mika's surprisingly strong grip held her elbow and guided her into the hall.

She couldn't bear to leave the dark, beautiful man behind. Without a word, without knowing who he was. And Master Robert's brand on her skin, making her shaky with unslaked desire. To be sent away like this!

Mika led her silently back to her room, and for the first time Cassandra could see what it looked like. It was lovelier than she had imagined when she'd been blindfolded and drifting to sleep the night before. The stucco walls led to high, beamed ceilings, and a fireplace took up one corner.

The same arched windows she'd seen from outside were covered in heavy wood plantation shutters. The room was dominated by a four-post bed, an enormous piece she recognized as being Spanish, and probably an antique, as was the high bureau in one corner. The silk and velvet patchwork bedding, all in shades of deep golds, browns, and reds, added a luxurious touch of color.

The only other furnishings in the room were what she thought of as "play" furniture: a leather-covered spanking bench—she recognized it from stories she had read—stood at the foot of the bed, while a heavy-timbered frame against one wall had several sets of thick metal hooks from which hung leather cuffs. Just knowing she had slept in a room with such objects made her shiver in delight.

Mika guided Cassandra with a hand on her back to sit on the edge of the bed. When she started to lie back, Mika quickly grabbed her arm. She took that to mean she was to hold still. Mika left the room then, with one last glance over her shoulder.

Cassandra waited, her sore bottom tingling and raw against the bedspread. She wanted to lie back on the bed, to rest. She was so tired from her busy morning. And there was so much to think about she didn't know where to begin.

She had lived with this void inside of her for the longest time, had felt these urges since childhood. She remembered being perhaps twelve or thirteen years old, remembered that first awakening of herself as a sexual being, becoming aware of what she wanted when the priest or one of the teaching nuns paddled her. And once she recognized her desires, no amount of petting with clumsy teenaged boys could quench the pure need raging inside of her.

Her college boyfriends had been no better. After she'd asked one of them to spank her, he'd told her she was a freak and never called her again. And that's how she'd thought of herself for a long time: a freak. It had been a relief, finally, to find other people like her on the Internet and in the books she'd read. People who felt these same dark urges, who needed the same things she needed.

But now she knew. She knew what she wanted, and it appeared as though she was going to get it—in ways she hadn't even imagined.

This was a revelation. The full weight of what she was doing hadn't really struck her until Master Robert had her over his lap. That sense of yielding she'd felt with him was so much more than she could have hoped for. That sense of giving over control. She felt more a woman than she ever had before. And she felt more natural about the yearnings that had haunted her all of her adult life.

And then there was the mysterious stranger. Would she ever see him again? With all that was happening to her, all she was already discovering about herself, why was it *him* she couldn't get out of her head? Even as she re-membered the sensation of Master Robert's hands striking her naked flesh, the sense of pure freedom it brought along with the pain and the pleasure, the other man's face lingered in her mind's eye.

Finally Mika came back with a bed tray and set it over Cassandra's lap. A European-style breakfast was set on fine china of the purest white, with one narrow black line around the rim. The tray held a croissant, some cut-up fruit, a small ramekin of yogurt, and a cup of tea.

Suddenly she was famished, and she ate everything on her plate while the petite Japanese woman stood silent sentry by the door. After she finished eating, Mika lifted the tray and motioned her into the bathroom. When she came out the tray had disappeared and Mika took her to the bed, snapped the cuffs to the chains there once more, and left her alone with her thoughts.

She again had one moment of panic, left alone and helpless. She pulled against the restraints, but of course they held tight. The idea that she truly couldn't escape calmed her somehow, and as she drifted helplessly toward sleep, she thought of the stranger. Of his strong features, his clear golden-brown eyes, of his touch as he wiped her tears from her cheeks. What an unusual thing to do. What an unusual man. Even now, her body craved his touch, his presence.

She must see him again! But how? She wouldn't even be allowed to ask his name. The sense of helplessness, of letting go of all power, still came as a relief. Yet at the same time, it brought a pain she knew wouldn't leave her until she saw her stranger again.

CHAPTER THREE

MIKA GENTLY SHOOK CASSANDRA AWAKE AND once again she was fed, then bathed by the two blond women while the late afternoon sun filtered in through the shaded windows. Their soft, careful hands were a sweet caress on her sensitive skin. The flesh on her bottom was still sore to the touch, and they rubbed a cooling, lavender-scented cream there.

No blindfold, and so she was able to watch them as they worked. Though she had never before felt any attraction to women, she saw them now with new eyes. The taller one had truly spectacular breasts; large and pendulous when she bent over, with pale pink nipples that stiffened noticeably when she touched Cassandra's skin. She was surprised to find herself wanting to smooth her hands over that full, soft female flesh.

The smaller of the two had a lovely figure. Her breasts were small, which suited her petite form. And she saw again how the little blonde was completely shaved, her sex peeking out enticingly in pink, velvet folds.

By the time she was taken back into her room she was thoroughly aroused once more. From looking at the two women, from the sensation of their hands on her, and from the entire ritualistic tone of it all. The bathing, the way they treated her as an object: treasured, yet still an object.

She loved it all.

Mika came in with a wooden tray of cosmetics and had Cassandra sit on a small chair by the window. She worked on her face for perhaps thirty minutes, then started on her hair. When she was done, Mika led her to the mirror which hung on one wall.

Mika had transformed her. Her hair hung in russet curls about her shoulders, part of it piled atop her head in delicate coils and held in place by a series of pins decorated with tiny, golden butterflies. Mika had shadowed her green eyes in gold, as well, and used a golden-sheened powder to accent the high, rounded curve of her cheeks, her collarbones, the tops of her breasts. Her lips were glossed pink and layered with something gold and iridescent. She looked exotic, decorated.

When Mika stood behind her and reached her arms around her, Cassandra caught her scent. Something floral and subtle and clean. When the woman's tiny, delicate hands came around to her stomach she held very still. And as Mika fastened a fragile gold chain around her waist she felt a surge of pure lust. A need for her small, clever hands.

But she was immediately distracted by the sight of the gold chain in the mirror. It made her look entirely different. Or perhaps it made her feel different. More decorated, somehow. But also bound, owned. Her whole body shivered and her sex plumped between her thighs.

Behind her, Mika's gaze met hers in the mirror and a small smile played at the corners of her serious little mouth. Cassandra smiled back. She couldn't help it.

Their eyes locked in the mirror. Mika snaked a hand up and tweaked her left nipple, just hard enough to hurt. Her smile broadened when Cassandra gasped.

She was absolutely soaked instantly.

What was this sudden lust for women? Was it really about the women, or more about the constant, steady atmosphere of sensuality? But she hardly had time to think about it before Mika led her away.

When they reached the door of what Cassandra had come to think of as the living room, Mika gave her the now familiar signal to lower to her knees, then left her there, kneeling in the doorway. Curious, she peered into the room, took in the elegant décor, the amber light cast from several lamps, the faint scent of good Scotch whiskey.

Master Robert sat in his brown leather chair, one ankle crossed over his knee, in that attitude of repose only the most confident of men adopt. He smiled a little when he saw her at the door.

"Very pretty, Cassandra. The gold suits you. Enter."

She did so, on her knees, not even lowering her hands to the floor, but keeping them clasped behind her back, thinking this might please him. She stopped in the middle of the Persian rug, on the very center of the design. She thought proudly for a moment of how the gold decorations on her body would match the colors of the rug and the velvet drapes that lined the tall, paned windows.

But where was the other man, her dark stranger? A tug

of disappointment tightened her stomach, even as a surge of adrenaline flowed through her. But Master Robert was there. And even though she didn't feel the intense attraction for him she had for the stranger, he was the man who would train her. That alone made her yearn to be near him, to please him. It was still damn exciting.

"Yes, lovely," Master Robert murmured. "Stand for me."

She rose to her feet, a sudden surge of dizziness unbalancing her. But it wasn't from standing up too fast. It was excitement, anticipation of what was to come. And the overpowering presence of Master Robert as he sat watching her with those wise gray eyes of his that matched his perfectly groomed hair.

He stood and took both of her hands in one of his, drew them high up over her head, then stepped back. She left her hands in the air, twined together above her head, while he made a circle around her.

"Hands clasped behind your back now."

She complied, the motion making her breasts thrust outward. They were tingling already, sensitized and full, the nipples taut beneath his gaze. She felt no embarrassment. There was something so utterly freeing about giving over all control to him. Her body was his to do with as he wished. She thought it had been from the moment she'd met him at that café in Santa Monica.

He reached out with both hands and lightly caressed her nipples, which came up hard and pulsing at once. Her sex swelled and pounded with heat.

"Before we begin tonight I want you to talk to me. I'm going to ask you a few questions. They won't be complicated, but they will be of a personal nature. I want you to reveal yourself to me. While you are naked, vulnerable, under my command. Do you understand? You may speak to answer me."

"Yes, Sir. I understand." But did she? What was this? Her heart was fluttering again.

"Tell me what brought you to me, what attracts you to this life."

It was hard to think, already sunken into the dreamy state of arousal as she was. But Master Robert required an answer. And the answer was so much a part of her, she trusted her mouth to find the words, to express the thoughts she'd had nearly her entire life.

"It began a long time ago. I almost can't remember a time without it, without this wanting." She paused, licked her suddenly dry lips. "I've had an eternity of people telling me what to do, of following their commands blindly, because I didn't have a choice. Now the choice is ultimately mine. Do you understand how important that is for me?" Her eyes burned with tears, her throat tight.

"I know exactly what you mean, my dear."

Again that surge of gratitude.

"I have spent most of my life striving to please those who can never be pleased, for whom I will never be good enough, perfect enough, no matter how I try. And here, for the first time, I feel accepted as I am. That's an epiphany for me, yet somehow I knew that's the way it would be if I came here, if I entered the BDSM lifestyle. Everything I read told me so. So did my instincts, on a very deep level. I don't know how to explain it."

Master Robert caught her gaze, delved deep into her eyes. "You explained it perfectly, Cassandra."

She smiled. The tears still threatened, but she was suffused with happiness at his simple words, at the pleasure and freedom of opening herself to him, as he had said.

"Now for a more basic question." Master Robert smiled, and said in his elegant voice, "Have you ever worn nipple clamps before, Cassandra?"

"No, Sir." Her voice was barely above a whisper, her heart and her sex instantly throbbing.

"You are about to."

While she stood, trembling, he pulled a pair of small clamps from his pocket. Unlike the chrome clamps she had seen on the Internet these were gold in color, with a thin chain running between them that matched the chain about her waist.

She shivered. The clamps had evil-looking little teeth. Her breasts ached for them.

She took a deep breath and waited, her nipples stiffening more with each moment.

He began with the right one, tugging and pinching it until it was as hard as it had ever been, the tugging going straight to her pulsing sex. She struggled to hold her hips still. Then, pulling her nipple out, stretching it, he opened the dangerous looking teeth of the clamp and let it close around her flesh.

The pain was exquisite, lancing through her body like white heat. The pleasure was just as intense.

Her head felt light and she was breathing in hard, short pants. Master Robert's hand came around to the back of her neck, steadying her.

"Long, deep breaths, Cassandra. Convert the pain to pleasure. Take it in, then breathe it out."

She tried to do as instructed, but she was totally over-whelmed by sensation.

"Concentrate."

His hand was still on her neck, and she thought of it as an anchor in the storm of sensation. Eventually she calmed and was able to breathe normally, even though the pain was still there. Pain that was pleasure at the same time. This was different from being pinched or spanked. It was more, for one thing. And deeper, somehow.

It was really doing a number on her head.

While she was still trying to sort it all out, he grabbed her other nipple, drew it out long and hard, and clamped it.

The pain was just as searing as the first one had been. Maybe even worse, as though now that her body recognized the pain, it fed it even more. Her breathing once again came in gasping pants while she tried to get a handle on it. A rush of wet heat between her legs made her squirm despite her efforts not to.

"Still, Cassandra."

She stopped, gritting her teeth, trying to control herself. For him. Her nipples burned, her sex burned, and her entire being was suffused with pleasure. And with gratitude once more.

Tears welled in her eyes, spilled over finally, and ignoring her instructions to be silent, she whispered, "Thank you, Sir."

As a reward for her errant behavior, Master Robert gave a sharp tug on the chain running between the clamps. She yelped aloud, which made him chuckle. After a pause he did it again.

Deliciously evil man.

He stood back and looked her over once more. "We're having company tonight. I am counting on you to behave as a good slave should. These are your rules. First, you will look no one in the eye unless asked to. You will not speak without permission. At all times while standing, you will clasp your hands behind your back as they are now. You will immediately comply with any command given to you.

"When not asked to stand, you will assume the classic submissive position. Down on your knees, and I will instruct you."

She sank down immediately, her head spinning with all the new sensations and new information. Other people were to see her like this! To perhaps touch her, punish her! And maybe he would be there, her mystery man. She went hot all over.

"On your knees, Cassandra. Yes, that's it. Now, spread your thighs wider and sink back onto your heels. I want your hands resting on the tops of your thighs, with your palms up. This is a position of supplication, you understand? Your head should be down, eyes on the floor. Yes, perfect. Very nice."

The position was utterly submissive. It made her feel beautifully humble. She trembled with heat, desire, and the sense of gratitude that was becoming familiar already.

"I like you this way. I think I'll leave you here until our guests arrive."

A flash of panic as he moved away from her. But she forced herself to calm, to sink into herself, into the sensation of yielding. Every nerve in her body was alive. Her poor, tortured nipples sang with pain. Her sex pulsed with need.

She waited.

Marcus paced the length of floor-to-ceiling windows in his house high in the Hollywood Hills. For once he didn't even notice the view of the city he so loved. He was too much inside his own head.

Confusion raged through him, which was totally unlike him. He was a man who always knew what he wanted, knew exactly what was best for him. He made his own decisions, about his finances, his portfolio, never leaving it up to his team of accountants and advisors, as the rest of his family did. No, he was involved in every aspect of his wealth. Since his tyrant of a father had died ten years ago, he had been completely in control of his own destiny. And of every other aspect of his life. Hell, he'd taken command of his life when he'd left his father's house at fifteen and come to live with Robert, his mother's brother. Why was it that suddenly a woman was throwing him off balance?

This was unacceptable. He had to get himself under control. He wasn't even certain he'd hidden his reaction well from Robert. His uncle was used to reading people's body language. And Marcus had been steaming with lust as soon as he'd set eyes on Cassandra.

Christ, she was something. That wild red hair and big green eyes, like a pair of flawless emeralds. Not to mention her perfect skin, her firm breasts tipped with plump, luscious, pink nipples. He was getting hard just picturing her in his mind.

Robert's newest girl. He'd do well to keep that point in mind. *Robert's.*

He crossed his living room in long strides. At the wet

bar he pulled out a crystal tumbler, filled it with a few fingers of a fine malt Scotch. The faint burn going down centered him a little. And reminded him that if he were to attend Robert's coming-out party for his new slave tonight, he'd better ease up on the booze. He had to remain in control. That was his life mantra. He wasn't about to screw up in front of Robert and the others, that was for damn sure. And not over a woman.

He was an experienced trainer himself, although he didn't have the years Robert and some of the others had. But he was disciplined. Always had been, which is why Robert had approached him about joining him in his "little hobby," as he had so charmingly referred to it at first, when Marcus was only eighteen.

Now, at thirty, Marcus was one of the youngest trainers in their small but powerful group. A group of old-school, formal Doms and Dommes. People who conformed to the strict rules of slave-training that had been in practice for hundreds of years. A discipline that required absolute control over not only the slaves, but over one's own urges and desires.

He downed the rest of his Scotch. Damn it. He'd better watch himself. Because this new girl had thrown his control right out the window.

CHAPTER FOUR

Her fatigued thighs trembled. And still she waited. It had been perhaps half an hour. The exquisite anticipation alternated with fear. What would happen to her tonight? And would her dark stranger be there? The trembling in her thighs turned to a liquid heat that made her weak all over at the mere idea of him.

The clamps pulled and pinched at her nipples with every breath she took, keeping her focus on that one part of her body. The pain reminded her of where she was, and of her purpose. If not for the pain of the clamps her mind might have wandered too far. Being made to stay in one position was a sort of meditation, a state she could easily become lost in. But that sharp pinch kept her grounded in her body. That and the sensual images of the man whose face she couldn't get out of her mind.

God, if he were to be allowed to spank her tonight! Her sex squeezed tight as she imagined his hands on her bare ass, stroking and tormenting her flesh.

Yes.

The temptation to press a hand to her aching sex was torture in itself.

She pictured his dark hair, a little wavy, a little too long. His strong jaw, his deep, gold-tinted brown eyes. She could have gazed into those eyes forever.

A sigh escaped her lips. Her yearning for this man's touch was like a solid weight in her body, in her swollen, expectant sex. She almost moved to squeeze her thighs together.

Footsteps.

Her pulse fluttered, her heart tumbled in her chest. She kept her eyes cast down and tried to breathe.

Voices, both male and female. They had arrived.

It was a strange sensation, kneeling naked on the floor, silent and waiting for someone to notice her. How could they not notice her? But these people would be used to such things.

More guests arrived. They moved around her as though she were merely a piece of furniture, there only as decoration. But wasn't part of what she wanted that feeling of becoming lost in the most extreme of objectification? Her heart pounded in her chest.

From the corners of her eyes she caught sight of expensive shoes and trouser cuffs moving around her. Drinks were poured. Ice tinkled in crystal glasses. She could smell it: the sharp, acrid bite of good gin, the more aromatic scent of Scotch whiskey, the perfume of red wine.

She wasn't sure how long she was there before Master Robert moved her hair aside and stroked the back of her neck. She knew it was him, knew his touch, his unique scent already. She shivered beneath his hand.

"My sensitive girl," he said with a quiet laugh.

The conversation in the room faded and died. Robert signaled her with a small squeeze on her neck.

"On your feet, my dear."

She rose slowly, her knees a little stiff and her heart hammering a thousand miles an hour. She had to face these people!

She could feel Master Robert behind her. His hand slid down to one shoulder, steadying her. "Lift your eyes now, Cassandra, and meet our guests."

She struggled for a moment before doing as he asked. She tilted her chin up, fluttered her eyes open, and saw them all.

Perhaps a dozen people, all well dressed in different ways. Designer clothes, the best in leather and fetish wear. Most were men, but there were a few women, too. Several slaves knelt in various positions around the room. They were all naked.

She pulled in a deep breath. Suddenly, this all seemed more real to her. She moved her gaze from face to face, searching for her stranger. He wasn't there.

Still, she was filled with a jumbled mass of confusion and exhilaration. The crowd had started to talk again in hushed tones. And then a very distinguished-looking man with thin, gray hair approached her. He smiled over her shoulder, at Master Robert, she imagined. And then he reached out and ran a finger over the curve of one breast. She was surprised by the sudden touch. And her sex went damp when he gave that same flesh a sharp little pinch.

"Beautiful," he murmured.

More people approached, touched her, pinched her

breasts, her thighs. Master Robert turned her around, and somebody's hand swatted her buttocks and the back of her thighs, making her tremble with need and nerves.

The touching, spanking, and pinching went on, none of it very hard, but it was overwhelming, all of these different hands on her. And it was that sense of being overwhelmed that helped her to let go, to yield, to sink into it.

Master Robert turned her around again to face a tall, slim woman in a long, narrow black skirt and a red leather corset. Her black hair was piled in a loose tumble on top of her elegant head.

"What do you think, Delphine?" Master Robert's voice came from behind Cassandra's shoulder.

"Lovely girl. And so responsive." The woman's voice was low and smoky. "I would love to call in that favor you owe me, Robert."

"Certainly."

What did this mean? Was she to be given to this woman to play with?

Master Robert went on. "But she's brand-new. Are you sure you wouldn't rather wait until I've worked with her a bit first?"

The woman grinned. Her lips were painted perfectly in bold scarlet. "You must be joking! Virgin flesh is our favorite. Don't be greedy, Robert."

He laughed. "You may as well have her now, then."

Now? But before she had time to think about it the woman's hand was around her wrist and Master Robert whispered into her ear, "Go with Mistress Delphine and obey her as you would me. You will refer to her only as Mistress if you are spoken to. Be a good girl and perhaps you will be allowed some release later. Then again, perhaps not." He sent her off with a chuckle and a gentle push toward the woman who waited to torment her.

"On your knees, pretty girl," Mistress Delphine's voice was in her other ear. "You will follow me on your hands and knees."

Cassandra obeyed, even as her heart pounded, her limbs going weak. What would this woman do with her? But it was all she could do to keep up with the black stiletto heels peeking from the hem of the Mistress's black skirt.

They crossed to the other side of the room, the wool rug rubbing against her knees. There, a naked male slave helped her to her feet and stood her beneath a crossbar hanging from a chain overhead. She caught his eye as he steadied her with a hand on her arm. Blue eyes. And brown curly hair, a pretty-boy face. He gave her a small smile as he fastened heavy leather cuffs around her wrists and drew her arms over her head. She heard the metallic clink of chain links as her cuffs were fastened to a pair of clips on the bar.

"Beautiful," Mistress Delphine said quietly.

She circled around Cassandra, stroking her skin here and there, making her shiver. The male slave handed the woman a small, black leather slapper, a device made of two wide strips of stiff leather perhaps five or six inches long, fastened together with a metal ring at one end. The Mistress used it to caress Cassandra's skin, to prod the full flesh of her breasts. When she swiped it between her thighs Cassandra went wet again.

"Spread your legs. That's a good girl."

She moved her feet apart. She found herself wanting to please this wicked, beautiful woman as much as she wanted to please Master Robert. In fact, it was difficult to think of anything else.

The woman moved until she stood close behind her. Cassandra could feel the heat emanating from her body, caught the faint scent of feminine perfume. A soft hand snaked around and cupped her breast, gave a small squeeze. She whispered in Cassandra's ear, "Breathe in, girl, then blow it out."

The order was followed by a small slap of the leather on her buttocks. It stung, but not nearly as much as Master Robert's hand had during her spanking.

Mistress Delphine moved her hand up to the delicate gold chain hanging between Cassandra's breasts and gave it a painful tug, sending a hot wave of pain and pleasure through her. She smacked her again with the slapper. Cassandra loved the dual sensations, tried to ignore her still-fluttering nerves to focus on what was happening to her. She was vaguely aware of the other guests gathered around to watch. Why did that make it more exciting?

The Mistress smacked her again, and then again, harder each time. The blows heated her skin, sensitizing it, and she loved each sharp contact. She couldn't help but move her hips back an inch, toward the lovely sting.

"No, Cassandra. Hold still."

The blows started then in earnest, a sharp rain of smacks that grew progressively harder. All the while the Mistress tugged on the golden chain, causing titillating lances of pain to stab through her nipples. It was almost too much, but it was good at the same time, every bit as good as Master Robert's spanking had been. She squeezed her eyes shut.

She couldn't help the moan that escaped, or the writhing of her hips. The flesh on her ass was on fire with sensation, her nipples were hard and hot, and her sex was full and aching. God, she needed to come! If only someone would touch her there.

As if by magic, her fervent prayer answered, a hand slipped between her thighs. Her eyes fluttered open as pleasure flared and heat raced through her body. Her gaze was met by whiskey brown eyes, deep eyes set in a beautifully masculine face framed in jet-black hair.

It was *him*.

～

Marcus couldn't believe he'd walked up to the girl while Delphine was playing her and touched her, a breach in scene etiquette. But he hadn't been able to help himself, and Delphine had done nothing more than smile at his unspoken request.

One brief stroke of her slick, plump pussy, then he pulled away. Even though his hand rested at his side, he could swear he smelled the sweet scent of her on his skin.

He had to smile at the surprise in her green eyes. Eyes that burned with the fire of lust. She was obviously fairly deep into sub space already. He could see it in her glassy gaze, in the rhythm of her breathing. He berated himself for arriving late, for not being the first to play with her.

But why shouldn't Delphine have that honor? Why was he thinking so differently about this girl than about any of the others he'd played and trained over the years?

She was Robert's discovery. Why should he think for one moment that he would be the first to be given the girl to play with?

Because I want her more.

Christ.

He moved away. The girl's eyes remained on him. Burned into him. He walked off to get a drink.

At the bar he focused on ignoring the soft moans coming from the girl's lips as Delphine continued to torment her. He ordered a sparkling water with lime. No more alcohol for him tonight. His control was shaky enough. He took a sip of the water, pulled in a breath before he turned back to watch.

The crowd had pulled in a little tighter around the action, but he could still see her. Could still see that she was deliciously sensitive, as responsive as any bottom he'd ever seen. Her breasts were hanging ripe and full, the golden clamps a perfect accent. The front of her slim thighs were pink where Delphine had hit her with the slapper. He was getting hard just looking at her.

Robert approached him. "What do you think of my newest acquisition, Marcus?"

He cleared his throat, keeping his eyes on the red-headed beauty. "A gorgeous girl."

"Yes, she is."

"Special."

"Do you think so?"

Marcus gestured with his chin. "Christ, look at her. The way she moves. The way her body answers every touch. She loves the pain. She's brand-new and going under already. She seems to understand how to convert the pain automatically. Incredible."

"Quite."

He turned to find a smirk on his uncle's face. "What?"

"I don't think I've ever seen you so smitten."

Marcus's blood went hot. "I want her," he stated simply.

"Then you shall have her next."

Cassandra was weak-limbed and warm from the endorphins flooding her system. But mostly from knowing *he* was in the room with her. And he had touched her!

God, the way he had touched her. He was her wildest dream come true. And he was still there somewhere, watching her as Mistress Delphine spanked her with the evil leather slapper, pulled on her clamped nipples, while she writhed in pleasure.

The Mistress had stopped, giving Cassandra time to catch her breath. The slave boy had checked her wrists for circulation, given her a small drink of water, asked her if she was cold. Cold! She was burning hot with desire and anticipation, pleasure and pain.

Her head was whirling. She could barely think. Her skin sang with heat, her nipples burned, and even while Mistress Delphine had played her so expertly, all she could think of was *him*.

The Mistress had left her side and the slave boy stood by, as though guarding her. She glanced around the room. Faces smiling at her. Where was he?

She caught his scent first. He was standing behind her.

She knew it was him. That woodsy, fresh scent. And when a masculine hand smoothed her shoulder, she felt his touch as though she'd known it all her life.

"I am Marcus, but you may call me Sir."

His deep voice crept over her like a blanket of velvet. She shivered deep inside.

Marcus.

He trailed his fingertips over her neck. Goose bumps rose everywhere on her body. She was shaking so hard inside she couldn't have managed to stand if she weren't bound.

His voice was a low murmur. "You are beautiful, Cassandra. Like some piece of art. Like one of Rodin's finest erotic sculptures. Do you know art? Do you know the great masters?"

She nodded, took a breath. "Yes, Sir. I do."

"You look like his *Danaid*, all fluid lines."

"*The Torso of Adele*," she whispered.

He laughed. "You do know, don't you? Yes, exactly, suspended as you are, your body stretched out this way. And like the female figure in *Eternal Idol* when you're on your knees."

She could not believe she was having a conversation with this man while she was bound and strung up like this! But she was unsurprised, for some inexplicable reason, that they had this love of art in common.

Marcus quieted as, with his other hand, he made an exploration of the small of her back, the curve of her buttocks, then down to her thigh. His hands were hot on her skin, his fingers smooth. She couldn't believe he was touching her.

"You're nicely warmed up. But your time with Mistress Delphine is only the beginning of what will happen to you tonight."

Her breath caught in her throat. *Yes.*

His hand slid over her stomach, down, and her sex clenched in anticipation as he brushed the curls at the apex of her thighs. If only he would slip a hand between them as he had before. With her legs still spread it would be so easy. . . .

Oh, God.

But he moved his hand away to explore the other curves of her body. His touch was a fiery, sensual pleasure unlike any she had felt before. And when he gave her a sharp slap she barely flinched. He laughed low in his throat, and slapped her ass again, and this time she moved into it. Only a fraction of an inch, but still he scolded her.

"I see you haven't yet been taught how to hold still." He smacked her again, and again her body surged into his hand.

This time his voice held an air of absolute command that made her knees go even weaker. "Cassandra. I want you to listen to me. You will hold absolutely still. No matter what I do, you will not move. Is that clear? You may answer me."

Somehow she found enough breath to speak. "Yes . . . yes, Sir."

No more words, just a quick volley of stinging slaps on her buttocks and thighs. They came so fast, so furiously, he must have been using both his hands. Her damp sex grew heavy with need, every muscle in her body strained with the effort not to move. And with every panting breath she could smell his scent, mixed now with the faint musk of sexual arousal. But whether it was his or her own, she couldn't tell.

The slaps grew harder. Her skin was on fire, absolutely burning. With pain. With desire. A drop of moisture trickled down the inside of one thigh.

She wanted to see his face. But she didn't want him to stop spanking her, even though her skin was so tender she wasn't sure she could take any more. And then he did stop.

Her own ragged breath was like thunder in her ears. Marcus came around to stand in front of her. God, he was beautiful. Power and confidence emanated from him. He was all she could see in the crowded room, all that mattered.

"Very good, Cassandra." He sounded a little out of breath himself.

He reached out a hand and cupped her chin, tilted her face up, and locked his gaze on hers. Cassandra shivered. There was so much happening in her body, in her mind. His golden-brown eyes were glittering darkly. Magnetic. Enigmatic. What was he thinking?

With his gaze still locked on hers, he cupped her breasts, weighed them, squeezed. Cassandra shut her eyes for a moment, trembling at the pure pleasure of his touch.

"No. Look at me."

She opened her eyes. His were like dark topaz, deep, mysterious. He said quietly, "This is going to hurt."

In one quick motion he squeezed the nipple clamps open and pulled them off. Pain surged through her breasts to gather in intensity at the hard peaks. She groaned. Her head spun with a blissful mixture of agony and endorphins. Marcus was holding her chin again, making her look at him, forcing her to focus on his face as the pain lanced through her in sharp waves.

When his other hand slipped between her thighs and probed the swollen folds of her sex she almost came undone. She cried out as he pushed his fingers inside of her. It was too good, with her nipples still singing in pain. Her hips bucked and she needed to come, but the moment she felt that first spasm approach he withdrew his fingers from her.

A sob escaped her. She couldn't help it. It was too good and too awful all at the same time. She needed him to touch her! Her whole body was on fire.

He still stood before her. And she could see that he was breathing hard, his wide chest rising and falling beneath his black silk shirt. What would his body feel like? Naked, against hers?

Oh, God.

She groaned again in frustration as he turned and walked away.

CHAPTER FIVE

Marcus stalked from the room, out into the wide, cool hallway. Robert followed him.

"Marcus. What happened in there?"

"She's done."

"I can see that. Mika and the girls are taking her down. But I meant you." He could hear fury in his uncle's voice. "You are far too experienced a trainer to simply walk away and leave her for others to attend to without a word. You want to tell me what the hell that was about?"

Marcus shoved his hands in his pockets. "I don't know."

Robert was quiet a moment. "You lost control in there."

Marcus ran a hand through his hair. Of course Robert was right. But he couldn't explain it to him any more than he could to himself. He said quietly, "Yes."

"You know as well as I do that we cannot allow that to happen. Control is everything, Marcus. It is our first responsibility."

"I know that! Don't you think I know that?"

Robert's voice was as calm and cool as the ocean one

could almost see from his house. "Remember who you're talking to, nephew."

Marcus drew in a lungful of air, blew it out. "I'm sorry. Damn it. I don't know what's wrong with me."

"Is it her? Cassandra? Or is it something deeper?"

"I don't know. I need some time to figure it out."

"I'd like for you not to miss her debut at The Lair next weekend. But you've got to get a hold of yourself if you're going to be there."

"The Lair? You're taking her there already?"

"Her needs run deep. And we are here to serve their needs, are we not?"

"But she's new. She's not ready." He was fuming and hot all over. But was it really on her behalf? Or did he simply not want anyone else to touch her?

"You saw for yourself how ready she is, Marcus."

He paced the hallway while Robert stood waiting patiently. Finally, his uncle said, "Perhaps you need something to distract yourself with. I can send Jacqueline home with you for a few days."

The petite blonde had served Marcus before, and he had enjoyed her. But he didn't want her right now. The only one he could think of was Cassandra, and he knew his uncle would never give such an inexperienced girl to anyone else so soon.

But the moment he thought of it, of having her to himself, the idea became all-consuming. To have her in his house. That silken flesh, those incredible, full breasts, that wild red hair in his hand . . . *his* . . .

But she was not his. That was the point. And perhaps the problem.

"I won't need Jacqueline, thank you, Robert."

His uncle raised his dark, gray brows. "You're sure?"

"Yes."

"Do whatever you need to do to get ahold of yourself, Marcus. You cannot let this girl go to your head. Then come to The Lair on Saturday evening."

But it was too late. She had already gone to his head. She was all he could think about since the first moment he'd laid eyes on her. And that brief exchange, their small conversation about art, that had really gotten to him. That she had a mind under all of that pale, tempting flesh. But she was not his. *Not his. Not for him.*

He would have to keep telling himself that. Because deep in his soul, he knew otherwise.

❦

Cassandra had slept hard after the party. She barely remembered the two blond girls taking her to her room, bathing her, putting her to bed. Now, with the morning light filtering in through the wide slats of the plantation shutters, the entire episode seemed like a dream.

Marcus. That was his name. She savored the feel of it on her tongue as she whispered it to herself.

He was the most fascinating man she had ever met. A perfect example of dark male beauty, and something else, something essential about him . . .

She loved his commanding presence, something he shared with Master Robert. But with Robert it was cooler, less passionate. Marcus was all fire and heat where Robert was calm, cool control. It was his fire that touched her.

And he had spoken to her. Why did that seem so significant? Despite that she was a slave in this place, he had talked to her. Had recognized her for more than what she offered of her body. She loved the duality of that moment.

She hated that she had no way of knowing when she would see him again.

Mika came in on quiet, bare feet, carrying a breakfast tray.

"Good morning, Cassandra."

She blinked in surprise. "You . . . I thought . . . we aren't supposed to talk."

Her voice was soft and sweet. "You go home today. It is part of the transition back to your normal life. You may ask me questions, if you like. But first, sit up and have something to eat."

Mika plumped her pillows and Cassandra sat upright in the bed. Mika laid the tray over her lap and poured a cup of fragrant tea.

Cassandra sat back against the pillows. "I have so many questions. I don't even know where to start."

The other woman smiled. "Start anywhere. We have time."

"How long have you been here?"

"I have been with Master Robert for three years."

"And you live here all the time?"

"Yes, all the time. I have given myself into his service."

"But do you never go out?"

Mika laughed, a gentle sound. "Of course. I go to the market, and to take care of whatever other errands Master has for me. And Laura and Jacqueline and I go to the beach sometimes."

Cassandra sipped her tea. "Laura and Jacqueline? They are the others?"

"Yes. They both live here, also. Laura is the taller of the two. Jacqueline, the girl with the piercings, goes to college part-time."

"It's so strange to be here and to think of the outside world at the same time. It's as though the two exist on different planes."

"This is why you will be treated as a guest here before you leave today. It takes some time to switch gears in your head. Being back in the world often comes as a shock, especially when you're new to this."

"I can't even bear to think about leaving." Tears stung her eyes and she set her cup down on the tray.

"You will be back next weekend, yes?"

Cassandra nodded.

"You need time in between your visits here to decide if this is what you really want, and how far you want to go with it. Living as a submissive is very different from visiting this lifestyle, Cassandra. You need time to figure out what will work for you. Master Robert spoke with you about these things at your first meeting."

Cassandra nodded. "But talking about it and living it are two different things."

"He knows. That is why you will only come on the weekends for a while. Is there anything else I can tell you?"

"Mika . . . do you . . . do you ever feel this sense of sort of falling in love with whoever is dominating you?"

She shrugged. "We all do. I think it has to do with our innate desire to please. The dominant is meeting a need in us no one else can meet, both physically and emotionally."

"It's overwhelming."

"It can be. This is one of the reasons why it is so important that you play only with people who are well-known and respected within the BDSM community. But you are in Master Robert's care now. You won't need to worry about that. He will only give you to those people he trusts utterly."

"And Marcus?" She shivered at the sensation of his name coming from her lips.

Mika nodded. "Marcus di Sante. He is Master Robert's nephew. He is young, but he is very good at what he does. Master trusts him as he would his own hand."

She thought of Marcus's hands on her and trembled, her sex clenching. She wanted to ask more about him, but she didn't dare. And she would have so much to think about all week as it was. But she knew Marcus's face wouldn't leave her thoughts until she saw him again. No, she corrected herself. His face would be in her thoughts always.

Coming back to her apartment in Santa Monica was a shock. She almost felt as though she were sneaking through normal society, just walking through the underground parking garage and taking the elevator to her floor. She was relieved to slip into her apartment and shut the door behind her.

It was the same place she'd lived in for five years. All of her belongings were there: her red velvet sofa, her antique lamps, the tall wooden shelves overflowing with the books she loved. Yet it all seemed alien to her, as though she'd been gone for months instead of three days.

Her high black heels clicked on the hardwood floor as she wandered into her bedroom to unpack her small bag. She set it on the antique Victorian dresser and caught sight of herself in the oval mirror above it. Her hair was a bit wild, the dark red curls falling around her shoulders in a state of disarray. She moved closer. Her eyes were huge, luminous. Did she see something in them that hadn't been there before? Or was she imagining it because she felt so different? She was not the same person who had left this room last Friday. She'd experienced so much in the last few days, she knew it had changed her forever.

Every single fantasy she'd ever had had come true. And a few she didn't even know had existed: being touched, stimulated, by women. The heightened excitement of being watched by the crowd while Mistress Delphine had played her. And while Marcus had played her, but she had been far too focused on the fact that it was *him* to be more than marginally aware of anyone else.

A small rush of heat flooded her body as she thought of him. Of the way he had touched her. His hands had been like fire dancing over her flesh. And when he had spanked her . . .

The insistent ringing of her telephone brought her head up and she grabbed the receiver from her nightstand.

"Hello?"

"Cassandra?"

A deep voice, familiar somehow . . .

"Cassandra, it's Marcus."

She was too stunned to speak. Could it really be him? Her body instantly went warm all over, her sex clenching with damp heat.

"Do you remember me? From Master Robert's house."

"Yes, of course." Remember him? She had thought of little else since the first moment she'd seen him.

"I wanted to talk with you."

"What about?" Her pulse was speeding, pounding. She wanted to drop to her knees.

There was a pause, then, "I want to know what you're thinking, feeling, about all of this."

"Oh . . . Well, I . . . it's all very new. I think I'm flying still. My mind won't stop turning it all over, analyzing. And maybe . . . I'm a little sad that it's over."

"That's normal. You'll feel better by tomorrow."

They were both silent a moment, then he said quietly, "The truth is, I couldn't stay away from you for a week."

Had he really just said that? She pushed her heavy hair from her face, sat carefully on the edge of her bed before her legs went out from under her.

He went on. "I shouldn't be calling you. You belong to my uncle, no matter how conditionally at this point."

"I'm glad you called. I wanted you to, wished for it." She was trembling all over. She could not believe they were having this conversation!

"I need to see you, Cassandra."

"Yes!"

He paused, and she heard him blow out a long breath. "It would be ignoble of me to ask this of you now, before you've had a chance to calm down, to think. But do think about it."

"Please, Marcus. Sir. I know what I want."

Another brief silence. "God, to hear you call me that . . ."

His voice was low, rough with desire. "Tell me why, Cassandra."

"Why I want to see you? Because even among a group of sensually sophisticated people, as they all are at your uncle's house, you stand out to me like a beacon. Because my body seems to know you. I don't know how to explain it." She felt that she could say anything to him, that she could tell him every thought in her head, that she was safe with him in this way.

"No, I understand completely. My body does know yours, in some inexplicable way. But what I want now is to know *you*, your mind."

"I'll tell you whatever you want to know." Her blood was singing in her veins, her heart clenching.

"Why this? Why a life of submission?"

"Because I've always wanted it, even when I didn't know it. Because now that I have experienced this, I know it's exactly what I've craved all these years." The words were tumbling out of her, she didn't even have to think about what she was saying. She was simply telling him the truth. "Because while I am long tired of always having to be the good girl, this way I can be both good and bad at the same time. It fills my need for rebellion from my repressive upbringing, and at the same time provides me with a punishment for my sins."

"Do you really believe what we do is sinful?"

"Yes and no. But I get a sort of dark pleasure from thinking of it that way. From imagining this is what will cleanse me. I suppose I have the classic twisted Catholic girl's perspective."

"Yes. But you're more intelligent about it than most slaves are. More thoughtful."

She blushed all over with his praise.

"And you, Sir?"

"I do this because I love it. It's as simple as that. My uncle raised me after I ran away from my father's house. He wasn't a very nice person. I was fifteen. Shortly after my eighteenth birthday, Robert revealed his life to me, a life he had put on hold to raise me to adulthood. He has my utter loyalty for that, which makes my talking with you behind his back such an unforgivable sin."

"Then we sin together," she said quietly.

"Yes."

She could swear she heard a smile in his voice. Pleasure suffused her; she knew she had pleased him with her answers.

"And I suppose . . . there is something perverse in me that loves the sin of it, as well." He paused, then, "Tell me Cassandra, how you know the name of Rodin's sculptures?"

"I love art. I always have. And there's something about the stillness, the starkness, of sculpture that speaks to me."

"Yes, that's it exactly. And black-and-white photography, for much the same reason."

"Yes, I love photography, whether it's Ansel Adams's scenics or more obscure work. Do you know Jan Saudek?"

"Brilliant figurative photographer. I can't believe you know his work."

"It's erotic, beautiful, even when it's crude."

"Yes, exactly." She heard Marcus take a deep breath.

"I'm sorry—I'm talking too much."

"No. I love to hear your voice. To know what you think, what you're interested in."

She warmed all over at his words. And they brought home to her that the connection she had felt with him before was amplified now, almost unbearably intense because that connection ran deeper than the mere physical.

"I want to see you, Cassandra. But I'm going to be responsible, as I should have been from the beginning, and give you time to think. It's the least I can do."

She wanted to be with him *now*. To talk with him, to feel his hands on her flesh, his lips . . . But she wasn't about to argue. She was far too intrinsically obedient to do that.

"Yes, Sir."

"I should see you next weekend at some point. And then we will talk again. About life. About art, which is often the same thing for people like us, I believe. I'll be thinking of you."

He hung up.

She stood, holding the phone in her hand, wondering if it had all been a dream. But she remembered every single word they had spoken to each other.

Her body burned for him. And her heart yearned. But only her body's needs could be slaked for now, even though Master Robert had ordered her to abstain from reaching orgasm during the week. He wanted her in a state of arousal when she returned to him. So, she would be the sinner again.

Moving to stand in front of the mirror on her closet

door, she cupped her breasts in her hands, but it only made her need worse. She squeezed, kneaded, imagining it was Marcus's hands there. She quickly unbuttoned her blouse and pulled it off, and then her bra. Her nipples were stiff and dusky pink, and needed to be touched. To be tortured.

She ran her fingers over the hard tips, and pleasure spun through her system. She pinched them, rolled them between her fingers, all the while thinking of Marcus's face, of his beautiful hands. Her sex began to pound with the need for release. She wanted to lie down on her bed, put her hand between her legs, and bring herself to orgasm.

She glanced at her bed. The fluffy white quilt, the pile of embroidered white and blue pillows, looked so inviting. But she was fascinated with watching herself in the mirror.

She slid her skirt down over her hips and kicked it off. She stood before the mirror, naked. Her skin was flushed, her eyes glossy. She moved her legs apart, slid her hand down to the dark chestnut curls there, and pressed hard. She couldn't help it.

A wave of pleasure rolled through her. She needed more. And the sight of her naked and aroused body in the mirror was thrilling, somehow.

Still watching, she used her fingers to part her lips, saw the tiny nub of her clitoris, and teased it with one finger while imagining Marcus's face, his touch. Her clit came up tight, a hard nub beneath her fingertip. She moved her hand over it, brushing, teasing, until she couldn't stand it any longer. She pushed a finger into her soaking wet cleft, felt her inner walls clench around it as the heel of her hand pressed into her aching clit. She was so damn excited it hurt.

Moving her fingers inside herself, she used her other hand to pinch one of her nipples, hard. There was no pain, only a deep pleasure that jolted through her body like an electrical shock, making her come hard. She ground her hips into her hand, driving her orgasm on in shattering waves that made her head reel.

She fell against the door frame of the closet, panting, and caught sight of herself in the mirror. Her cheeks and her breasts were flushed a bright pink; her eyes glittered. Her whole system still hummed with pleasure, but it wasn't enough. She would need to come a hundred times to quench the need that speared every nerve ending in her body.

She needed to go back to Master Robert's house. Needed to see Marcus again. That would be her only relief. She would admit her transgression to Master Robert. He would punish her. *Yes.* She needed it, craved to be punished. Mere orgasm was not enough for her now. She needed to be dominated, controlled, tortured with pleasure.

She couldn't wait to go back.

CHAPTER SIX

The Lair.

Could there really be such a place? But then, only in Cassandra's wildest dreams did a place like Master Robert's home exist. And now he was telling her about an even larger private house that was made to be a playhouse for those people whose tastes in sensual pleasure ran to the extreme.

People like her. Like Master Robert. Like Marcus.

Even now he was at the forefront of her mind. But Master Robert was talking to her again. She shifted in the leather chair in Master Robert's elegant, book-lined office and focused.

"As we discussed at our first meeting, Cassandra, ultimately nothing is done without your consent until, and unless, you make the decision to sign a contract to stay with me. And so I need to know if you are willing to come to this place with me tonight." He leaned forward in his chair, folding his hands on the enormous oak desk.

"There will be a large group of people, perhaps as

many as fifty, a hundred. They are an exclusive group, all of them very well versed in the BDSM lifestyle, all practicing the same rules and the same philosophies I live by. But you would be lent out there, as you were here last weekend. I'd like for you to go, but you must separate your own needs from my desires."

"But I am here to serve your desires," she said quietly. "That *is* what I need, Sir."

Except for that one enormous transgression of her feelings for Marcus. But she was certain Master Robert would, unknowingly, punish her for that.

He smiled. "An excellent answer, Cassandra."

She smiled back, happy she had pleased him, and her mind whirling with what this new place he was taking her to might hold for her. Is that where she would see Marcus? But she could hardly ask.

"Mika will take you to your room now to prepare."

"Yes, Sir."

He smiled at her and she shivered with pleasure just knowing she had made him happy. Yet at the same time, her need for Marcus tugged at the back of her mind, sending guilt twisting through her.

Mika came in immediately, as though she'd been waiting just outside the door. She probably had been. Without a word she gave a small bow to Master Robert, took Cassandra's elbow, and guided her into the hallway and to the room she had begun to think of as hers.

There she was undressed by Laura and Jacqueline, then bathed by them as she had been before.

It took a long time for Mika to do her hair and makeup. Cassandra tried to lose herself in the ritual, but her heart was pounding too hard. Her mind was absolutely spinning with possibilities, and always the first one: *Would Marcus be there?*

Finally she was ready and Mika took her, naked and decorated in silver this time, to the living room.

Master Robert was sitting in his usual chair. "You look lovely, Cassandra. Perfect. Except for this one last detail."

He stood and she saw for the first time that he had a heavy, white leather collar in one hand. "Hold your hair up, that's a good girl, and bend your neck forward. Beautiful."

She felt beautiful. Treasured. *Owned.* The collar was a symbol of everything she had dreamed of. It was hard and soft around her neck all at the same time. Safe. And it made her want to drop down to her knees and kiss Master Robert's hand in gratitude. But he was moving away from her.

"We'll go now. Mika, call the car, please." He stood up. "To the front door, Cassandra."

Why had she thought she'd be dressed for this trip? But she did feel dressed, with the collar around her neck. And she was slipping down into that dark place in her mind already, even though she hadn't been spanked or pinched yet.

Everything was happening too fast for her to think about it. Mika held the front door open, and a cool breeze came in carrying the salt of the ocean. Master Robert took Cassandra's elbow and guided her into the back of a black stretch limousine. Hands helped her into a seat, and it took a moment before her eyes adjusted enough to see that it was Mistress Delphine and her pretty slave boy. Master Robert sat beside her, the door shut, and the car pulled into the night.

Cassandra was made to kneel on the floor of the car next to Mistress Delphine's boy, while she and Master Robert talked quietly among themselves. She didn't even try to listen. Her body thrummed with excitement as she wondered what might happen tonight. If Marcus would be there. A surge of panic moved through her when she realized he might not be. She took in deep, gulping breaths, trying to calm herself. She was wet with anticipation already.

The ride seemed brief, she'd been so caught up in her own thoughts. The door of the car opened and cool night air rushed in, bringing her out of her daze.

"Come, sit up, Cassandra."

Master Robert's hands on her waist, then Mistress Delphine's slave boy was helping her to step from the car. Cold pavement beneath her bare feet. She had a quick impression of a very large house—it could only be called a mansion, something of this size—with a wide, sweeping staircase punctuated by white columns. She didn't dare look up to see more, just followed the guiding hands at her waist to the top of the stairs.

There Master Robert told her, "On your knees now, yes, you know how this is done."

She sank down behind him instantly, suddenly very much aware of the collar around her neck, Mistress Delphine's slave boy beside her. The air here was different, less moist, and there was no smell of ocean in it. Here it was all new-cut grass and that unique scent of old mortar, like the sidewalks of her childhood in Connecticut after a summer rain.

She dared to glance up for a moment as two uniformed

servants opened a pair of heavy doors. She followed Master Robert's feet inside, onto a white marble floor. Then his hand on the back of her neck, just that familiar bit of pressure.

"You may look up now, Cassandra. I want you to see this place. To see the grandeur of it. To see the fantasy we are about to walk into."

She did as he asked. They appeared to be in some sort of anteroom. Another pair of enormous doors were in front of them, and these doors were flanked on either side by what she at first took to be statues. But after a moment she realized these were people, slaves like herself. Well, perhaps more so. There was a man on one side, a woman on the other, each in a tall niche. And they were entirely naked, except for the heavy, gleaming chrome manacles at their wrists and ankles and a fine silvery-white powder all over their skin. They were chained to bolts in the niches with arms and legs spread wide. Both of them had their heads bowed. She wanted to see their faces, they were so beautiful in their silent poses. In their stillness. Just like the statues she and Marcus had talked about. For some reason she couldn't explain, tears stung her eyes.

And just as suddenly, fear pierced her heart. What kind of place was this? What would happen to her here? She could not be chained to a wall and left all night, as these two had been! Too awful, to be objectified to the point of being a part of the architecture.

But isn't that exactly what you wanted?

No. Well, perhaps, but not to this extent. No, she had never, ever imagined anything like this.

But wasn't that the attraction of it all? The mystery

that both terrified and intrigued her. And confused her. She hardly knew what to think.

She glanced out of the corner of her eye and focused her gaze on Master Robert's black wool pant leg. He would take care of everything, she silently reminded herself. She wouldn't have to think.

Her neck muscles loosened and she pulled in a deep breath.

The pair of heavy, white-painted doors between the lovely, bound slaves were pulled back and Master Robert's hand on her neck told her to crawl through them, to the other side. A brief moment of panic shook her, then she went through, eyes focused on her Master's Italian loafers.

Sound surrounded her, infused her senses. People talking, laughing. The tinkle of ice in glasses, the scent of expensive perfume. Exactly like a cocktail party, except for the occasional moan or the lash of a whip. The contrast was almost shocking, the formal setting and the sounds and the knowledge of what was happening here. She didn't really want to look up, to see it all, yet she couldn't help herself.

Her jaw almost dropped as she tried to take it all in. The place was indeed the mansion it had appeared to be from the outside. The ceilings were vaulted, so high she couldn't lift her chin enough to see where they ended. The room they were in was some sort of ballroom, or grand salon: enormous, surrounded by tall windows on either side draped in heavy gold brocade, closed against the night. The rows of windows were punctuated here and there by large paintings, gorgeously depicted erotic pieces done in a classical style. She had never before seen oil paintings of this quality showing this sort of subject matter.

But the people in the room were even more interesting.

Everywhere she turned were gorgeously dressed Doms and Dommes, many in leather, mostly in black, as the dominants so often were, but some of the women in particular were dressed in beautiful evening gowns in brilliant jewel tones. Many had whips and floggers and other implements of torture in their hands or hanging from their belts. And everywhere, naked and collared slaves followed them about on hands and knees, some on their knees with hands bound behind their backs. The slaves were so beautiful, all of them. Or perhaps they only appeared to be. The state of their submission was beautiful to her in itself. Beautiful and shocking, to see so many gathered in one place.

And she was one of them.

Oh, yes; she was hardly a simple spectator here.

Pressure on the back of her neck again and she realized she had stopped in the middle of the floor to gawk. She followed Master Robert's feet to a corner of the room, where he and Mistress Delphine settled on a long, low couch done in deep red velvet.

"Kneel here, at my feet, Cassandra."

She did so, wishing she could lean into his leg, wanting the reassuring warmth of him against her skin. But she knew better.

A naked young girl approached and took drink orders from the Masters. They seemed content to sit and talk among themselves for the moment, and she used the opportunity to look more at this strange and exotic place Master Robert had taken her to.

She let her gaze wander past the crowd, to the darker corners of the room, and saw finally the equipment placed at intervals here and there. Padded spanking benches of different designs were scattered among the large St. Andrew's crosses she had seen in books: tall X's made of wood with eye hooks to which a submissive might be bound at wrists and ankles. Several already were, splayed out for their Masters to torture.

In one area was gathered a group of slaves, all kneeling on the floor and wearing the most unusual masks. Some were in the form of horses, some were the faces of dogs. The masks, which came over the slaves' heads like hoods, were somewhat primitive and gilded in gold paint, like the masks common during the Renaissance in Venice. Those who wore the dog masks were all collared and leashed. One was being made to drink from a bowl on the floor while the Masters looked on, laughing and pinching the puppy-boy, prodding him with the tip of their crops. He had an absolutely bursting erection.

One horse-masked slave girl was hoisted onto a long wooden table, which was intricately carved and more heavily gilded than the masks. A large man held her head while a woman fit a bit into her exposed mouth and covered the mask with a leather bridle. The man settled a small pony saddle on the girl's back, buckled it around her waist.

Cassandra shivered, half in excitement, half in dread. Would this humiliation be forced on her? She didn't think she could bear it. Yet at the same time, her sex grew inexplicably damp. She liked to watch these others endure this torture.

Master Robert leaned down and whispered into her ear, "I see you looking at the pony girl. Perhaps we should fit you with a saddle, a bit. And of course with a tail."

Her eyes went immediately to the rounded buttocks of the girl wearing the saddle. A long tail of horsehair protruded from between her smooth cheeks. She understood instantly how the tail was mounted there. She trembled all over.

Master Robert put a hand on the back of her neck, calming her, even as he chuckled softly at her obvious discomfort. "Don't worry, girl, I have other plans for you tonight. Come, follow me." Then, turning to Mistress Delphine, he said, "I'll see you later in the evening. Enjoy."

He snapped his fingers and again Cassandra kept her eyes on his feet as he moved across the room. Where would he take her now? What other evil scenarios had this group of sophisticated sadists thought up? But even as she had the thought, she felt that soft, slippery sensation of her mind moving out of focus. Or not out of focus so much as very focused on whatever was most immediate, yet blurry around the edges. At this moment, the only things that mattered, really, were following Master Robert's feet, obeying him, pleasing him. And of course the question of whether Marcus would be here tonight, of how long she would have to wait to see him. And even as she crawled across the floor, had these thoughts, she understood on some deep level that simply being in this place was doing incredible things to her head.

Over the marble floor and down a long hallway, her knees moved quickly across a series of Persian rugs. She didn't dare look even to the side. She didn't need to know what was there, other than whatever Master Robert chose to show her.

Finally he guided her to the right and through a doorway.

"Up, Cassandra."

She lifted her head, taking in the room. Still large, although nothing like the scale of the grand salon they had just left, it was dimly lit by enormous, ornate chandeliers hanging from the vaulted ceiling. But she could see more tall, brocade-draped windows. The only other thing in the room was an enormous structure made of heavily carved and gilded wood. It was a beautifully made frame with complicated crossbars and posts, perhaps seven or eight feet high. Golden hooks protruded here and there and lengths of silky golden cord were strung between posts, in places in a complicated, weblike manner. Some of the bars at waist height were padded and covered in a deep black velvet. At one end was what appeared to be a long table, done in the same black velvet.

And standing in the middle of this elegant and wicked structure was her dark stranger, a stranger no more.

Marcus.

CHAPTER SEVEN

He was dressed in black leather pants, a white shirt with billowing sleeves, heavy black boots; what Cassandra thought of as classic BDSM pirate drag. One arm was held overhead, gripping a crossbar. The other held a long riding crop, which he was tapping in a slow rhythm against his leg.

Her mouth went dry, her sex went wet, and she was filled with longing, confusion, and a stab of lust so strong she knew if she'd been standing she would have fallen to the floor.

The big, black boots in particular really did something to her. She wanted to kiss them, to touch them. They were commanding in and of themselves, those boots. She looked up, into his face, even though she knew better. He was smiling just a little. His teeth were gorgeous, white and strong. His mouth was pure sex, lush and pink yet thoroughly masculine. His eyes were perfectly dark. She looked away, casting her gaze to the floor.

"Good evening, Marcus." Master Robert's voice appeared to boom out across the nearly empty room.

"Good evening, Uncle."

God, his voice was dark and smooth, like honey, like smoke over molasses. The tone of it made her nipples go hard.

She would die if he didn't touch her tonight. If all he did was watch as Master Robert played her.

"Delivery, as promised."

"Thank you, Uncle."

It was said too quickly for her to think about what those words meant. Movement in the room, then those big, black boots right in front of her. A hand under her chin—oh, God, *his* hand!—forcing her gaze upward, until she couldn't help but look into those bottomless eyes. His gaze was steady, concentrated.

"Tonight, Cassandra, you are mine to do with as I wish. Are you ready?"

She opened her mouth to answer. Nothing came out.

He slapped her lips with his fingertips. It didn't hurt much; it was just hard enough to wake her up. And just enough to make her insides go soft and molten, that little hurting tap of his fingers and his commanding intent.

Where had the man gone who had spoken to her so civilly on the phone? But it didn't matter, really. She knew that was a part of him, and so was this commanding Dominant. It was the combination that had drawn her in completely, that made her heart surge as much as her sex.

"Yes, I'm ready, Sir."

He smiled, looking pleased, his gaze resting on hers perhaps a little too long.

Was she really to be handed over to him for the evening? She would be grateful for even an hour. Torture, not knowing. Of course, mind-fuck was half the power of BDSM, she was coming to discover.

He was still looking at her, smiling at her, when Master Robert leaned down and spoke in her ear in his smooth, sophisticated tone. "I am giving you to Marcus for the night. You are his, understand? You will obey him as you do me. I will come to collect you when I'm ready. And I will have a full report, so you must be on your best behavior. He will not tolerate any infraction of the rules, and he will punish you for misbehavior. You haven't been punished yet. I guarantee you won't like it. Pain without pleasure. Is that understood, Cassandra?"

She nodded, barely able to speak. "Yes, Master Robert."

Marcus flicked his eyes to his uncle. "I don't like the nodding. A posture collar will cure her of that."

"Do as you will, Marcus."

She heard Master Robert's footsteps as he left the room. Marcus tapped the top of her head lightly with the crop.

"Into submission pose, Cassandra."

She knew what he wanted, but it was a moment before she could make her muscles obey. Suddenly she was terrified at the idea of being left alone with him. She knew what that would do to her head, to her heart. And then she would be sent home with Master Robert. Unbearable.

A quick, hard smack of the crop on her right breast got her moving. She sat back on her heels, spread her thighs, laid her hands there, palms up, and bent her head, which was filled with the sound of her own breathing.

"Stay there. I'll return in a moment."

She held as still as possible, shivering just a little all

over. She could not believe she was to be his tonight! The idea was intimidating. What if she didn't please him? It seemed hugely important that she did.

He was back quickly, leaning over her from behind so she couldn't see him. He whispered in her ear, "I wanted to be sure he was gone before I told you this: that you have no idea what this does to me, knowing you are in my hands tonight. This is not the time to talk, as much as I want to hear your voice again. Tonight we are at The Lair, and we must use this place as it's meant to be used. And I will use *you* as you are meant to be used. Thoroughly. Lovingly. Tell me you want this."

Her insides shivered at the sound of his voice, at his meaning. "I want this. I need this. I need you."

"As I need you. Lift your hair, my sweet Cassandra."

She did. He unfastened Master Robert's collar from around her neck without ever touching her skin. Her stomach did a little dip of disappointment. But very quickly the narrow leather collar was replaced with something very tall and stiff, built almost like the cervical collars people wore who had strained their necks. He buckled the device at the back of her neck, which felt stretched out, luxuriously elongated. A strange sense of panic washed over her when she found she could barely turn her head, or move it in any direction at all.

He laid his large, warm hand on her shoulder. "Calm, Cassandra. It's alright. You'll get used to it in a moment. It will make you feel safe."

She didn't know about safe, but she was flooded with lust at that slight touch on her skin.

More.

When his hand slid down her arm she closed her eyes, breathed in, trying to catch his scent. Yes, there it was, that woodsy scent which smelled like the deepest part of a forest to her. That deep, dark, dangerous place in the very center, where anything can happen.

Then he was leaning in closer, until his breath warmed her hair. He whispered, "You are in my hands, Cassandra. You are mine tonight. *Mine*."

Her thighs trembled. His scent was driving her crazy. And in her mind was simply the word again, *yes*.

"Come, on your feet."

She stood, swaying just a little. Then his big hand slid around her wrist, and for the first time she was able to get a real sense of how tall he was, at least six feet, perhaps an inch or two more. But his presence, his essence, was enormous.

He took her to the wooden frame. Up close she could see the intricate carvings of flowers and vines, and here and there a phallic symbol or a couple in a sensual embrace woven into the pattern. The work was exquisite. But she didn't have time to think about it.

Marcus brought her to the long, velvet-covered table at the far end of the structure and had her lie down on her back, the velvet soft beneath her naked skin.

"Bring your arms over your head for me and spread them for me. Yes, and now spread your legs wide."

She did as he asked, her heart pounding so hard she could barely breathe. He buckled her wrists into heavy leather cuffs, amazing her by kissing each wrist before he bound it. Her heart swelled. If she hadn't been bound she would have wrapped her arms around his neck, demanding to be kissed.

But no, this was Marcus—she would never do such a thing with him.

He attached her ankles to the velvet bed in the same way as her wrists. She was spread-eagle, open to his searching gaze. The vulnerability of her position was sending her to some trancelike place already. She watched him from beneath half-closed lids. His bone structure was unbelievable, like some classic statue. And his mouth was impossibly lush for a man's. She didn't dare try to look into his eyes.

When he ran one finger lazily down between her breasts, she gasped. His touch was like heat lightning, burning her flesh. Her breasts immediately began to ache, her nipples coming up hard and tight, pulling against the silver clamps there.

As though reading her mind he gave the chain between the clamps a small tug, sending a burst of sensation through her nipples. She let out a moan.

"I love that you're so sensitive."

She groaned when he slipped his hand between her thighs and thrust his fingers inside her. She was wet, aching. Her sex convulsed around him. She could not believe it was him touching her like this.

"God help me, Cassandra," he muttered.

She could barely stand it, his voice, his pained expression. She had to fight not to move her hips, to thrust into his hand. But after a moment he started himself, sliding in and out of her at a slow, agonizing pace.

"Oh, God," she groaned, ready to come.

"Not yet." His voice was firm, commanding, but ragged around the edges.

He continued to stroke her, angled his fingers to slide against her g-spot. She bit her lip as pleasure built in her, a tight coil of heat and need.

Not yet, not yet.

But then he took her chin in his other hand, forced her gaze to his. His eyes were intense, hazed with emotion or lust, she didn't know which. She was too filled with both herself. Her head was spinning, out of control.

"Not yet, Cassandra. Hold it back. *For me.*"

She gulped in a breath, bit her lip harder, squeezed her eyes shut. Her body teetered on the edge of climax. But she held it back for him.

For *him*.

His fingers pumped harder inside her and tears fell from her eyes, slid over her cheeks.

"Do not come. Not until I tell you to. I can see that you want to. That you want to please me."

The pleasure was overwhelming, but yes, anything for him. Her head strained against the tight hold of the posture collar with the effort to hold her climax back. Her sex, her breasts, ached, burned. Her arms and legs pulsed with need. The brink of climax was knife-edge sharp, until it began to feel like an orgasm in itself; one long, drawn out wave of almost unbearable pleasure.

He pumped his fingers faster, kept his gaze on hers, forcing her to focus on nothing but his face, his voice, his fingers inside her.

Marcus.

When his thumb hit her clit she almost lifted off the table.

"Now, Cassandra. Come for me."

Her body let go with a torrent of pleasure. Sharp, stabbing through her system at a hundred miles an hour, dragging her over the edge, hurtling her into darkness. Her sex clasped around his fingers, holding him tight inside her. Her thighs shook, pulling against the bonds as her entire body convulsed. She cried out.

Wave after exquisite wave, it seemed to go on forever. Her breath came in ragged gasps as her climax subsided, a little at a time. When he finally slipped his fingers out of her body, her sex was still clenching. She was dripping wet.

"And now we begin," he said softly, holding her chin, still. Holding her gaze. His eyes were glittering, bottomless. She could drown in them and never come up, happy to do so.

She hadn't yet caught her breath when he started in with a small flogger that appeared in his hand as if by magic. Soft strokes of the leather over her skin, all across the front of her body, her belly, her breasts, her thighs. The strokes quickly became harder, the leather tails biting into her sensitized skin.

Oh, he was wicked. She was still half-coming, and the flogger felt like heaven to her, even as it burned her flesh. It was even better when he brushed her skin with his fingertips in between the lashes, one stroke of the whip, one stroke of his hand. His touch on her was gentle, in stark contrast to the evil little whip, making her feel each ripple of sensation even more.

"That's it, Cassandra, take it all in."

She realized vaguely that she was overloading. The lovely touch of his hand, the bite of the flogger, she didn't know which was which anymore. She didn't care. She just didn't want him to stop.

When he did she was only very dimly aware that she was totally out of her head, dreamy, drifting on the pain.

It wasn't long before he started on her again, this time with a small bristle brush. He dragged it over her body, sometimes softly, sometimes so hard it felt like sandpaper on her skin. Over her breasts, her rib cage, her stomach, then down over her thighs, her calves, even the tops of her feet. She loved the feel of it, loved the way it made her skin quiver all over, even as it hurt. And it did hurt; he made sure of it.

He kept on with the brush for what felt like a long while, until she was in an almost meditative trance. Her skin was really burning now, absolutely on fire. And she was floating; her head, her body. Her eyes fluttered closed.

His scent brought her around enough to take in what he was saying.

"I'm going to really whip you now."

Marcus couldn't believe how incredibly responsive she was. She shivered at the mere sound of his voice! He loved it, that he could affect her in this way. She would make a perfect slave with a little training.

Not your slave.

No, but he could borrow her, as he had tonight. He knew already it would never be enough.

She was panting hard as he unbuckled the cuffs which held her to the table. Her glazed eyes were a gorgeous flash of green fire. The front of her body was crisscrossed with fine red welts. Beautiful. She let out a quiet moan and his gaze moved to her mouth. Her lips were a dark pink. Soft, tender-looking.

Kissable.

Restrain yourself. Impossible to kiss her here, where Robert could walk in at any moment.

Instead, he went about the task of getting her to sit up, then to stand, so he could move her to another area where he bound her hands in black leather cuffs, then clipped them to a heavy golden chain hanging from one of the crossbeams on the play structure.

Concentrate on the task at hand.

Difficult, when the task was Cassandra. When he wanted to kiss her, to hold her in his arms, every bit as much as he wanted to spank her. When his mind was whirling, wondering why she made him feel this way.

Focus.

He checked her bonds to make certain they were secure, then left her for a moment and bent over the leather bag on the floor that held his equipment. He found the three-foot-long single-tail whip he wanted. From what his uncle had told him, no one had used such a toy on Cassandra yet.

Nothing like virgin flesh. It was always an honor, and frankly a thrill, to be the first to do something to a new slave. Even more so because it was her, the first woman ever to enchant him. He knew on some level he was dangerously out of control when it came to her. But he was not going to pass up an opportunity to play her.

He held the whip in his hand, ran his palm up the slender length of it. Black and wicked-looking, the single-tail was a high pain toy. It delivered a unique sensation that started as an intensely sharp sting at the point of contact, then slowly spread outward, so that the effects of each strike took a full minute or two to ride out. He normally would use it only on a more practiced bottom, but he had a feeling she could take it. He was rarely wrong. And he wanted to give her that extreme sensation experience. He wanted to give her everything she desired.

He moved around behind her, coiled the single-tail in his hand, then flicked his wrist. The whip snapped in the air.

Cassandra jumped.

He smiled. He could see the goose bumps rising on her flesh already.

He moved in, laid a hand between her shoulder blades, felt her shiver beneath his touch. Christ, her skin was like pale satin. The skin here was almost as silky as the slick folds of her hot little pussy. His groin tightened just thinking about it, remembering the texture and the scent of her, his fingers buried inside her.

He said quietly, "This is going to hurt quite a lot."

Again that silent shiver from her.

"You've already been taught about converting the pain. But this will be a real test, this whip. It's called a single-tail, or a snake whip. In the end you'll have a burst of endorphins like nothing you've ever experienced before. You'll never forget this little toy. I'll take you through it. You will follow my direction. Do you understand, Cassandra?"

"Yes . . . Sir." Her voice was a breathy whisper.

He came around to the front of her body. Her eyes were

cast down. He lifted her delicate chin in his hand, as much as he could with the posture collar on. Her eyes were still glazed, unfocused. He could see she was deep down in sub space. Her features were so sweet, so innocent-looking in comparison to her lush body; the full breasts, the curve of her hips.

But it was her mouth he kept going back to.

He leaned in and kissed her. Just a small brush of lips against lips. But it went through him like a shock.

Christ.

She hadn't even kissed him back. But he felt like he'd been slammed in the chest with a sledgehammer. This girl did something to him . . . God, he couldn't stand that she could never belong to him.

He was angry with himself suddenly. Angry that he seemed to be unable to resist her. Unable to behave as a proper Dominant should. With respect for another man's property, at the very least.

Fuck.

He stepped back, ran a hand through his hair.

He was here to give her what she needed. That was his job. But who the hell was he kidding? She was here with him because he wanted her. *Her*, Cassandra. Plain and simple. And devastating to his way of life if he didn't get himself under control damn quick.

Just play her, damn it.

He pulled in a lungful of air, pushed it out on a harsh breath. He took another step back, moved around behind her. Lifted his arm and swung.

CHAPTER EIGHT

Cassandra floated on a cloud of sensation, completely inside her own head, yet acutely aware of every inch of her own skin. And just as aware of Marcus, standing behind her. His scent filled her nostrils, swam through her body, saturating her system.

There was no conscious thought; she had no control over her body anymore. She was a being of pure desire, of want, of need. And no matter how he touched her, hurt her, it was never enough.

She had heard his warning, had trembled with the desire to feel that pureness of pain he was promising her. But she was too far gone to even tense in expectation.

The blow came, a lancing sting that almost felt as though it had cut into her skin.

"Take it, Cassandra. Breathe into it. Yes, inhale, exhale."

She did as he said. The sting intensified, became so razor-sharp she had to pull in a gasping breath.

"Yes, good, keep breathing. Follow my voice."

The pain moved, spread, through her buttocks, her legs, her torso, through her breasts in an aching stab of pleasure. Her sex pulsed in response, keeping beat with the pain thundering through her body in a hammering rhythm. It was almost too much, nearly unbearable—yet exactly what she needed, had always needed.

"Feel it, Cassandra. Move with it. Move into the pain."

Impossibly, the sensation increased. She groaned.

"Breathe, my girl."

His hand curved around her body, came to settle on her belly. And with his touch came a roar of fiery pleasure, exploding in her head, in her flesh. She trembled with the force of it, her sex clenching. When his hand slipped down between her thighs and pressed into her clit, she came hard, harder than she had ever thought possible. Pain and pleasure combined, fused, burned through her in a molten torrent.

Her mind slipped away and everything went black.

It must have been only seconds before she opened her eyes and found Marcus staring into her face. It was another moment before she realized he had her chin in his hand, one strong arm holding her waist.

She was suffused with gratitude and with the after-effects of orgasm. She felt loose, weightless, and filled with a great, inexplicable pleasure.

"Ah, there you are. Back with me."

His smile was like the light of heaven to her. She smiled back.

"God, you're beautiful," he murmured.

He reached out, stroking her cheek, and she realized he had removed the tall collar that had held her so firmly in its embrace. She turned her head into his palm and kissed the soft flesh there. She couldn't help herself.

"Ah, Cassandra."

Nothing but pleasure hearing his voice like this, feeling his hands on her body, her face. And then the strangest thing happened. He was kissing her face, small, fluttering kisses over her cheeks, her chin, her eyelids, and finally her lips.

Her heart twisted, surged with longing. To touch him, to be with him, to feel him inside her body. She didn't understand everything he made her feel. She couldn't think now.

He tasted like wild honey.

When he pulled away she was panting with an entirely new kind of need his kisses had stirred in her. Unfathomable tears stung her eyes.

He was watching her.

"What is it, Cassandra? What do you need?" His voice was so gentle it hurt.

She could only shake her head, mute.

"Then I will have to figure it out." He paused, searched her face. "I will figure you out. I will come to know you inside and out, until I know everything about you. Every dark secret, every moment of yearning."

He was speaking so quietly she wasn't sure he intended for her to hear him, for her to answer in any way. She stood quietly, waiting to see what he would do next. Happy to be in his presence, under his hands, under his care. She would accept anything this man did to her right now.

She was more than half in love with him, but it was more than the things he did to her with his hands, with the wicked little single-tail whip. It was the thoughtful way he looked at her, as though he really were trying to figure her out. It was the sharply planed, male beauty of his features, the graceful way he moved. It was that one precious conversation, and the way he spoke to her when she was under his command. He was the first man who truly cared what went on in her head. Irresistible.

She tilted her head to see him better and felt the soft brush of her own hair across the back of her shoulders. A small shiver went through her.

She wanted more. She wanted this to go on forever. And just as she was thinking it, he reached out and swept one hand very slowly down the front of her body, beginning at the hollow of her throat, over her rib cage, her belly, stopping just above the triangle of curls at the apex of her thighs.

She sighed, lowered her eyelids, let her head fall back, taking in the sensation of his hand on her flesh. Blood rose to the surface of her skin, as though to meet his touch.

"I want more of you, Cassandra. Now. Tomorrow. Next year. But all we may have is tonight. And since we are not alone here, I can't have you the way I really want you, in my bed, in your body. Will you take what I can give you here? In the only way I can feel you in my arms?"

She lifted her head and nodded. She couldn't help but smile. She was as happy at this moment as she had ever been in her life, even though she wasn't sure if, or when, she would see him again. She understood his loyalty to his uncle, understood her own loyalty to Master Robert. But she couldn't bear to think about that now. It was too complicated. For now, she would take what she could.

"Please, Sir . . ."

He reached up and unfastened her wrists. He was pressed right up against her as he worked the metal buckles free. She could smell him, the manly scent of sweat, a little musk of arousal along with that woodsy fragrance he wore. She inhaled deeply, trying to pull something of his essence into her lungs, to keep him with her.

He led her to a low, velvet-covered bench and immediately pulled her over his lap. His thighs were strong and hard beneath her stomach, her breasts pushed into his steely flesh. She loved the crush of his body against hers, wished he were as naked as she was. Before she had a chance to settle in, he smacked her bottom with his hand. One hard rap, quickly followed by another. Hard slaps coming one after the other, so quickly she couldn't catch her breath in between.

It hurt. But as always, the pain morphed quickly into pleasure, so that it was no longer pain, except that it was, in a way she could never explain to herself. She wanted it, craved it. And even as she surged into his hard, loving hand, she squirmed to escape.

Soon she was panting, barely able to keep up with the pace he set. The slapping never seemed to stop, to pause even for a moment. But the pace itself forced her to become lost in it, in the pain, in the desire flooding her sex, her breasts, her mind.

She heard herself panting, moaning, over and over. God, it hurt. She was drowning in a pool of sensation. She needed to come.

Finally he stopped. She heard his ragged breath. It matched her own. She groaned her need one more time.

He turned her over with oddly gentle hands until she

was cradled in his lap. He ran his hands over her shoulders, her arms, her thighs.

His voice was rough, husky, still breathless. "I want to hold you, Cassandra. I want to spank you some more. I don't fucking know what I want anymore. What have you done to me?"

He gazed into her eyes. She was too far gone to understand what she saw there. His expression was pained, his eyes almost black. He blinked hard. Reached out to touch her hair, pulled back. The intensity of his gaze was making her heart ache.

Finally, he shook his head. "Damn it, Cassandra," he muttered.

Her heart fluttered, stalled in her chest. Had she not pleased him?

"I don't know what it is about you. You make me lose control. This isn't right. I shouldn't be doing this. The more I touch you, the more I need to. And you are not mine." He paused, shook his head. "We're going to stop right here. Now. I'm handing you back over to Master Robert."

❧

"No!"

Marcus had his hands on her shoulders, ready to bring her to her feet. That one word stopped him short. He was shocked. By her refusal to go back to her rightful Master. By the way he was feeling about her.

He watched her face, searched her emerald eyes. She was deep down in sub space, must be after all the play she'd had tonight, especially the single-tail. Yet somehow she was right there with him. He hardly knew her, but the look in her eyes lanced straight into his heart.

"You don't know what you're saying, Cassandra." His mouth was so dry he could hardly get the words out. What the hell was wrong with him?

"Yes, I do." She paused, biting her luscious lower lip, then, "I want to stay with you. Please, Sir."

He shook his head.

She whispered, "Please let me stay with you."

Her words ripped at him. This situation was impossible. But his desire for her had turned into a sharp, aching need. There would be no turning back.

She was warm in his lap, light and supple and utterly yielding to him physically, even if she was talking out of turn, going against the most basic rules set down for a submissive. But he wanted her to speak, to hear her voice, to know what she had to say.

He must be losing his mind.

She was still staring up at him with glazed, green eyes. Her pale cheeks were flushed, her full mouth a delectable pink. The curve of her breast was pushed up against his arm, right at that point where the cuff of his sleeve had fallen back. He could feel the heat of her skin against the back of his wrist.

He wanted to touch her, too badly. That was the whole problem, wasn't it? This girl was irresistible to him, in every way.

"Please," she murmured again, curling more closely into his chest, then tipping her head back to look up at him.

Her lips parted as she took in a sighing breath. He

thought he saw a mist of tears dampen her eyes. He couldn't stand it any longer. He bent his head and pressed his mouth to hers.

She opened for him immediately. He'd meant it to be a brush of lips, just to taste her. But as soon as he felt the whisper of her sweet breath in his mouth, all reason left him. He plunged into her; that was the only word for it. She was all wet sweetness on his tongue. She was kissing him back, fervently, eagerly, so full of heat he could feel it through his clothes. Her body was absolutely on fire. And so was he, on fire with a bottomless need for her.

He pushed farther into her mouth, twined his tongue with hers. She was squirming in his lap, panting beneath his lips. Hell, so was he. Like some kid making out for the first time. His groin tightened, filled to bursting. He'd never felt so out of control.

Control. Hell.

He pulled back regretfully. He was supposed to be in command here, damn it! And he was definitely out of control, way out. He'd never let things go like this before, never with anyone else. But he didn't want to stop. He had to have her. Whatever the cost.

He stroked her hair, looked into her eyes once more. She was totally gone, caught up in desire, in the chemicals surging through her body. But was it really him? Or was it the setting, the play, the pain and pleasure he had given her tonight? He had to find out.

"Cassandra, listen to me." He held her face in his hands. Her cheeks were like warm, flushed silk in his palms. "I want you to come and be with me, alone, at my house. Not tonight. Another day."

"Yes. Please, Marcus! Sir," she added.

Her face held a blatant expression of urgency. He would choose to believe it for now.

"I am going to call you at home next week. We'll talk about it. Do you understand what I'm saying? Why are you crying?"

"Because I can't wait until next week."

God, he could hardly stand it. She was so open, so vulnerable. Vulnerable, yes. Was he taking advantage of that? Perhaps, to some extent. But that's why he would call her during the week, to talk to her when she was in a more stable state of mind.

And when she is not in service to Robert.

Yes, that too. He knew he was doing something very wrong, on several levels. She did not belong to him. He had no right to poach on his uncle's territory. His own flesh and blood, for God's sake!

None of it mattered right now.

"I need to take you back to Master Robert now."

She started to shake her head, but he stopped her with a firm hand on her chin.

"I will call you in a few days. I will come to get you if that's what you want. But now I need to turn you back over to him."

Before he did something he would regret. He had to get some distance, think this through.

But he knew the only thing that would stop him from having her was if she didn't want to be with him. He would never force himself on her, not in that way. Looking into her eyes, holding her in his arms, he felt he understood what was in her heart, and he knew already she would never refuse him. Whatever demon possessed him now possessed her, too. They were meant to be together, somehow. And he meant to make it happen. Damn the consequences.

He helped her to her feet and pulled a cord on the wall, summoning a trio of slaves to take her away to care for her and return her to her Master. His arms felt empty the moment he let her go. His chest tightened when she looked over her shoulder at him, her expression imploring. He knew just how she felt.

He moved to the long windows, pulled the heavy drapery aside, and peered out into the darkened garden, running a hand through his hair. Two days. Two days before she would be away from his uncle's house, before he could safely contact her. He had a lot of thinking to do between now and then, once he'd had a chance to calm down. He could barely think straight now. Not after having his hands on her, inside her, his mouth on hers.

His erection gave a jump at the thought, but there was a hell of a lot more to it than that. More to her. He couldn't explain how he knew it. But she'd felt as though she belonged to him from the first moment he'd set eyes on her.

Meanwhile, he would suffer. He would go home, stroke himself to orgasm thinking of her. But he wouldn't be satisfied until he'd talked to her. *Talked* to her, for God's sake! Since when did he care what any slave had to say, as long as they were beautiful, obedient?

He had to get out of The Lair, to leave this place. He couldn't stand to face his uncle right now.

Quickly packing his equipment in the leather bag he

always carried, he made for the front door, hurrying past the main ballroom, where dozens of guests were still gathered.

Cassandra was probably in there now with Robert and that wicked bitch, Delphine.

No, don't think about it.

Nodding at the doormen, he didn't bother to ask for his car to be brought around, but walked down the wide driveway to where his black Porsche was parked.

Rain fell in a barely discernible spatter as he threw his bag onto the passenger seat, got in, and turned the key. The engine roared to life, and he felt the power of the car beneath his hands as he pulled out onto the street.

His head was still filled with images of her, her pale, smooth skin, her lush mouth, the taste of her, damn it. He hit the gas harder and sped through the night, down the twisting roads of Bel Aire. Past the homes of people who thought the way he and his uncle lived was sinful, depraved. Fuck them all.

His tires squealed as he took a hard turn, and there was an accompanying flash of satisfaction. But it lasted only a moment. And he realized that no matter how fast he drove, no matter how hard he ran, there was going to be no escaping his sweet Cassandra.

CHAPTER NINE

Sunday afternoon. Cassandra had been home for half the day and her mind was beginning to work normally again. At least, she thought it was. But so much had happened to her over the weekend she couldn't be certain. Her body was sore in so many places, gloriously sore, and she loved that reminder of what had been done to her.

All she could really think of, though, was Marcus.

He would contact her this week, but how long would she have to wait? Absolute torture.

She sat back into the pile of brocade pillows on her red velvet sofa. Pulling one into her lap, she curled her legs beneath her and brooded.

She had never experienced anything as intense, as overwhelming, as she had when she was under Marcus's command in that room at The Lair. She'd been in total sensory overload, she knew that. But half of it was because it was *him*.

She enjoyed everything Master Robert did to her, everything Mika and the other girls did, even the wicked

Mistress Delphine. But Marcus made her lose her head altogether. Her head, her body, her senses.

Was she foolish to think there was some deeper connection there? Maybe. But she was convinced of it, convinced he felt it, too. That much she could read in his dark eyes, knew it when he talked to her, with that desperate edge to his voice. She felt it, too.

It didn't make sense; they barely even knew each other. She didn't know if he could overcome the idea that he was betraying his uncle in talking to her outside the realm of his uncle's house, outside of those times in which his uncle had given her over to him. And if he couldn't . . .

Her stomach clenched. She had to see him; she yearned for his voice, his touch. At the same time, guilt gnawed at the back of her mind. Master Robert had brought her into the world she had craved for so long. She hadn't yet signed a slave contract with him, but still, she knew what she was doing with Marcus wasn't right. The sinner once more. But she wasn't going to turn away from him.

When the telephone rang she jumped, her heart pounding. She took a deep breath, picked up.

"Hello?"

"Cassandra."

Her whole body surged at the sound of his voice in her ear. "Yes."

"It's Marcus."

"Yes, Sir."

"You don't have to call me that now, alright? Right now we are just two people, talking."

Not possible.

"Yes, S . . . Yes, Marcus."

"That's better." A small rush of pleasure at the approval in his voice. "I need to talk with you, to see you. I saw in your file that you work at some sort of clothing boutique. Can you get away today?"

They kept a file on her? But she would think about that later; she had to keep track of what he was saying to her.

"Yes. I've taken some time off work. I needed some space to process everything."

"Come to my house, then. I'm in the Hollywood Hills." He gave her the address, which she scribbled on a pad by the phone. "Can you come now?"

"Now? I'll be there as soon as I can."

He hung up. Her hands shook as she set the phone down. She sat, unable to move for a moment, her pulse hammering so hard she could hear the roar of her own blood in her ears. But she quickly realized she had much to do to prepare herself for him, to present herself to him properly.

She pushed up from the sofa and headed for the bathroom and a quick, hot shower.

She was going to see Marcus, to be entirely alone with him. Her whole body trembled with desire at the mere thought. She wasn't sure of what to expect, didn't really know what was happening. But the important thing was that he wanted her. And along with that hot surge of desire was her heart fluttering in her chest. A flutter made of anticipation, and something else that almost made her want to cry.

She dressed carefully in her Roissy Academy outfit: black skirt, fitted white blouse, thigh-high stockings, and black stiletto heels. She felt completely, gloriously, naked beneath without her bra and underwear. Her body was humming with nerves, singing with lust already. In less than half an hour she would be with him.

Marcus looked out the window, watching Cassandra park her car in the driveway. She got out, moving gracefully in her short, floaty skirt. He'd never seen her in heels before; the girl had gorgeous legs.

His heart skipped a beat when she knocked at the door. Was he ready for this? For this woman who tied him up in knots? He had to grimace at the irony.

He gripped the knob, opened the door, and there she was, every beautiful inch of her. He could remember instantly the texture of her naked skin, covered now by her clothing. He could change that quickly enough, could order her to strip right there on his doorstep. But he wanted to talk to her first.

"Come in."

"Thank you."

He caught her scent as she moved past him and into the house. She smelled of something faintly floral and fresh, something with a touch of innocence about it, just like her.

But this girl was hardly innocent, was she?

When he gestured for her to sit down, she did, on the edge of the brown leather sofa. Her hands gripped the cushion on either side of her thighs.

Oh, God, don't think of her thighs now.

He sat down next to her, but not too close. "Cassandra, it's alright to talk to me. You don't have to be afraid."

"I'm . . . I'm not." She fidgeted, looked away, then back at him, catching his gaze. She smiled beatifically, and everything inside him went soft at once. "I can't quite believe I'm here."

"I'm glad you came. I had to see you. To talk more with you. I still want to tie you up and torture you; that hasn't changed." A small smile from her at that. "But I want . . . more."

"So do I." Her eyes were shining, her expression so trusting, it hit him like a blow.

He didn't understand it, didn't understand a lot of things. But he had to pull himself together, to talk to her, as he'd wanted. There were so many things he wanted— needed—to know about her. Where to start?

He reached out and took her small, warm hand in his, felt the trembling in her fingers. "Tell me, Cassandra, how did you come to find my uncle?"

"I was looking on the Internet for . . . people who thought the same way I did. For someone to show me all of the things I'd only ever thought about."

She bit her lip, her small, white teeth coming down on the tender skin. Made him want to kiss her. But not yet. If he kissed her it would all be over, this talking.

She went on. "I was surprised, to find someone so real on the Internet. But there was his ad . . . did you know about his ad?"

"Not this one in particular. But that's how he found Jacqueline and Laura."

"And Mika?"

"Delphine found her. She was a gift, of sorts."

Cassandra nodded her head, her russet curls falling

around her shoulders. "I have to tell you, I had no idea this would all be so . . . overwhelming. I thought I would be brought into it more slowly."

He laughed. "My uncle doesn't do anything on a small scale."

She was quiet a moment, then said soberly, "You love him, don't you?"

A small dropping sensation in the pit of his stomach. "Yes. And I respect him."

"He took you in."

"Yes."

"You didn't tell me why."

This wasn't something he normally discussed, not even with Robert. They'd both been there; there was no need to talk about it. But he found he wanted to reveal himself to her. He didn't understand it. But with Cassandra, he was operating so much on pure instinct. He was letting that dictate his behavior more than he was logic.

He pulled in a deep breath and began. "My father was a Hollywood stuntman, an adventurer. I think I inherited that, the need for extreme thrills, even if I get mine in a different way. I was always trying to impress him as a kid. I broke my arm sailing off the roof of our house on my bicycle when I was eight years old. Stupid. But nothing was ever good enough for him. This life is what I'm good at, finally."

He paused for a moment. This was the part of his history he'd detached himself from a long time ago. Talking about it now made him feel raw, open. Hell, everything about Cassandra opened him up. But he wouldn't fight it now. "When my mother died I was ten. He never got over it. He was angry. Even worse when he drank. At fifteen I left, came to Robert. He took me traveling with him, to Italy to see our family there, to London, to Switzerland. We spent my eighteenth birthday in Paris. That's when he first showed me. We went to a club there, a small, private place, where I saw a woman bound and spanked on a stage. I'd never seen anything like it. I loved it immediately. Less than a year later I had my first slave."

"Oh." She turned away, but he could see the color rising in her cheeks.

He reached over, took her chin in his hand and forced her to face him. "Don't worry, Cassandra. She's long gone. Right now I'm only interested in you."

"But why?" Her eyes burned. With anger? With passion?

He let his hand fall away. "It's something I feel on a very subtle level, except when the chemistry is hitting me like a blow to the chest. When I can smell your scent. When I'm close enough that I can feel the warmth of your breath. When you are naked beneath my hands. But I feel it just sitting here, talking with you, too."

Her pupils grew as he spoke until they were so large and dark, the green of her eyes was obscured, like a lunar eclipse. She was shivering faintly all over. His groin tightened along with his chest.

"Why are you here?" he asked quietly.

"Because I couldn't stay away. Because of all the same things you've talked about: the chemistry, the inexplicable connection between us, the need to be together."

"I wanted for us to talk. I pictured the two of us sitting here together, being very civilized." He brushed her hair from her face. It was like dark, gilded silk in his fingers. "There is nothing civilized about what I'm feeling right now. I'm bending the rules, having you here with me like this."

She nodded. "I know."

"But I can't seem to care. Betraying my uncle seems less important than being with you, which is awful, really. I understand that this is a risk for you, too. If this doesn't feel right, you are free to go. I won't make any demands of you. I won't keep you here unless you want to be here. And you have to understand that even though you have not yet signed a full slave contract with my uncle, you *are* his right now, until—if and when—he offers you the contract, to accept or refuse." His heart was pounding, hammering in his chest. "You have to know that this is wrong of me. That I feel I'm taking advantage of you. It tortures me. But not as much as being apart from you does."

"I understand. I want to be here." Her eyes were locked on his. "Don't ask me to leave. Please."

There was strength in her voice. He knew she understood what they were doing. That was all he needed to know.

❦

She waited to see what he would say, her blood hot in her veins, her head spinning. Yet at the center was a well of utter calm. She knew this was right, being here with him.

But he didn't say anything. He sat and looked at her, silent, brooding. A thousand emotions flitted through the depths of his whiskey brown eyes, but they moved too fast for her to read them. She waited, almost holding her breath. She let it out on a long sigh when he moved in slowly to kiss her.

She expected a tentative kiss, but there was nothing tentative about it. He crushed his mouth to hers, opened her lips, slid his tongue inside. She opened for him, almost wanted to cry again. Why did this man bring up so many emotions in her? Then his arms went around her, pressing her in close to his body, and she stopped analyzing everything.

The kiss was deep, feral, and she felt it all. Warmth suffused her; desire lanced through her system. She wanted to be naked with him, could hardly stand to have clothing between them.

He angled his head, deepened the kiss even more. His hands came up, cupped her cheeks, holding her so tightly it almost hurt. She didn't care. All she knew was that despite the social constraints, the logical reasons why she couldn't possibly feel so much for him, this was right.

His hands were everywhere, roaming her body, exploring every curve. His palms against her breasts with the cloth of her blouse between them was unendurable.

"Marcus, please . . ."

He seemed to know what she was asking for. He unbuttoned her blouse, stripped it from her shoulders. Her skirt came next; she didn't even know how he managed it, exactly. All that was left were her stockings and heels. His hands found her naked breasts, covered them, caressed, pinched. Then he replaced his hands with his hot, wet mouth and she thought she'd lose her mind.

She moaned when he drew one nipple into his mouth,

his swirling tongue sending ripples of desire through her body, bringing gooseflesh up on her skin.

"God, you taste like candy, so sweet."

He pulled away and she thought he might begin to play her, to use pain to excite her. But he caught her gaze and stared into her eyes. His were a dark, stormy brown, the gold washed away by lust, by emotion. She was desperate for him to kiss her again, to drink in everything he was feeling. To feed her own emotions with his.

"Cassandra . . ." He was nearly panting, his voice rough. "All I want right now is to touch you, to make love to you. I don't need the rough play. I just need you."

"Yes, I don't care about the rest of it now."

He stroked a finger over her cheek, her lips, before letting her go long enough to strip off his clothes. As each piece of clothing came off, his body was revealed to her for the first time. He was even more beautiful than she'd imagined. His skin was a dark golden brown, a sprinkling of hair on his chest, denser around the dusky nipples. Muscle rippled in his broad shoulders, his chest, his abdomen. Finally his slacks followed, and she saw his gorgeous erection, full and heavy, the skin beautifully textured. She could hardly wait to touch it, to have him inside her body. She reached for him and he came to her, pushing her down onto the couch.

He kissed her mouth, her chin, moved lower to rain kisses over her aching breasts, her stomach.

"I've been waiting to taste you from that first moment," he murmured, before moving even lower to spread her thighs and brush his lips against her curls.

When his tongue flicked out at the tip of her clit her hips came up off the cushions. He used his hands to press her down, exerting just enough control to feed that need in her to be dominated.

He went to work right away, using his tongue and his hands, stroking her clit, his fingers driving inside her. Her sex swelled, pleasure flowing through her, into her limbs, her mind. He was doing the most incredible things to her body, and knowing it was him, *Marcus*, made it even better.

When he began to suck on her clit in earnest, all the while moving his fingers inside her, her climax came fast and hard, shattering her, making her call his name. And when it was over he moved up her body to kiss her mouth, soft kisses, over and over. Still shaking from her climax, she was a jumbled mass of desire and need and the blossoming of love.

"I need you inside me. I need to feel you that close to me."

"Yes, now, Cassandra."

He held his body over her, supporting his weight with his arms. She could feel the heat of him before he lowered himself, slipped between her thighs. The head of his magnificent cock nudged at her opening, and already pleasure was shooting through her. She looked up into his face. God, he was almost too beautiful to bear. But she couldn't pull her gaze away. His expression was intense, his eyes dark liquid. She wrapped her arms around his neck, watching his face as he entered her, one torturous inch at a time. And every inch was sheer pleasure, making her body soar higher and higher.

"Christ, Cassandra," he rasped. "If I'd known you

would feel this good, I would have taken you in that first moment. You are so beautiful. So hot inside I can hardly stand it."

Finally he was buried deep, filling her completely. He leaned down and kissed her, a long, wet kiss, a hungry kiss. Everything he felt, everything she needed to know, was in that kiss, in that moment.

He began to move, each thrust of his hips driving pure pleasure into her body. Her hips arched to meet him, wanting to take him in as deeply as possible, wanting everything he offered. She trembled on the edge of orgasm. When he angled to hit her g-spot, she moaned, bit into the soft, sweet flesh of his shoulder. He drove into her, began to shudder, and she let it go, coming as he came inside her, the two of them shaking in unison. Coming apart, coming together. Entwined, body and soul.

CHAPTER TEN

THIS WAS THE THIRD MORNING IN A ROW Cassandra had woken up in his bed, in his arms. *Marcus.* Their days and nights together had been blissful, intense. And in between all of the wicked things he'd done to her, they'd talked for endless hours. They'd lain in each other's arms. She had first seen him only two weeks ago, yet nothing had ever felt more right to her.

She looked at him, at his closed eyes, noticed the tiny lines at the corners. Reaching out, she touched her finger there, lightly traced the planes of his face.

"Marcus . . ."

"What is it?" His voice was soft, sleepy.

"What happens now? What does this mean? What are we to each other?"

His eyes fluttered opened, the deep brown lit with gold. "Much of that depends on you. The bottom always has the most power, isn't that what they say? It's true. But I want to be with you. It's crazy, but something about you . . ." He stroked her hair, tangled his fingers in the curls. "If you decide it's too complicated, I will be crushed. Devastated."

"So would I." She couldn't imagine being without him.

"I know this is all happening fast."

"It is. And I've been lying here thinking that I have to stop and question whether the circumstances are adding to the intensity."

"Relationships in the realm of BDSM are always intense. But that doesn't mean it's not real."

"It feels real."

"Yes." He picked up her hand, brushed a kiss across her knuckles, making her shiver. "We've been avoiding this conversation. But I think it's time we talked it all out."

She nodded. He was right. Her pulse stepped up a beat.

"You have to tell me, Cassandra, if you are willing to give up my uncle's training to be with me. Because frankly, I can't stand the idea of anyone else's hands on you. But I am a trainer myself. I can fill that role, in between these moments when we are simply together. But you have to decide what you want."

"I want to be with you—even if it means breaking the rules. You must know that by now. But what will he do to you?"

"I could be cast out from the community—"

"No!"

"Yes. And my uncle could disown me, but I'm willing to take that chance. I'm even willing to hurt him, if that's the only way I can have you."

"But I can't put you in that position, to make that kind of choice!"

"Don't you understand that I have no choice? I need you, whatever the cost. You are well worth it."

"No one has ever thought so before." Tears stung her eyes.

"Then it's about time someone did." He kissed her hand again, turning it over to press his soft lips to the tender flesh of her palm. He said quietly, "I know it's crazy, but I am falling in love with you, Cassandra. And that's never happened before. That's worth everything to me."

The tears fell over her cheeks, onto his hand that still held hers. "I thought it was only me."

"It's *us*." He caught her gaze, looked into her eyes. "I want to be with you, to love you, to hurt you, to tame you. I want you to be mine."

"I am yours, Marcus."

He kissed her then, tenderly, lovingly. When he pulled away he said, "We need to tell my uncle. I'll talk to him."

"No, I need to go with you."

He nodded. "I understand. Tonight, then."

◈

Mika, dressed in her collar and her tattoos, silently let them in and led them to Master Robert's office. She left them at the door. Cassandra tried to stop her hands from shaking. So odd, walking through this house fully dressed. She was grateful for Marcus's reassuring hand pressed to the small of her back.

Master Robert sat behind his enormous desk. Imposing, both him and the desk. Marcus had called and told his uncle he had to speak with him right away, but the older man's brows shot up when they came into the room together.

Marcus guided her to one of the chairs in front of the desk, then sat in the other. Robert leaned forward in his chair, steepling his hands.

"Good evening, Uncle."

"Is it? Why don't you tell me why you are here together. Although I think I can guess."

"We came here to ask you to release her."

"She has no contract with me." But his voice was deep, stern. He was plainly angry.

"Not as such, but we both know there is an implied contract even now."

"Hmmm, yes." Robert leaned back. "When did this happen?"

He was looking right at her, making her shiver. She still wanted to please him, even now; she felt a sense of failure that ultimately, she hadn't.

Marcus answered, "From the first moment we saw each other."

"I knew you wanted her. I've never seen you react in such a way to any woman. I should have seen this." Robert paused, his dark gray brows furrowed. "Do you understand how serious this is?"

"Of course, Uncle."

She could see the pain in Marcus's face as he spoke. Was Robert really going to disown him? He was Marcus's family, all he had left, from what he'd told her. How could she do this to him? Her heart fluttered frantically in her chest.

"Marcus, there can be no actions in this life that do not carry consequences."

"I understand that."

"Is she worth it?"

Oh, God. This was too awful. She stood.

"No. No, I'm not."

She ran from the room.

He caught up to her at his car, parked in the driveway of his uncle's house. She didn't even know where she'd been going. He grabbed her arm.

"Cassandra!"

She turned to him, wiped the tears from her face with one hand. "I can't do this."

"What do you mean?"

"I can't let this happen to you. I can't let you make these sacrifices. Not for me. I'm not worth it. I'm not."

"You are worth everything to me!"

She shook her head, blinded by tears. "How do I know? How do I trust that? We haven't even known each other two weeks. And if this is some fleeting thing, is that worth losing your uncle over? Being shunned by your community?"

He paused, drew in a deep breath, blew it out. "I love you, Cassandra. I know you were raised to believe you don't deserve it, but that's bullshit. I'm here and I love you, and you're going to have to deal with it."

He grasped her arms, held on tight, whispered again harshly, "I love you."

A sob rose in her chest, choking her. She could almost believe him. Maybe, with time, she would know the truth of his words in her own mind, in her soul.

Robert's voice came from the doorway. "Love, is it?"

Marcus turned to him. "You know I would never do this to you for anything less."

They both waited, watching Robert's stern features. Marcus's grip on her arm tightened, and her heart went out to him.

"Cassandra." Robert's voice was still harsh, cold. She shivered.

"Yes, Sir."

"Do you love my nephew?"

"Yes!" Tears blinded her momentarily. More threatened when Marcus wiped them away with a tender hand.

There was a long pause. "Then you are already his in the only way that counts. In the truest way. I could never give that to him. Take her, Marcus. Treasure her. You hold a gift beyond imagining."

She felt Marcus relax beside her, his muscles loosening.

Robert stood up a little straighter, gestured to Marcus with a raised chin. "And when you two have come up for air, come back to my house. You will both be welcome here."

"Thank you, Uncle."

She looked up to see Marcus smile, read the relief on his face. She knew he'd been ready to make this sacrifice for her. She was grateful he wouldn't have to.

Robert turned and went back into the house, closing the door. Marcus turned to her. Even in the pale moonlight, she could see his eyes blazing with pure emotion. With love. God, she loved him, as impossible as it seemed. And if that was possible, to fall in love with someone so quickly, so deeply, then maybe anything was possible.

The tears were spilling over onto her cheeks, blurring her vision. She wasn't perfect. Yet he loved her, anyway. Her head spun with the realization that she could have this life, she could submit to him, and it was something beautiful and almost sacred, because he loved her. There was nothing sinful about it, except in the most delicious way. And despite the confusion in her head, the struggle, her heart knew she really had no choice but to be with him. She needed him more than she needed to continue punishing herself.

He pulled her close, held her in arms rough with passion. And when he kissed her, the rest of the world faded away. Her years of guilt, of shame, all of it was dissolving beneath the force of his love, of her love for him. Nothing else mattered.

Marcus pulled his mouth away and whispered into her hair, "There's so much I want to show you. The sensual pleasures you came here for, and so much more. We'll make these discoveries together."

Yes, it was time to stop seeing everything as punishment for her imperfections, to allow herself to enjoy her dark side without needing it to be sinful. Marcus would help her. Together they would figure it out, would learn how to love each other in the midst of these sinful pleasures they both so craved and adored.

Since discovering this shadowed and voluptuous world, she had found joy in fulfilling the needs of her body. And now, unexpectedly, she had found what she needed to fill her heart.

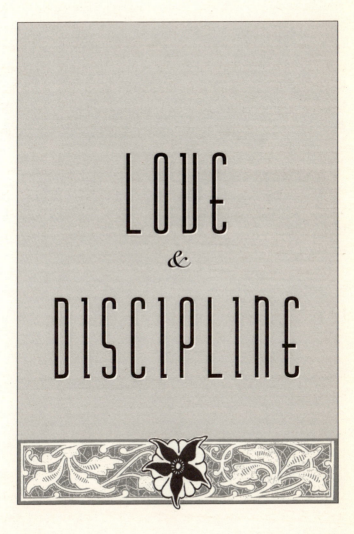

LOVE

&

DISCIPLINE

CHAPTER ONE

WHEN HE WALKED INTO THE RESTAURANT BAR for their appointment on Friday afternoon, the first thought Maggie had was that the phrase "tall, dark, and handsome" had been invented just for him. He approached the table with cool, leonine grace. When he was close enough, she could see his eyes were hazel, a luminous combination of gold and silver. Amazing eyes. Mesmerizing. Power emanated from this man in almost palpable waves. Her stomach twisted into an odd little knot as she stood to greet him.

"Mr. Knight?"

"Ms. London, nice to meet you. But you must call me Damien."

He took her hand in his, his grasp warm, firm. Heat flared in her palm at the contact. Yes, definitely a handsome man, with his tall build, his head of dark, luxurious hair, and those eyes. He could hypnotize a woman with those eyes. The hustle and noise of the lunchtime crowd faded into the background, along with the dark paneling, the red linen tablecloths, the scent of garlic bread.

He came to her side of the table and held her chair while she sat down, flustering her. So few men in New York knew anything of these old-world manners. To find it in a man here in San Francisco was just as surprising. Perhaps in Europe . . . yes, he was very European. Something about him. The way he dressed, in casual elegance, the way he moved and spoke. A bit too formal for a man of his age, which she guessed to be late thirties, forty at most.

"Thank you for meeting with me, Mr.—I'm sorry. Damien."

"Shall we order? A drink for you? Yes."

He motioned to a waiter. The man came almost at a run. Utterly confident, this Damien Knight, and commanding in a way people probably responded to almost without realizing it, as the waiter had.

"I'll have a Glenlivet on the rocks. What do you drink, Ms. London?"

"Maggie, please." Good lord, had she just heard a hint of flirtation in her voice? This would never do. She never flirted with her research subjects, and this was work. But a drink would not be overstepping the boundaries of professionalism. "A glass of white wine. Nothing too sweet."

His gaze held hers. "Yes, nothing too sweet for you, I imagine."

What was the intimation in his tone? "Excuse me?"

"You don't seem the kind of woman who enjoys too much sweet . . . anything."

What was he implying? And why was his strangely insightful remark making her blush? It was true, she wasn't crazy about sugar, chocolate. She didn't care for those sweet, girlish things so many women loved. No kittens and bows for her. She certainly wasn't the kind of woman most people would call "sweet." Competent, in charge, perhaps a little bossy, even. But never sweet.

She didn't know what to think of this man.

His fine, long-fingered hands on your skin . . .

She really had to stop that!

She cleared her throat. "Thank you for coming to do this interview with me."

"You're the one who came here from New York. I came only a few blocks. You're still expecting this to be a series of interviews?"

"Yes. I thought this subject might require more than one meeting."

"You're right. It will. There are many different aspects to the BDSM lifestyle. It's not something one can learn about in a single conversation. Tell me again the name of the magazine you write for?"

"*Citi.*"

He lounged back in his chair, the picture of cool confidence. "A women's magazine, is that right?"

"I suppose. Although it's more sophisticated, more thoughtful, than the usual fashion magazine. We approach tougher subjects, are more liberal than most other women's magazines, more forward-thinking. Hence my sex column. Our demographic is working women, metropolitan women. Women who are unafraid of the world."

"As you are?"

Was that a small smirk playing at the corners of his mouth?

It was a strong mouth, the mouth of a man who knew exactly who he was. His stance, his walk, everything about him conveyed the same message.

Their drinks arrived and she took a grateful sip, wishing she'd ordered something stronger.

He held his drink in his hand as he did everything, with grace and a casual strength, his fingers sensually caressing the glass. "So, Ms. London, tell me, what is Maggie short for? You don't look like a Margaret."

"No."

"Then what?"

She was silent for a moment. His gaze on her was more than scrutinizing somehow. She moved her fingertips around the rim of her wineglass, shifted in her chair. "Magdalena."

"Your mother was Italian?"

"French. I was born in Italy."

"Your parents traveled?"

"My mother did. I thought I was conducting this interview."

His silvery-gold gaze rested on her face, held there. He watched her, silent. This man obviously justified himself to no one. She reached into her briefcase and pulled a notepad out, a pen. "I hope you don't mind if I take notes?"

"London doesn't sound either French or Italian."

She sighed. How was she ever going to get control of the conversation with a man like him? "It's not. London is my father's name. He's American."

"And you were born in Italy why?"

"You really aren't going to stop until I've answered all of your questions, are you?"

He took a swallow of his drink. The sound of the ice moving in his glass seemed abnormally loud to her, the faint clink as he set the glass down on the table.

He shrugged, broad shoulders moving beneath the finely made black cashmere sweater. "I'm curious about you."

"Why?"

"Because a woman who makes a living writing about sex is fascinating by nature. You were about to tell me what your mother was doing in Italy when you were born."

She shook her head. "My mother is an artist. She went to Italy to paint, to Tuscany. And to have me. She said she wanted me to be born into beauty."

"And so you were."

By the look he gave her she was fairly certain he didn't mean the Italian countryside. Her face was hot. She took a sip of her wine.

"What about your father?"

"I never knew him. Can we get back to the interview, please?"

Where had that "please" come from? He really did inspire a sense of yielding in people; she'd seen it with the waiter. But Damien Knight would soon figure out that she was as strong as he was.

Then why was her breath tight in her chest? Her neck still on fire, her hands shaky?

"Certainly." He was all acquiescing grace suddenly.

This was better, back to business. In business mode she

should be able to ignore the strange effect this man was having on her.

She wrote his name at the top of her pad of paper, cleared her throat. "Can you give me a simple definition of the term 'BDSM,' for my readers?"

"BDSM stands for bondage and discipline, domination and submission, sadomasochism. But it can be any or all of those things."

Why did hearing him say these words make her go hot all over?

Focus!

"And, um . . . what is it you do when you're not . . . practicing the BDSM lifestyle? What do you do for a living, if I may ask?"

"I'm an independent consultant. I handle acquisitions and mergers for large corporations."

"Then I imagine you went to college?"

"I have a degree in business, and one in law. Is this information important to your article?"

"I'm trying to draw a profile. Do you enjoy your work?"

"Yes. It's exciting. Almost as exciting as talking with a beautiful woman."

He caught her eye, his gaze glittering. She looked back down at her pad of paper, cleared her throat once more. "So, how long have you been involved in BDSM?"

"Since I was fifteen years old."

"Fifteen? That can't be true."

"Oh, I didn't know enough to be serious about it. But even then I spanked my first real girlfriend, pinched her thighs. I was doing these things months before we had sex."

Her cheeks were heating again. To do these things as a teenager! She was no prude, but it was hard to think about him ever being a teenaged boy, never mind putting some young girl over his knee and . . . good lord, he'd never said that. Where was she getting this stuff?

"So, when did you understand what you were doing, what it was you wanted, exactly?"

"It takes most of us a number of years to know exactly what we want. That applies to any area of our lives, don't you agree, Magdalena?"

"Maggie," she corrected automatically, then felt foolish. Why did it mater what this man called her?

"Of course. Maggie."

There was that twinkle in his eyes again. Was he making fun of her?

"You were saying?" she prompted.

"I was saying that it takes a while for each of us to know ourselves. Sometimes we're well into adulthood before we know our own hearts, our own desires. But I figured mine out early. By the time I was eighteen I knew. I understood that I found a deep pleasure in bringing pain along with pleasure to the women I was with. That I loved the sense of power I felt when dominating them. That it was natural for me. Looking back I can see that it's always been there. I'd been able to get my way with teachers, other children. The way I see it, turning to a life of dominance was simply living the truth of who I was. Who I am."

She realized when he stopped talking and grew quiet that she was leaning toward him, the edge of the table pressing into her ribs. She sat back in her chair, made a few quick notes.

"Do you always use a steno pad to take notes when you're interviewing someone?"

"What? Yes. I know, it's old-fashioned. But I feel more in touch with the words this way than I would using those electronic gadgets everyone is so fond of." Her cheeks went hot again at that admission. She didn't even know why. Maybe because it was personal? But he was dragging as many personal things from her as she was from him.

"There's a certain kind of charm in being old-fashioned about some things. Not everything, of course." He smiled at her. Strong white teeth, almost too perfect. "Your job is certainly not old-fashioned, and yet, I find you utterly charming."

Her whole body went hot, a liquid flush that began in her face, moved down over her belly, spread to her arms, her legs. She didn't know what to say.

He sat and watched her. His face was perfectly serious; he wasn't mocking her. After a moment he said, "Shall we continue with the interview, Magdalena?"

God, she really had to get ahold of herself.

"Um . . . I had some questions . . ." She scrambled through her briefcase for the list she'd made before she left New York. After five minutes with him she had a whole new list of things she wanted to know. Like how he looked through her the way he did, as though he could see what was going on in her head. X-ray eyes.

"Why don't I just talk to you?" he suggested. "You can find your questions later."

"Yes, sure. Okay."

She held her pencil over her pad of paper, feeling foolish, totally off balance. She had never before met anyone who could do this to her. She didn't like it.

He took a calm sip of his drink. "If we're going to do this interview, if my words are going to be in print, I want you to understand a few things. We are not simply a bunch of perverts. There's more to this life than that. It's not just sex. It's nothing so simple. Yet at the same time, it's a very basic need we fill by doing the things we do.

"I believe this is a world of overstimulation. We are bombarded on every side; traffic noise, neon lights. It's a neon world we live in. I believe it takes more and more simply to make us feel anything at all. We are sensual extremists. But I believe we are indulging a need a lot of other people have, but don't admit to. I think much of the rest of humanity is bored."

"And you're never bored?"

"Never."

"I don't see how that's possible. It's an exaggeration."

He shrugged, drank again from his glass. The ice cubes had melted into tiny pebbles. "You can't possibly understand without having experienced what we experience."

"I'm here for you to tell me. To make me understand."

"I can try. I will try. Because I'd like for people to know what we're about, we sensual extremists."

"So you have an agenda in talking to me?"

He leaned forward, his hands clasped on the linen-draped table. His eyes were on her again, those intense, elemental eyes, and she couldn't look away. "Yes. But I have to admit to you that since meeting you, my agenda has taken a different turn."

Her pen clattered to the table. She didn't pick it up. "What do you mean?"

"I no longer want to tell you what this is all about. I want to show you."

CHAPTER TWO

HE SAW THE PUPILS OF HER GRAY EYES WIDEN, the only thing that betrayed her sense of shock. On the outside she appeared to be as cool as ever. Her look was cool in itself; pale blond hair cut into a sleek bob that grazed the underside of her delicate chin, those pale gray eyes. Everything about her was long and graceful. Her legs, her neck, even her hands. And her demeanor was of someone utterly in control of her world. But he was someone who had spent his life training himself to pick up on the subtleties of human behavior. It was a large part of what he did as a dominant.

He knew right away she had understood his meaning.

"I am here to conduct an interview, Mr. Knight. Not to become . . . involved with you on a personal level."

Back to "Mr. Knight," was it? Oh, yes, she was absolute stone now. What would it take to soften such a woman? He wanted to do it, knew he could if she would allow it. The idea of conquering that restrained aloofness was exciting.

"This is a very personal subject, Magdalena."

"I write a sex column. All of my subjects are personal."

"Yes. But talking to a manufacturer of vibrators is more about a product than it is a person. BDSM is highly personal. It's about what happens in our heads, even more than what happens on a physical level. The entire history of our lives comes into play in this arena. We all have to ask ourselves: What makes us like this? What makes us want to do these things other people consider deviant? Well, so do we. But we revel in it, anyway."

He could tell she was trying to absorb all of it. But she was still thinking about his half-veiled suggestion. So was he. She bit her lower lip, her teeth sinking into the soft pink cushion of it. Gorgeous, her mouth. Not a bit of lipstick, yet it was pink and full and glossy.

A part of him wanted to slip a gag between those lovely lips. Another part of him simply wanted to kiss her.

Totally unlike him to think about kissing a woman as much as he did about dominating her.

She said quietly, "I don't like what you're suggesting."

"I am suggesting this for personal reasons, of course. I did say this was personal." It was true. He had to get his hands on all that pale, silky flesh. His body was buzzing with lust, his groin tight just looking at the way she held her head on her slender neck. He slipped his hand around his glass, the dewy moisture cool against his fingertips, but he didn't want to take his eyes off her long enough to lift his glass and sip. "If you really want to know what this life is all about, the only way to truly know is to experience it yourself. Otherwise all you're doing is quoting me. That interview could have been conducted by phone."

His reasoning was every bit as true as his desire for her.

"I'm perfectly fine with quoting you."

"If you were writing an article about Australia for a travel magazine, would you do it without first going there? Would you simply talk to people, do research on the Internet?"

"No, of course not."

"Then why treat this issue in such a cavalier fashion?"

She paused, bit her lip again, pushed a lock of her sleek blond hair behind one ear. He could tell she was mulling the idea over. She seemed like the kind of woman who would brave almost anything rather than do her job poorly. The kind of woman who would step up to a challenge. But he knew he didn't have her yet.

He reached across the table, covered one of her small hands with his. Fragile bones, almost birdlike. "Magdalena. I know you want to do this right, thoroughly. I am offering you a way to do that. I can promise you there will be no sex. Unless, of course, you agree to it. Have you ever heard the saying that the bottom has all the power in a dominant/submissive relationship?"

"Maybe . . . somewhere."

"It's true. You set the rules, the limits. We will negotiate everything before we begin."

Yes, talk as though it were already a done deal. Manipulative of him, he knew, but he had to have her. Something about her cool reserve, every movement so controlled. And she was too beautiful. She was exactly the kind of woman he loved to bring to her knees, literally and figuratively. Oh, he was a sadist alright. But then, he'd never tried to deny it.

She took a long drink of her wine and set the glass

down, but her fingers remained twined around the stem. "What makes you think this would be effective in any way? I mean, this is not something I'm even interested in."

"Call it instinct. A lot of what I do in the world of domination and submission is instinctive."

"And your instincts are telling you I'll write a better article if I allow you to dominate me?"

"No. Logic tells me that." He leaned toward her, lowered his voice. "My instincts tell me that for a woman like you, so competent and so in control, letting it all go, yielding control to me, would be an enormous relief."

Heat rose in her pale, smooth cheeks. Her eyes were absolutely blazing. She was angry. But she was also interested. He could see it in the quick rise and fall of her breasts—spectacular breasts—beneath her black turtleneck sweater. He took a sip of his Scotch, giving her a moment to cool off.

"You're saying you think this is something I need? I'm capable of recognizing my own needs, and taking care of them. I'm a sex columnist, not some repressed prude who isn't even aware that alternative forms of sexuality exist."

"I never said you were a prude, or insinuated that you're repressed. But I think this could be a very interesting discovery for you. And I would be honored to be the one to take you there."

A pause, then, "You think you're very smooth, don't you?"

He shrugged. "Does that really matter? As long as I'm good enough at what I do. I can assure you I am."

She played with the stem of her wineglass, but her gaze was fixed firmly on his face. Still trying to cover her nerves, her excitement. "There is a fine line between confidence and cockiness, you know."

"I agree. You're not the first to accuse me. It doesn't bother me, this assessment. In this arena I am utterly confident. I wouldn't allow anyone less skilled, less experienced, to take you there."

"I haven't said I'm going."

"You haven't said you're not."

She stared him down, her gray eyes still smoldering. He knew she was moments from being in his grasp, under his command. His groin tightened at the idea. She really was lovely. Even better that she had a good mind to go with her regal beauty, a strong mind, a strong will. He waited for her answer.

~

She was absolutely on fire. How was that possible? She had never given much thought before to this whole issue of submission and dominance. But here he was, this stranger, offering her this experience. An experience she found intriguing despite herself. But why not? It wasn't as though she had anything to lose. And exploring sex was what she did for a living, had done for the four years she'd been writing her column for *Citi*.

She wouldn't have to tell her readers, her editor, anyone, that she'd done her research this way. But what an article this could make! That was part of the excitement of it, the attraction, although she had to admit most of it was him. All dark, cocky, male beauty. Sophisticated, elegant. Such a contrast to his deviant sexual proclivities, which made it even better, actually. She wouldn't be half as attracted to him, to the idea, if he was one of those more classic bad boys.

She'd known from the first moment he'd suggested this that she was going to agree to it. She just didn't want to give him the satisfaction of giving in too easily. For her own sense of pride, yes, but she gauged him as the kind of man who enjoyed a bit of a chase, a sense of conquering.

"I'm here in San Francisco for two weeks."

A lift of his dark eyebrow. "Oh?"

He wanted her to come out and say it, that she wanted him to touch her, spank her, whatever other sexual adventures he had in mind. Fine. She'd never had a problem talking dirty at the appropriate moment. She didn't want to question why it felt appropriate at this moment, in a restaurant, surrounded by people. Why it felt dirtier because of that fact. Why it made her shiver with lust. But she could answer him in civilized terms.

"I will come with you, let you show me this world of yours. I will submit to you, if only to see what I've been missing."

Brave enough words. So why was she shaking?

He smiled, his teeth gleaming like those of a predator. "Shall we begin, then?"

"What? Now?"

"The necessary negotiations take some time. I suggest we get that done today, in the interest of time."

"These negotiations—we just talk about what will happen?"

"We'll talk about your limits. I ask questions, you answer. Simple. Would you like to order lunch first?"

"No, thank you." She couldn't eat now if her life depended on it. Her blood was racing through her veins, her heart hammering. And between her thighs a desperate heat was growing. Impossible to ignore.

He nodded. "We'll begin, then."

She nodded, picked up her wineglass, and drank to soothe her dry throat.

"Let's start here. Tell me if you have ever done anything which might be considered kinky or outrageous."

"I'm a sex columnist. Of course I have."

"Like what?"

"You need to know my sexual history? Are you serious?"

"This is serious business. I have to know certain things about you, so that when you are in my hands, I can gauge what's going on in your head."

"In my head?"

"I told you earlier there's more to this kind of play than the physical aspects. Part of my job is reading your response to whatever it is I might be doing to you."

A small shudder of heat at those words.

"I'll need to know, without your speaking, what works for you and what doesn't." He paused. "Tell me."

His commanding tone sent another shiver through her. She could not believe this was happening, that they were having this conversation in the middle of this little Italian restaurant in North Beach.

"I've been with a number of men. And two women. I've had a ménage with two men. Used a large variety of sex toys." She could not believe she was saying this!

"Never any bondage? You've never tied a lover up in silk scarves, had a man spank you?"

Her sex went damp. God, would he do these things to her? Did she actually want him to?

"No. Never."

"Have you ever played with pain in any way? Pinching, that sort of thing?"

"Just rough sex. Nothing different from what a lot of people have done."

"And did you like it?"

She held his gaze. "Yes."

He leaned back in his chair, his stance casual, confident as always. "I thought so."

"Is this part of it? Mocking me?"

"I'm not mocking you. I'm simply pleased that my assessment was correct." He finished his drink, waved the waiter over, ordered a glass of sparkling water for each of them. "No more alcohol for this kind of discussion. Or when we play, ever. This will be a sensory experience and we must both be able to feel everything fully."

"You keep calling it 'play,' yet at the same time you talk about how serious it is."

"It is serious play. The things we do can cause damage to the bottom, or submissive. We sadists, we responsible citizens of our community, love to hurt people, but we never want to cause damage."

"I see." A hard lump was gathering in her throat. This was all a little scary, yet she was too drawn to him, to the challenge, to the idea of doing such taboo things, to back out now. Maybe the fear was part of the attraction? She didn't like to think of that. It seemed too strange.

"I'm going to ask you a series of questions about what

you might want to try, what is definitely out of the question, and what you might consider at some point. Answer me with a yes, no, or maybe, alright?"

"Yes. Sure."

"Would you allow me to tie you up? To bind you in other ways?"

"Yes. Why not?"

"To blindfold you?"

"Um . . ." Why did that idea seem frightening? But deliciously so. "Yes."

He smiled. Those flashing white teeth again.

All the better to eat you with.

She really had to focus!

"What about a little pain play? Spanking, pinching?"

Her heart gave a quick, sharp thump in her chest. "I . . . I don't know."

"Honest answer. Very good. This is something we can explore as we go."

Good lord, he was going to spank her! Her hands twisted her napkin into a tight knot in her lap. Her panties were suddenly drenched.

"What about nipple clamps?"

"How am I supposed to know these things if I've never tried them?"

"Is that a no? Or a maybe?"

"I don't know . . ."

"I'll take that as a maybe. What about being made to serve me? To obey orders."

"Serve you? Obey? In what way?"

"To kneel on the floor, to clasp your hands behind

your back. To strip your clothes off." His tone had low-ered again, a sexy rumble in his chest. "To do as I tell you. To serve me drinks, to bend over my lap."

God.

"Yes." The word came out on a whisper.

"Excellent. There are a number of things we'll table for now: electrical play, piercing, anal play. You're too new. We'll begin slowly."

God, God, God! What was she getting herself into? But her soaking panties were a clear indication that she would enjoy this. Wanted this, even though it had truly never oc-curred to her before. What had he said about letting go of control being a relief? She didn't know about that. All she knew was that the thought of doing these things with him turned her on, made her hotter than she'd been in a long time.

He stood, took his wallet out of a pocket, and threw some cash on the table.

"Shall we begin?"

CHAPTER THREE

"Now?"

"There's no time like the present, as they say. Do you need to go back to your hotel room for anything before we go?"

"I assumed we would be going to my hotel room."

She had to get a handle on this situation. Some semblance of control. He was too controlled, too calm.

"We could, but I don't make a habit of carrying my equipment with me. Of course, I could make do with my bare hands and a few belts and scarves, but I prefer to do things properly."

"Wait. I . . . I just need a moment."

He came to stand behind her chair. He leaned over her, closer, until she could feel his breath warm on her hair. "If you give yourself time to think about this, to analyze it, to break it down, you will talk yourself out of it."

"Maybe that would be a good idea." But the scent of him had every nerve in her body on red alert. He smelled as elegantly sexy as he looked; something dark and smoky, like his voice. She pulled in a deep breath, held it in her lungs.

His voice was almost a whisper now. "Don't let fear force you to miss this adventure, Magdalena. And I promise you, this will be an adventure, the likes of which you have never experienced before."

She was shivering all over, a faint trembling running through her body like an electric current.

"Are you ready, Magdalena?"

"Yes. I'm ready."

"Then we'll go."

His hand was hot on the small of her back as he walked her out of the restaurant. She felt as though he'd already branded her flesh with his name. In front of the restaurant he stopped and turned to her. "You have a cell phone, I imagine?"

"Yes, of course."

"Do you have a friend you can call? Anyone whom you can tell exactly what's going on?"

"Why?"

"Because you are about to get into my car, to come to my home. Someone should know who you're with, where you're going."

She stared at him. Why was he saying these things to her? Yet she realized this was noble of him, protective. She'd never met anyone like him. "I could call a friend in New York. He'll understand. I think he will."

"Then do it."

She shook her head as she pulled her cell from her briefcase, dialed Jet's number. She waited while it rang. Jet Jackson was her best friend. He handled the music column at *Citi*. He was tall, gorgeous, darkly exotic, and decidedly homosexual.

"Jet here. Speak to me."

"It's me."

"Maggie! Darling! How is San Francisco?"

"It's . . . interesting. Look, Jet, I don't have a lot of time to explain now, but I need to give you some information."

Damien nodded his head, and handed her a card with his name, telephone number, address.

"Ready and waiting, doll."

"I'm going to be spending some time with Damien Knight, the man I was sent here to interview. I thought you should have his information, know where I am."

"I can get it at the office, from Delia."

"No, I want you to have it."

" 'Curiouser and curiouser, said Alice.' You're going to have to explain this later. In great detail."

"I will, I promise." She read him the information from the card. "I'll call you tomorrow, okay?"

"Okay, honey, see that you do that. Is he gorgeous?"

"Yes."

"Then good for you!"

"I have to go now, Jet."

She hit the off button, stuffed the cell phone back into her briefcase, and looked at Damien.

He nodded his head. "Very good. This way."

His car was parked right in front of the restaurant. Leave it to this man to find a parking place in San Francisco, a city where that was a nearly impossible task. He drove a sleek black BMW sedan. A modern gangster's car.

He held the door for her—all old-world gentleman, if she didn't know what he was about to do with her. She slid onto the cream-colored leather, and waited while he came around the car to get into the driver's side. She was quiet while he started the engine, shifted, and pulled out into the street.

Block after block went by in a blur. What the hell was she doing, anyway? But she was no prude, as she had said to him. She'd been with plenty of men in her time. Her body buzzed with an exquisite anticipation. The attraction was far too intense to resist. The challenge was too good to resist. Still, her nerves were drawn tight. She didn't dare talk to him on the ride across town. Respecting her silence, he turned on some music, a familiar, classical symphony. No rock music for him. She would have been shocked if that was what he'd chosen.

They headed west and south, out of North Beach, down to the Embarcadero and along the edge of San Francisco Bay. The view was spectacular, even with the usual year-round fog floating in wisps over the gray-blue water. The air would be cool and damp outside, but in the car she was warm. She glanced over at his strong profile, at the line of his jaw, at his hands on the steering wheel. Her thighs tensed, quivered. Heat crept through her system in curling ribbons.

They drove past Aquatic Park, with its joggers, people flying kites, doing tae kwon do on the long expanse of lawn, and the view of the Bay really opened up. He continued west, then made a left turn and they climbed up a hill, into an area she wasn't familiar with. The houses were spectacular, in a variety of architectural styles. All million-dollar homes or more.

A right turn onto a side street where the homes were even more regal, more beautiful; mansions really.

"This is where you live?"

"Another block."

She should have guessed as much. A man with his grace, his manners, his natural aura of power, had to live in some mansion on a hill, far above the dirt and noise of everyday life.

She felt as though she were in a story about someone other than herself.

They rolled to a stop in front of a three-story house of red brick, covered in climbing ivy. Lovely, intricate iron-work graced the paned windows, as well as the gate that rolled away to reveal a short driveway when he pushed a button on his key ring.

They drove in, and the gate slid shut behind them. Already she had a sense of isolation, of being in another world. Her body was doing strange things, filling up with a kind of melting sensation that made her weak all over.

He drove into a dark garage. Dim lights came on and the wide door rolled down behind them. Totally alone with him now, cut off from the world. She shivered, and almost jumped when he laid his hand over hers.

"Stay here, I'll get your door."

Yes, definitely full of old-world charm. She loved it despite everything she'd taught herself about being an independent woman.

He held his hand out to her, helped her from the car,

and took her briefcase out of her hand. Then he led the way through a side door and into the house.

They came into a narrow hall that opened into an airy foyer. The floors were marble—marble, for God's sake! There was a gorgeous piece of modern sculpture on a columnar stand, a sinuous twisting of stone that was clearly erotic.

She didn't have long to examine it before he led her across the foyer and into what must be the living room. One wall of floor-to-ceiling windows was set off by banks of bookcases. She itched to get closer, to see what sort of books he read. Later, maybe.

The room was decorated in clean neutrals: sandstone, warm whites, touches of rich browns and golds, a touch of black here and there. A large Persian rug covered the gleaming wood floor. The furnishings were surprisingly contemporary for such traditional architecture, but the overall effect was pleasing, sophisticated in a simple way.

"Please, sit down." He gestured to one of the long white sofas. "Would you like something to drink?"

"No. Thank you. You know, this is all so oddly civilized."

"I'm a civilized man, if a little depraved." He gave her a crooked, sexy grin. "Did you think I'd live in some dark, underground hole, with chains dangling from the walls?"

"Maybe."

"I do have an underground chamber. Perhaps if you're well-behaved I'll show it to you."

She couldn't tell if he was joking, but desire stabbed through her at the images he conjured. Her hands gripped the edge of the sofa cushions. Where was this coming from?

He went on. "We need to discuss safe words. Are you familiar with the term?"

"I think it has something to do with my telling you when I've had enough of . . . whatever you may be doing."

"Yes. But we should be specific here. If you feel that what's happening is too much for you to take, emotionally or physically, and you want me to slow down or back off, but you don't want the scene to stop, you say yellow. If you need everything to stop, you say red. I promise you I will respect these words and will not try to argue or cajole you into continuing. But do not use these words unless you mean them. And if you need to use them, don't try to struggle through. Don't prevent yourself from using your safe words because of some sense of pride. Understood?"

"It seems simple enough."

"Do you understand, Magdalena?"

A firm tone, yet nothing condescending there. Simply commanding.

"Yes, I understand. But I have to tell you, Damien, I have no idea how I'll respond to being . . . given commands. I've never done anything like this before, and while I'm willing to try, this is very much counter to who I am."

"It's people like you, the strong ones, who most need to let it all go. Trust me. You're in my hands now. Alright?"

She nodded, blew out a long breath. "Alright."

"And Magdalena? From now on, you will call me 'Sir.'"

❧

"What?"

He saw the shock in her eyes. Oh, yes, she'd been

interested enough, fascinated even, until things had really begun to happen. Now she would struggle. He'd expected it, had wanted to shock her a bit. Not simply for sadistic pleasure, although he couldn't deny he derived pleasure from it. But because he felt it was the only way to take her into this. She was not the kind of woman to handle with kid gloves. She was too strong for that. He had to catch her off balance, had to unsettle her, break through her reserve, through the wall she kept around her.

"We will begin now."

He could see the storm rising in her eyes, in her flushed cheeks, and he loved it. He could feel the excitement beneath her rage, and it fed his own, fed his need to touch her. "You're angry. That's fine with me. Your anger is the only place right now where you can show your emotions. Because despite your claims to sexual sophistication, despite all of your experience, this is utterly new to you. And the only way it will really work is to break through those boundaries, to reach that buried place of passion. Don't worry. I know just how to do it."

"You are unbelievable!" She rose to her feet. "You are the most self-satisfied human being I've ever met! To think you can manipulate me like that—"

"You have to understand that this is my job. Domination is more about mind-fuck than anything else, if you'll pardon my language."

"You brought me here simply to fuck with my head?"

Her gray eyes were absolutely blazing with fury. God, she was beautiful like this. He stepped closer.

"I brought you here because I wanted you here, Magdalena. And you wanted to be here. You can't deny it.

Because there is something electric in the air between us. And you are as anxious to explore it as I am."

"How dare you—"

He dragged her body in close to his and kissed her. He meant to silence her, to help her convert her temper to desire. But he didn't expect the raging surge of lust that roared through his system at the sweet crush of her lips beneath his.

He pulled away. What had happened? He could swear he felt dizzy. The scent of her lingered in his nostrils. Something dark and spicy, definitely nothing sweet and innocent about the way she smelled. His cock twitched in answer to that lovely, feminine scent, demanding to be sated.

Lord help him.

"I . . ." Her eyes were glazed now, the fiery silver sparks a muted gray.

He had to pull himself together. Control was key.

"Have you changed your mind, Magdalena?" he asked softly.

She shook her head. "No."

He reached out, rested his hand on her shoulder, felt her tremble. He could almost smell the fear on her. But she was going to do this, anyway. He admired her strength, her resolve.

"Come with me."

With a hand at her waist, he guided her back out into the foyer, down the hall. At the end was a door. He opened it, flipped a switch that turned on the lights, took her hand, and led the way through.

"Watch your step."

Down the stairs with her hand warm in his. So small, so fragile. But there was nothing fragile about this woman.

Another door at the bottom of the staircase. He stopped and turned to her.

"This is where it all happens, on the other side of this door. This is your last chance to back out. Tell me, Magdalena, once more. Do you want this?"

She looked into his eyes as though she were searching for something. Reassurance, perhaps? He gave her hand a squeeze. "I can promise you an adventure like none you've ever experienced before."

Images flashed in his mind: of her, naked, bent over his lap. Of his hands on her perfectly rounded ass, bringing the welts up on her skin . . .

She nodded her head, her blond hair sweeping her cheek. "I want it."

"Then you shall have it. A true sensual fantasy."

He paused, stroked her face. Her skin was as smooth and cool as porcelain, except for her cheeks, which were flushed with heat. He wanted to stop and question his tender treatment of her, what it was about her that brought out such unusual behavior in him. But now was not the time. Now he would introduce her into his world, a world of secret desires brought into the light. He swung the door open, and smiled when he heard her gasp.

CHAPTER FOUR

THE ROOM WAS DIMLY LIT WITH SOFT RED AND amber lights, enough to illuminate the large space filled with pieces of equipment she'd only ever seen in movies. Images of medieval torture chambers flashed through her mind. Yet everything was clean, elegant, luxurious. Padded benches of different heights, covered in deep red velvet, were hung with golden chains and gold-plated manacles. The walls were draped in gold damask. Handcuffs made of red leather and lined in fur dangled from chains in the ceiling. Gilded cages in various shapes and sizes sat on white fur rugs on the floor. A fairyland of torture devices. A playland for the rich and deviant. A perverse sense of irony about it all.

Her knees went weak.

She had never seen anything like it. She was about to enter this place, had agreed to it. And she wanted to.

"Inside now, Magdalena."

She could not get her feet to move.

He said softly, "Do it now, or I'll make you enter on your knees."

That was all she needed to hear. She stepped into the room. He was right behind her, closing the heavy door. She felt absolutely cut off from the world. She should have been frightened; instead she was as turned on as she'd ever been in her life. Even better when he smoothed his hands over her shoulders, standing behind her still. She couldn't see him, but she could smell him, that dark, masculine scent. And she could *feel* him. His presence alone was a palpable thing. Electrifying.

He leaned in and whispered, "I'm going to undress you now."

She started to shake her head. But he moved in closer, held the edge of her turtleneck down with his hand, and kissed her just below her ear.

That kiss went straight to her sex, which filled, swelled, pulsed with need. When had she ever known a man who could do that to her with nothing more than a small kiss?

His hands were everywhere, gentle, exploring her curves, yet never quite touching her breasts, her bottom. By the time he slipped her sweater over her head she was ready, wanting him to do it.

"Ah, such lovely skin." His voice was low, soothing.

He stroked her bare skin with his hands, still not crossing the boundaries of her black lace bra. Her breasts ached for his touch. In any other circumstance she would have torn her bra off and demanded what she wanted. But not now, not with him. This was different. Frustrating, in a keenly exquisite way.

He smoothed his palms over her shoulders, her back, her belly.

Lower, yes . . .

As though he heard her silent plea, his hands dipped lower, unbuttoned her wool slacks, let them slide down her legs.

"Christ, Magdalena, but you are gorgeous. Every silken inch of you." He moved his hands down, over her hips, her thighs. "Your skin is so polished. Unmarked. Virginal. But I'll take care of that eventually."

She shuddered. What would he do to her? Her nerves were strung tight. Combined with her increasing arousal, she could barely stand still.

He came around to the front of her body, ran one finger over the curve of her breast, and her nipples peaked. "Spectacular. Have you ever had your nipples pinched hard enough to hurt? Really hurt?"

Oh, God.

Her nipples hardened even more.

"That's only one of the things I will do to you. Maybe not today, but eventually." He paused, smiled. "Or maybe today. One thing I can promise is to keep you guessing. You should know, for your article, for yourself, that that's a part of it. The element of surprise. The wondering. The small heartbeat of fear about what might happen next. The anticipation for the bottom. The smug satisfaction for the top. Yes, we can be evil in that way. You will learn to love it, if you don't already. But I think you might have discovered the pleasure of the unknown even now. That little thrill."

He moved around behind her again, lifted her hair,

stroked the back of her neck. She felt as though his fingers were between her thighs. Her sex went damp. She pressed her thighs together.

"No, Magdalena. In fact, let's have you spread your legs for me."

He couldn't be saying this to her, couldn't be asking her to do this!

His mouth was right next to her ear. "You will do it, Magdalena. For me."

His hands slid down over her lace-clad buttocks, his fingers brushing the back of her thighs, then insinuating themselves between them.

"Spread for me. *Now.*"

His voice was harder than it had been before. Her legs were shaking. She moved them apart a little and his hand immediately dove in to cup her damp mound.

"More. I know you want to. My hand is right there. I can feel your heat, your need. You're soaking wet and I've hardly touched you. Do it, Magdalena. Don't fight me."

Her mind whirling, she did as he said. She couldn't manage to think about it. What was happening to her?

"Ah, much better."

Why did she feel pleased at the approval in his voice?

"You see, it's an easy thing to do, following orders. You simply need to hand yourself over to me. I'll take care of everything. Now, down on your knees."

"What?"

"Shh. No talking back. Just do as I say."

"But I can't—"

"You can. And you will." He pressed his hand to the

back of her neck. Not enough to hurt, but it was clear he would force her down if she didn't go on her own.

She sank to the floor, her heart slamming into her ribs.

"That's it. Now spread your knees apart. Place your hands on the top of your thighs, palms up."

She did it, hardly believing this was her on her knees on the floor, doing whatever this man told her to do. And enjoying it. Yes, something inside her was breaking apart, opening up already. How much more would he put her through before this was over? How lost would she become in what was happening here?

"I'm going to go over the rules now. The most important thing for you to remember is that I am in charge. You will not speak unless I tell you to. And when you do, you will address me as 'Sir.' You will do as I tell you, obey me without question or pause. You may wonder why I ask certain things of you. Trust that I know exactly what I'm doing, that everything has a purpose. You will come to understand eventually. Meanwhile, if you have questions, you will ask them once the scene is over. When we are no longer in role, you may speak to me as you normally would. Is that understood? You may answer me."

She nodded, a strange sense of liquid heat infusing her limbs. It became all too real at this moment. "Yes. I understand."

He reached out and buried the fingers of one hand in her hair, pulled tight, until her scalp burned just a little. But he'd made his point.

She gasped at the small shock of pain, and at the way her sex clenched in response. "Yes, Sir."

"Excellent."

He let her go, turned, and she watched him walk to a high, carved, antique armoire set against one wall. He opened the doors. Inside was an array of leather items, some with dangling bits of metal. There were also chains and lengths of rope, coiled and hung from hooks. The same heat that had coursed through her body earlier turned to fire. Her head was spinning.

He came back to her. "Lift your hair for me."

She complied. He bent over her and fastened a leather collar around her neck.

She felt . . . she wasn't sure what exactly. There was a tightness in her body. Reluctance? No, more than that. Fear? Panic?

Tears stung her eyes. She shook her head, biting her lip. She whispered, "I cannot do this. Please. I can't."

He went down on one knee so he could look her in the eye. He held her chin in his hand, forcing her to meet his gaze.

"You can. I know what you're feeling. You're fighting it. But your body has already proven that you want this. Just let it go. Stop struggling. You can do this. You can allow yourself to have this. Don't you understand this means you don't have to be responsible for anything while you're with me?"

She shook her head again, unable to speak.

"Do you realize that even as you fight this, you have not broken your submissive pose at all? Your hands are back where I told you to place them, palms up on your spread thighs. Your mind might want to be in charge, but your body has already given itself over to me."

She took in a deep gasping breath. What he said was true!

One stray tear spilled over and crept down her cheek. He gently wiped it away with his thumb.

"I will take care of you, Magdalena. Cry if you must. But let it happen."

She nodded, her eyes still blurred.

He stood. She didn't watch this time as he walked away, moved about the room. He came back and stood behind her once more.

"Stand, my dear."

He helped her to her feet, and pulled her arms behind her back. A moment later the soft grasp of leather closed around her wrists, then she heard the clink of the buckle.

Panic set in full force and her pulse raced through her veins. He rubbed the skin just below the cuffs with his thumbs. "Shh, it's alright. You're fine. Take a few deep breaths. Clear your mind. Clear yourself of the fear."

She tried to do as he said, drawing in a deep breath, blowing it out, but her chest still felt as though it were weighted down somehow. Was this her standing here nearly naked, collared and bound? She couldn't believe it. Yet at the same time her nipples were hard and aching, her sex swollen with need. Her mind and her body battled; she still didn't know which would win.

He led her to a waist-high bench, pressed gently between her shoulder blades with his hand.

"Bend over this now. Don't fight me, Magdalena. Just do it."

She went over, doing her best not to put too much thought into it. The velvet was soft against her skin and she thought vaguely that it must be of the highest quality, silk velvet maybe, since it didn't feel scratchy on her bare flesh.

She felt completely vulnerable, bent over, her hands fastened behind her back.

"Lovely," he murmured. "You have one of those gorgeous, heart-shaped asses. It begs to be stripped bare. To be beaten."

She flinched. A small laugh from him.

"But not yet. We'll take things slowly."

He brushed a hand over her back, a light, feathering touch. His fingers moved over the lace of her panties, down to the back of her thighs, behind her knees. His touch was sensual, gentle. And everywhere he touched a trail of desire lit her skin, making her tremble inside.

If she spread her legs just a little he could slide his hand between them again . . .

When he slipped his fingers beneath the edge of the black lace, she drew in a sharp breath and her legs moved apart of their own accord.

"Eager, are we? That's exactly what I like to see."

Again that wash of pleasure at the tone of his voice, at his approval.

His fingers slipped to that juncture at the inside of her thigh. So close.

"You're burning hot. Do you know what that makes me want to do to you?" He paused. "Everything. But I will honor our agreement, even though I'm as hard as I've ever been in my life."

Oh, God . . .

His voice lowered until it was almost a whisper. "Our contract doesn't preclude me from doing this."

He slid his fingers into her wet cleft. She moaned. He went to work right away, pushing his fingers into her while he wrapped his other hand around her waist to dip down and massage her clit.

Her hips bucked into his hand, the pressure building inside her immediately. She could feel his breath hot in her hair. The vulnerability of her position made every sensation more intense. The sense of helplessness.

"Come into my hands. Come, Magdalena."

Her climax hit her, fast and furious. Pleasure rolled through her, crashed over her. Her body shuddered, her legs shook, her sex clenched and squeezed at his fingers still pumping inside her.

It seemed to go on forever. He didn't stop until the last quivering spasms had subsided. When it was over he trailed hot kisses down her spine.

"That was perfect."

This time she let herself revel in his pleasure, in her own. She was in no condition to fight anything now. At least, that's what she told herself. But the truth of it was her body was half in love with this man, who could take her over in this way, bring her such incredible pleasure. Her mind wasn't far behind.

Oh, he'd gotten her too easily. But she didn't really care right now.

"Your skin is flushed. So beautiful," he murmured almost reverently. "The only thing that would make it look better is my handprint on your ass."

Had he really said such a thing? But of course, she knew he was perfectly serious.

"Are you ready for your first spanking? Because I am dying to give it to you. You may answer me."

Was she ready? Her body was ready for anything he wanted to do to her. But she felt she should at least think about it, make some sort of decision rather than allowing her body's needs to lead the way.

"Don't analyze this. Follow your instincts."

He stroked a hand over her ass. God, she wanted to feel his clever hands on her skin. The lace was only in the way. Yes, she wanted him to spank her, to touch her. How he did it didn't matter.

"Yes," she whispered.

"Yes what?"

"Yes, please, Sir." A pang at having to use that formal title. But she was too turned on to care.

"Much better."

He moved his hands over her bottom again, sliding them down to the underside of her cheeks. The skin there was tender, sensitive. He gave a little pinch. She jumped.

"You must do your best to hold still. No matter what I do to you."

There it was again, that small threat beneath his elegant tones. It made her heart beat faster, her sex pulse with need.

His voice in her ear again, the dark scent of him surrounding her. "I'm going to strip you bare now. And then I'm going to spank you. It's going to hurt. It's going to be the most wonderful thing you've felt in your life. Get ready."

CHAPTER FIVE

He saw her tremble, felt it beneath his hand resting on the back of her neck. Yes, she was scared. Of course she was. But she was also in a high state of arousal, which would make it easier for her to take. And her fear, her excitement, went right into his bloodstream, heating him up inside. He couldn't remember ever having such a strong reaction to a woman, to her inarguable beauty, her responsiveness. He couldn't wait to really get started.

He slid his palm down her spine. Some day he would flog her long, lovely back. But not today.

By the time his hand had reached the top of her curved buttocks, her breath was coming in sharp little pants. She gasped when he grabbed the edge of the black lace and pulled.

Her naked ass was as gorgeous as he knew it would be. He had to take a brief moment to admire it before sliding the scrap of lace down her legs, then helping her to lift her feet to step out of the pretty, bad-girl underwear.

He moved his hands up and cupped her heavy breasts. Even through the fabric he could feel the taut peaks of her nipples, the heat of her rolling off her body in waves. God, she felt good, all hot and soft but for those hard nubs of flesh. What would they look like, taste like? He almost groaned aloud just thinking about it.

This woman was shattering his self-control suddenly. What was it about her? She was gorgeous, all pale skin and cool blond hair, those calm gray eyes. Virgin flesh was always the most entertaining. There was nothing like the novelty of being the first one to deliver a spanking. But he'd played beautiful new submissives before. None had affected him the way she did. It was always exciting, but his cock was absolutely straining to get at her.

Perhaps it was the way she thought, the way she spoke. She had a brilliant mind, he could tell that already. And she was feisty. How clichéd that such a word, such a thing, should stimulate him as it did. But he knew that was part of the attraction. An attraction that seemed to be turning into obsession already.

He decided not to risk taking her bra off. It was bad enough looking at the smooth curve of her ass, knowing he was going to touch it. Knowing that if she parted her legs a bit more he'd see the pink lips of her sex peeking through.

Christ.

It was almost too much for him. When was the last time that had happened? Maybe never.

He took a deep, calming breath, redirected his mind to the responsibility at hand. To be her first. He had to make it good, had to make it perfect for her.

He feathered his fingers over her skin, tracing the outline of her cheeks. Yes, that perfect heart shape, too sweet. And untouched. Until now.

He gave her a small swat. She jumped.

"Calm, Magdalena. That didn't even hurt. You're just surprised."

Another swat, a little harder this time. Her skin showed a touch of satisfying pink already. He smoothed his hand over her skin, feeling the heat, then gave her a good smack.

"Oh!"

"Yes, that one hurt a bit, didn't it? Just move into the pain. Breathe into it. You can do it. You can love it."

Another smack, then another. He began to create a tempo with his hands. He knew it was always easier if he gave the bottom a rhythm they could sink into. He kept it up, a series of easy slaps on her flesh, not too hard, just hard enough to hurt. He could tell from her breathing, from the way she was beginning to surge back into his hands, that she was getting some good endorphins already. That she was sinking into sub space; that place in her head where the outside world ceased to matter.

He knew if he slipped a hand between those delectable thighs she would be soaked.

No, too much. Focus.

He slowed the rhythm down, paused to pinch the delicate flesh on the underside of those delectable cheeks. She gave a little jump, immediately surged back into his hands once more. Yes, he had her.

But for the first time in his life, for some inexplicable reason, she had him, too.

Lord, she'd never felt anything like this in her life! Her skin was warm all over, but absolutely burning where he'd spanked her. And her sex was on fire, crying out for release.

Please, please . . .

But she knew already not to say it aloud.

This was all so different for her. She could not believe she was doing this, giving over all control and loving it. But there was no doubt she was.

He'd stopped the spanking, giving her a moment to catch her thready breath. Then he smoothed his hands over her heated flesh. Yes, so good, his smooth palms sliding over her sore skin. Such a lovely contrast.

Then his hand moved between her thighs and his fingers probed her cleft, found her clit, tugged and pinched at it. She went off like a rocket immediately, her climax stabbing through her like a thousand shooting stars. Her body shook with the force of it, with the exquisite rush of pleasure.

By the time it was over she was trembling, gasping.

"You are too perfect, Magdalena." Was his voice a little shaky? Couldn't be . . .

He was sliding his fingers over her wet sex still, and the pressure was quickly building again. He worked at her clit with one hand; with the other, he began another slow volley of smacks on her ass. The sensation was intense, overwhelming. She didn't know what to do. She wanted to push into his probing fingers, into his punishing hand.

"Let it go," he whispered.

And she did, just let her body melt into the dual sensations, until the pain of the spanking and the absolute pleasure of his fingers working her clit, then sliding inside her, became all one thing. One sensation: pure pleasure. She rocked back into the pain, forward into the pleasure, not caring how wanton she must look.

Soon she was reaching that lovely peak once more. This time she took one deep breath and fell over the edge, into the shattering embrace of orgasm. Her body shook with the steep rush of sensation. And before the last ripple subsided, he was pulling her up, against his body. She burrowed into the heat of him behind her. His strong arm held her tightly around her waist. She let her head fall back onto the hard plane of his chest.

"Christ, Magdalena."

She smiled. She'd heard the ragged heat in his voice, felt the tremble of his body against hers. And knew a different kind of satisfaction.

Being upstairs, dressed again and sitting in his elegantly furnished living room, seemed surreal to her now. Too unbelievably civilized, given what they'd just done together.

Her head was still spinning a bit, her body light, weightless. She had to make an effort to keep a foolish grin off her face.

He stood against the fireplace mantel, a casual pose except for the betraying set of his shoulders. And he had a drink in his hand now. But she felt too smugly sated to be concerned about the tension held in his stance.

"How are you?" he asked. "Are you warm enough?"

"Yes, I'm fine. Wonderful."

"Do you have any questions about what happened?"

"I'm sure I will later. But not now. I feel too good."

"You do look like a cat with a bowl of cream." He smiled then, and the tension, whatever had been bothering him, seemed to wash away. His smile was as devastating as ever.

"I do have one question. Are you always so distant with your partners after you play with them?"

His dark brows furrowed for a moment, then he was at her side, sinking down onto the cushions beside her.

"Forgive me. I should be more attentive. Are you alright?"

"Yes, I'm fine. Really. I just . . ."

She shook her head helplessly. She didn't know how to explain it, this need to have him close to her. Was this simply an effect of what had happened to her? Or was it something else?

She would have to think about it later.

"I should have told you about this. Sometimes the bottom can crash. It's an emotional reaction to what your body has been through. A release of sorts."

"Ah, that explains it, then."

Did it?

He stroked her hair from her face, tucked it behind her ear. Such a tender gesture from him, the man of steel. Perhaps he wasn't so cool and steely on the inside after all?

But no, he was just being nice to her, doing his job. He was excellent at his job.

"I'm going to take you back to your hotel now. You

need to rest, to think about everything that's happened here today."

"Okay."

Why the hell was her throat tightening at the thought of his leaving her alone in her hotel room?

He helped her to her feet, showed her through the house, back into the garage, into the car.

He started the engine, pressed the magic button, and backed out of the garage. They rolled through the iron gates, onto the street. She was surprised to see the sky darkening already. How long had she been in his house? She'd lost all sense of time.

Fog was rolling in as he drove through the streets of the city. It was dark enough now that the colorful lights of neon signs stood out as they passed. She watched idly as storefronts, bars, apartment buildings slipped by outside the window. It all seemed a little less than real. And too cold out there, too unfriendly.

She turned to watch Damien's profile instead. He was so intent on his driving. But there was a vague softness about his mouth that hadn't been there before.

"Damien? Are we supposed to talk about this?"

"Yes, of course." He downshifted as the car climbed a hill. "We'll talk later. When you've had some time to normalize."

Why wouldn't he look at her? And why did that make her chest knot up? She wasn't the type to become emotionally involved. It must be that reaction he'd told her about. Because this loose-limbed woman on the verge of tears was not her.

She wasn't sure right now that she would ever be her old self again.

They reached the front of the sleek and thoroughly modern W Hotel on Third Street, and the doorman opened her door. Damien got out of the car, handed the man a tip, and told him he'd be only a few minutes. Then he was by her side, his arm slipping around her waist. He felt good. Strong.

"I'm going to see you up to your room. Do you have your key?"

She dug through her purse, handed him the plastic card.

"What room?"

"Fourteen twenty."

They crossed the slick expanse of black-tiled floor in the lobby, passed the curved check-in counter with its enormous bowls of green apples, and went to the bank of elevators. He kept his hand at her waist. She couldn't help but think of where else those hands had been today.

They rode up in the elevator quietly. But she didn't need to talk about anything right now. She was busy enough with the images of the day flashing through her head. Happy enough with his arm around her.

The elevator doors opened and he walked her out, found her room number, opened the door with the key. His hand still on the small of her back, he ushered her into the sparsely elegant room.

She assumed he'd leave right away, but he stood there, his arm still curved around her back. With his other hand he tilted her chin, forcing her to meet his gaze. His hazel eyes were burning.

"You sure you're alright?"

"Yes. Are you?"

He didn't answer her, just stared into her eyes with that intense gaze of his. He still radiated power in the same way he had when she'd first laid eyes on him. But there was more there now. Her body was heating up again, needing him. But he was going to leave her there.

"Magdalena . . ."

"What is it?"

He gave a small shake of his head, then moved in and kissed her, crushing her lips against his. Bruising, almost, but she wanted it, needed it.

He tasted faintly of the Scotch he'd had to drink. A little sweet, a little sharp. Masculine. He tasted even better when he opened her lips with his tongue, slipping right in, tasting, teasing. She moaned into his mouth, her body lighting up with need.

Just as quickly it was over and he was pulling away from her. His eyes were blazing with a dark golden fire.

"I have to go. You should eat something, maybe have a bath. I'll check on you later."

He moved toward the door, opened it, and slipped out so quickly she had to ask herself if she'd imagined that kiss. But the taste of him still sat heavy on her tongue. The heat of him was still on her skin.

She moved to the mirror over the dresser. Her reflection peered back at her. Her lips were full and looked a little swollen. Her eyes were huge, the pupils enormous. Her skin was pale, yet her cheeks were flushed a deep pink.

She looked different, felt different. She wasn't sure

what she thought about it yet. Yes, she needed some time to come back to earth, to dissect what had happened to her, figure out what it all meant.

The one thing she knew was that Damien Knight had touched a place in her no one else had ever reached before. In one afternoon, he had opened up a part of her she had kept tightly closed for years, had made her really let go. He'd made her feel the purest pleasure she had ever known, just as he had promised. What else would he do to her? Too deliciously frightening to think about.

But she wouldn't stop thinking about him. Oh, no, he had burned an indelible place in her mind already. And like a smitten schoolgirl, she found herself wondering if he felt the same way.

Silly of her, very much unlike her. But for tonight, she would indulge herself.

What was the calm and cool Damien Knight thinking? Because he certainly hadn't been calm and cool when he'd left her hotel room. Was it possible she had managed to shake up the one man who was, finally, stronger than she was?

CHAPTER SIX

DAMIEN SPED THROUGH THE CITY STREETS. WHAT the hell was wrong with him? His heart was hammering in his chest as though he'd just avoided a car wreck.

He'd certainly avoided what could have been a tragic mistake if he hadn't left her hotel room when he did.

Maggie. Magdalena.

He loved that she didn't like it when he called her by her full name. Even now it made him smile. God, he really was a sadist. But right now he was the one being tortured. By images of her long, sleek body, her polished skin, those enormous gray eyes that looked as though they were carved out of crystal. The woman was so incredibly responsive. The way she came into his hand, over and over . . .

His groin tightened, his thickened cock pressing against the fabric of his slacks.

She would be easy, physically. It was her mind he'd have to work with. She'd given in a bit too effortlessly today. By tomorrow her mind would be full of questions. Doubt. He would deal with it then.

Meanwhile, he had to put her out of his mind, some-how. He hadn't been so obsessed with a woman in a very long time. Not since his early days with Julia.

Stupid of him, to even think about Julia now. It wasn't as if he were going to marry Maggie. No, he'd never make that mistake again.

Why the hell was he even thinking about such a thing?

Maybe because she made his heart beat and his palms sweat as though he were twenty-one again, as he had been when he'd met his ex-wife. What a disaster that had turned out to be, and all of it his fault.

He revved the engine at a red light, tapped on the steering wheel with impatient fingers. He wanted to get home, have a drink. He wanted to drink too much, really. Take a shower so he could get the smell of her off his skin before it drove him completely insane.

He was being ridiculous. He wasn't twenty-one again. A man of his age, his experience, shouldn't feel like this, like he would come apart if he didn't see her again. Ridiculous.

But as absurd at it was, he knew when he got home he'd find some excuse to call her the moment he walked in the door.

❧

Maggie closed her eyes and leaned her head onto the rolled-up towel behind her. A glass of Cabernet was perched on the marble edge of the bathtub. She took a deep breath, the quiet scent of her favorite vanilla and am-ber bubble bath filling her lungs.

Her body was pleasantly sore all over, a sensation she

reveled in, as silly as it seemed. What had that man done to her head? She was thinking, feeling things, which were entirely new to her.

Had she really submitted to Damien Knight today? Had she allowed him to bend her over, to slip her panties off, to make her come for him while she stood there, helpless?

But she hadn't really been helpless, had she? She had done those things willingly. Hell, eagerly! And she wanted to do them again. For *him*.

She slid a soapy hand down her body, over her breasts, her nipples going hard instantly. Lord, he was more beautiful than any man had a right to be . . .

The phone on the wall above the bath rang, startling her.

Damien.

She picked up the receiver. "Hello?"

"There you are, darling. I'm checking up on you."

"Jet, hi."

"So, how was it? Tell me everything."

"Um . . . it was interesting. No, more than that. It was wonderful. Exhilarating."

"Did he hurt you?"

"Only a little."

"And did you like it?"

She was quiet a moment. Could she admit it out loud? But this was her best friend.

"Yes."

"That's it? Just 'yes'? No details?"

"I don't know what to say about it just yet. I'm still a little . . . floaty."

"I can't quite believe you did this, Maggie. Not even you, the infamous *Citi* sex columnist. I don't mean that as an insult, darling, but you're pretty much a control freak."

"It's okay. I know it. How can I not be?"

"Honey, the rest of the world is not your mother."

"I know. But she was so totally out of control. I feel safer if I know I'm in charge of my world."

"Maybe that's what this is all about for you. Letting it go for once."

"That's what Damien says."

"Oh, lord, you're not going to turn into one of those women who go around constantly quoting their boy-friends, are you?"

"Hardly. This is me you're talking to, Jet. Oh, hold on, the other line is beeping. In fact, let me call you back. It must be him."

"Whatever you say, darling."

She hit the flash button and switched lines, her pulse racing.

"Hello."

"Magdalena."

"Yes." A speedy flutter of her heart at the sound of his voice.

"I hope I'm not disturbing you. Are you resting?"

"I'm in the bath."

"Right now?"

"Yes."

There was a long silence. Then, "We need to make a time to meet tomorrow. I can pick you up at noon. We'll have lunch, talk."

"And then?" Was that her own voice, so breathless?

"And then, if you are still agreeable, we will come back to my house and explore some new territory."

"Oh." Her mouth was suddenly too dry to speak. And she was acutely aware of her naked flesh beneath the warm, scented water.

"Tonight I want you to rest, to eat a light meal. Sleep in tomorrow if you can. You'll need your strength."

That sounded more like a promise than a threat to her. And her body was responding once more to the command in his voice, her sex filling with need, her breasts aching. She didn't know what to say.

"Are you there, Magdalena? Are you listening?"

"Yes. I'm here." She smoothed her fingers over her breast, gave her nipple a small pinch.

Yes.

"I'll see you at noon. Meet me in the lobby."

"I'll be there." She would do whatever he wanted her to do, frankly.

There was a soft click, then a dial tone. She hung the phone up, sank further under the scented water. She slid her hands over her body: her breasts, her stomach, down between her thighs. Her sex clenched. She moved in, using her fingers to tease at the swollen, pouty lips. Her hips surged, her thighs tensed. God, just the sound of his voice had done this to her! But she needed this, needed some release. Yes, just a fast orgasm, to take the edge off.

She moved the fingers of one hand, slipped two inside her, let out a soft moan. With the other hand, she used her fingers to roll her clit, to tug on it, to pinch. Her breath came in short pants and her whole body was sizzling with need. Her hips tilted, and she drove her fingers deeper inside, angled to hit her g-spot.

She pictured his face, his large, strong hands. He had the long and dexterous fingers of a surgeon, a musician. But no, he used them for more decadent tasks. He'd used them on her.

Yes!

She rubbed her clit and moved her fingers a little faster, imagined it was his hands on her again, and came, hard. His face was in her mind as her body convulsed in pleasure. As her sex clenched around her plunging fingers.

Yes!

When it was over, she was left shaking and weak. Weak with desire for *him*.

Tomorrow couldn't come soon enough.

❧

Five minutes to twelve found her in the lobby of the W Hotel. She wore a simple black pencil skirt, a body-hugging black V-neck sweater, and tall black boots that hugged her calves in a simple silhouette. She often wore black in New York. Why did it seem to mean something else today?

She paced the gleaming black and white floor, checking the front door every few minutes. Then, not wanting to appear overanxious, she settled into one of the black, leather chairs.

She was trying very hard not to examine the thoughts whirling through her mind, trying not to think too much until she saw him, had a chance to talk this out with him, because the confusion she was feeling this morning was very disturbing, her thoughts convoluted. She didn't know what was normal under these circumstances, wasn't sure what she was supposed to be feeling.

"Ah, there you are."

"Damien, hi." Her pulse throbbed and she went hot all over the moment she saw him, heard his voice.

"No smile this morning. It seems we have things to talk about. Come."

He held out a hand to help her from her chair, those old-world manners again. Despite herself, she melted a little at his touch.

"There's an excellent place to eat right here in the hotel. It's called XYZ. Have you tried it yet?"

"No. This is the first time I've been in San Francisco in years."

"Really?" He placed a hand at her waist as he had the night before and steered her toward the restaurant. "Why is that? I imagine a journalist would have plenty of opportunity to come here. From one cosmopolitan city to another. Particularly in your area of . . . expertise. San Francisco is a city known for its sexual debauchery. A true city of sin."

"I suppose. I . . . I've avoided coming here, if you want to know the truth."

God, why had she admitted that to him?

"Let's get a table and then you can tell me why."

They moved toward the doorway of the restaurant. Inside, they were seated immediately at one of the black leather booths. The curtains around the booth, the low curved ceiling, gave a sense of privacy. The place had that hushed air about it very elegant restaurants often had.

The diffused light coming through the fogged-glass windows added to the ambience. The waitstaff moved in graceful silence over the glossy wood floors, serving small works of art to the patrons.

A waiter came to their table and handed them suede-bound menus. Damien ordered San Pellegrino for them both, waved the waiter off, and settled into the soft booth in his usual casual pose.

"Now tell me, why have you stayed away from San Francisco?"

"You get right to the point, don't you?"

"Yes. Tell me."

"This city holds . . . bad memories for me."

"A man? What did he do to you?"

"Why would you assume it was a man who drove me from here?"

"Because it usually is."

"True."

Their drinks arrived. The waiter placed their glasses and the remaining bottle on the table and asked for their order.

Damien spoke before she'd had a chance to make a decision. "I'll have the asparagus salad with quail egg and prosciutto. The same for my companion."

He raised a brow at her; she nodded her head. The waiter scurried off. Once more she had noted how the waiter deferred to Damien in a way which was slightly more subservient than was usual.

"Are you going to wait until our food has arrived before you tell me this story?"

"Are you going to give up if I make you wait longer than that?"

He sat back, took a sip of his sparkling water. A small smile quirked the corner of his mouth. "Of course not."

She sighed. "It's my mother."

"The French artist?"

"Yes." She picked up her glass, took a long sip, set it down again. Her throat was thick, tight, making it hard to swallow.

"Surely that's not all I get?"

"You don't want to hear this. It's not pretty."

"So much of life is not pretty. 'Pretty' isn't a requirement for something to be important or interesting."

She met his gaze, held it. "You're very much the philosopher, aren't you?"

"And you're stalling again."

She shrugged. "I don't talk about her much. My mother is a mess, to be honest. She's very bohemian. Or at least, that's her excuse."

"For what?"

"For being a flake. For spending her life flitting around the world, stopping only long enough to paint whatever strikes her fancy, eating and paying bills only when she remembers. Then moving on again."

"A hard life for a child, being moved from place to place."

"It wasn't all bad. Even I can admit that. I had seen most of the world by the time I was eight. She took me all over Europe, to Tahiti, to Thailand."

He leaned in to the table, closer to her, his voice low

and more intimate. His hazel eyes were on her. "A whirl-wind existence."

"Totally out of control. I never had a moment when I could just sit still, contemplate who I was, my place in the world. I had no place . . ."

She remembered the sights and scents of the cities to which her mother had taken her. The light on the water of Venice, the spices and flowers of Indonesia. The lack of safety in it all, being in those strange cities with her mother often gone for days at a time, run off with a man, or to paint something intriguing, leaving her on her own in a hotel room. She'd learned to be an adult at a very young age.

Damien's hand slid over hers, warm, reassuring.

"That explains why you're so completely controlled now."

She pulled her hand away. Why was there bile rising in her throat? "I wasn't so controlled yesterday with you."

"You're angry."

"Hell, yes, I'm angry," she hissed. Her blood was boiling suddenly.

He asked very softly, "Are you angry with me? Or are you angry that you allowed yourself to let go?"

She shook her head, trying to calm down. "Both, maybe."

"I understand."

That was all he said, just those two simple words. But they made all the difference in the world.

His voice was low, so soft she had to strain to hear him over the music filtering through the background of muted conversation, clattering plates. "Tell me what happened."

She stared at him for a moment. She was going to tell him. She didn't know why.

"I was eighteen. I was tired of taking care of her, of being the parent, you know? I couldn't do it anymore. I had to try to have a life of my own making. Some stability. We'd come here from London so she could see some gallery owners. And I was . . . I was so tired. I told her I wasn't going back to Europe with her."

"I take it that didn't go over well?"

"She became depressed." She stopped, remembered her mother as she'd last seen her, her beauty faded by sorrow and drink. "She was angry with me. Told me if I stayed behind, then I was on my own. Even though that was exactly what I wanted, it broke my heart that she would do that to me. Forsake me for growing up."

"It wasn't because you'd grown up. It was because she didn't want to be alone."

Was he right? Lord, the way he could see into her, know her life, without really knowing her at all.

He took her hand again, this time holding it firmly.

"You're safe here now. I won't let anything happen to you as long as you're with me."

But how long would that be? Another thirteen days and she would be gone. He would be nothing but a very interesting memory.

Too bad that was a blatant lie.

CHAPTER SEVEN

THE LIVING ROOM IN HIS HOUSE WAS JUST AS
she remembered it. Once again she noticed how the clean,
simple lines of the furnishings contrasted with the more
formal architecture. A lovely contrast, almost magically
beautiful, like something out of a magazine. It was perfectly silent, other than the sound of his shoes brushing
over the Persian rug as he moved to close the drapes, shut-
ting out the light of afternoon outside. Then he came to
stand behind her. She shivered simply knowing he was
there, that close to her. She imagined if she leaned back
just a little she could press against his chest, feel his heart
beat through his clothes.

She was very much aware that she was thinking like
some starstruck teenager. But she couldn't help it.

He slid his hands down her arms, and she could feel
the warmth of his touch even through her sweater. Her
breasts were already full and needy, her sex damp.

He moved in closer. "We begin now."

"What? Here?"

"We don't need the shock or the luxury of my little dungeon. Today, it's just the two of us, with whatever I have at hand. It will be a different kind of shock for you."

Her sex clenched. Why did she feel the need to argue?

"I don't understand. Why here, in this perfectly normal room? And don't tell me I can't speak now. We're not playing yet."

He was quiet a moment. Then, "Rest assured that I will work the anger out of you."

"Will you, now?" She didn't care that she sounded sarcastic.

His hands on her shoulders again, this time exerting a gentle pressure. She could sense the heat of him against her back, seeping into her spine. "I'm going to tie you up. To do some wicked, mysterious things to you. To make you come so hard you'll scream. And you'll love it. Before we're done you'll beg for it, for me to hurt you. For me to fuck you. And you won't be angry anymore."

His words enraged her. Inflamed her. She squeezed her thighs together. "Do you kiss your mother with that mouth?"

"My mother is long dead."

"Shit."

"Lovely language for such a sophisticated woman."

"God, I'm sorry." Her cheeks were burning, with shame, with lust. "About the language. About your mother."

"Don't be. She was a nightmare. And yes, that has plenty to do, I'm sure, with my sadistic tendencies toward women. A sort of divine retribution. Divine to me, anyway, to take that rage and turn it into something positive. To turn it into pleasure. Freud would have had a field day with me. But that doesn't make what I said about you any less true."

Her whole body heated, the heat turning to a molten desire that flooded her system. The way his mind worked, the way he spoke to her, was the biggest turn-on of all. Even knowing he was just as damaged as she was got to her.

But she hated that he was right about her. She knew it already, that if he touched her again the way he had yesterday she would scream, would beg for him.

God.

"And Magdalena?"

"Yes?"

"The scene starts now. Prepare yourself."

She swallowed, hard. But she didn't want to fight it.

She stood in silence as he went about the room, lighting small candles in glass holders: on the coffee table, the side tables, the mantel. The tiny flames cast a soft glow around the room, illuminating the space in a flickering play of light and shadows.

He came back to her and removed her clothes quickly, and as gracefully as he did everything else, every movement almost a dance. This time he took her bra off, then her panties. She didn't attempt to argue. She knew she wanted to be naked with him. *For* him.

He led her to one of the white sofas, sat down, then pulled her into his lap. She let her arms rest at her sides. She didn't know what to do with her hands. But that problem was solved for her when he reached behind him, pulled the thick satin cord holding the drapes back, and used it to bind her wrists. She bit back hard on the panic welling in her throat. Yet at the same time she was fascinated at the sight of her hands being bound in this way. And that silken cord was so much better than rough rope would be for her. Too perfect. How did he know these things?

His voice was low, soothing. "Don't be frightened by this. The rope symbolizes your freedom. That you are handing yourself over to me."

Somehow she knew exactly what he meant.

Once her wrists were bound, he raised her arms over her head and placed them at the back of her neck, allowing him full access to her naked body. Immediately he began to stroke her, running his hands over her flushed skin. Her sex was aching, needy, wet. When he brushed her nipples with his fingertips she let out a gasp. God, they were so swollen and full, it almost hurt. They did hurt when he pinched them, hard. She bit her lip and reveled in the pain.

"Ah, that's it. You can take it, you see? I knew you could."

With one hand he opened her thighs a little, enough to move down between them. He found her cleft, rubbed his fingers over her, shifted and pressed two fingers right into her.

She gasped.

"You're so wet, so ready. You need this, don't you?"

She couldn't say anything. Her whole body was wracked with a sharp, stabbing pleasure.

He pushed his fingers in deeper.

"Say it, Magdalena. Say you need this. This pleasure, this bit of pain."

She shook her head, wishing she could hide her face from him.

He pinched one of her nipples and she unconsciously arched into his wicked touch.

"Say it. Now." His tone was harder, inarguable, followed by another pinch as he shoved his fingers deep inside her.

"Yes!" Her body convulsed, on the edge of orgasm already. "I need this. Please."

"Good girl."

He reached to one side and pulled a small, white candle from the table. He swirled the melted wax around in the holder, watching the slide of it against the glass.

"I need you to hold as still as you can, Magdalena."

He fisted one hand in her hair at the back of her head, holding her firmly. It was a good thing, too, because the moment she realized what he was going to do with the hot wax, she wanted to run.

"This is going to hurt. But it will also give you an incredible release of endorphins. You have to ride out the pain, to breathe through it."

He tightened his grip on her hair, really holding her down. Then he lifted the candle and tilted it over her breasts.

The molten wax came spilling down on her, seemingly in slow motion, giving her time to become truly scared. The heat of it hit her skin, not even hurting at first, just a slowly spreading warmth. Then the burn kicked in.

She yelled, tried to jump, but he still held her firmly by the hair.

"Breathe, Magdalena. You can do it."

She tried, but all she could do was pull a quick, gasping breath into her lungs. She watched as he set the candle down and slipped his hand between her thighs to massage her clit. As it had when he'd spanked her, the pleasure fused with the pain, until it all felt good.

"That's better, yes?" He kept at it, until her sex was swollen and pulsing. "Let's try this again."

He picked up the candle, and this time she felt better prepared as he held it over her and spilled.

Once more the initial warmth that turned into an aching burn as the melted wax cascaded over her chest, onto her breasts. She breathed into it, as he instructed her. And this time she was able to convert the pain. Her head rushed with the lovely endorphins he'd promised her.

Again he set the candle down and slid his fingers over her wet cleft as she rode out the searing pleasure. Incredible, this sensation, once she allowed herself to give in to it.

When she was on the verge of coming, he moved his hand up to her breasts, kneaded the full flesh there, massaging the wax into her skin. Her nipples came up hard, needing attention. And as though he could read her every desire, he moved to roll them, one at a time, between his fingers. He tugged and pinched them, sending pleasure shafting into her body.

She squirmed in his lap and felt his solid erection against her hip. God, he was big, and so damn hard. What would it be like to feel him inside her? If only he would slip his fingers between her thighs again. "Please . . ." she whispered.

"No talking, now."

God, he really was a sadist, wasn't he?

Once more he lifted the candle and poured, the wax

coming down on her skin in a rain of blazing heat. This time the pleasure kicked in right along with the pain. She panted, hard, when he pressed the wax into her skin. The heat radiated, fusing with pleasure as it coursed through her body. She was dizzy with it all, overloading on sensation. And she wanted more. Needed it. Needed to come. She moaned, squirmed. She could not hold still.

"I know what you need, Magdalena." He pinched one of her nipples, hard. Another jolt of sensation shot through her.

"Oh! Please . . ."

"Patience."

Finally, he reached down and pushed his fingers inside her. Her sex clenched hard as pure lust stabbed through her.

"No, Magdalena. Not until I say you can."

He pinched her nipple with his other hand, a tight, punishing pinch. She could barely breathe, her head and her body buzzing. He shifted his hand and pressed on her clit with his thumb.

"Oh!"

"Not yet." His voice was very low. "Do not come yet."

She wanted to obey, was too far gone to question how much she wanted to comply with his demands. But her climax lay heavy in her body already. She arched her hips, moaned.

"No, Magdalena."

And again he picked up the candle and spilled the wax onto her breasts. This time, the molten wax pooled over her nipples, stinging and hot. She took in a deep breath, closed her eyes, concentrated on his fingers working inside her, rubbing at her clit. And on the singeing pain on her skin, her nipples. Her body was poised on the edge of climax, waves of preorgasmic pleasure washing over her.

"I . . . I can't hold on."

"You will obey me."

Yes . . .

She clenched her teeth against the powerful tide rising inside her. He pinched and tugged at her nipples, worked her clit. The pressure was building to dizzying heights. She knew she couldn't hold back any longer.

"Please . . ."

"Please what?"

"I need to come."

He paused. "Oh, really?" He gave her clit one hard pinch. The pain reverberated through her, making her sex clench with hot, surging desire.

"Yes!"

"Yes what?"

"Yes, please, Sir . . . please . . ." She was almost sobbing now with need.

"Tell me what you want." He shoved his fingers hard inside her, burying them deep.

"Please . . . let me come. Make me come."

He leaned over, his breath hot in her ear. "What is it you want? Is it this?"

He pinched her clit and her whole body clenched with nearly unendurable pleasure. Exquisitely painful.

She gasped. "Yes!"

"And what else?"

"Oh, God . . ."

He pushed his fingers in again, drew them out, leaving her empty.

"I want you to fuck me . . . please. I need you."

His cock twitched against her thigh.

He leaned over her and said quietly, "You have no idea how much I'd like to do just that. But fucking is not part of this game."

A small sob escaped her then. How could he do this to her? To make her want this, to make her need him, and then to deny her?

A tear fell onto the sofa cushion below her face.

"Such pretty tears. So pretty you deserve some sort of reward."

She clenched her eyes shut, trying to stop crying. He shifted her weight in his lap and reached down to pull something from between the sofa cushions. She tried to see what it was, but couldn't. Then she heard a low, whirring buzz. She almost cried again in relief.

"I have here a very large vibrator. I hope you can take it. Do you think you can?"

"Yes! Please."

"Are you sure?"

He pushed her thighs farther apart so that she was open to him. Then he touched the buzzing tip of the phallus to her hungry cleft. She moaned.

"Can you feel the size of it? Not yet, can you?"

He shifted her body once more, turning her facedown, then guided her up onto her knees. He had her spread her thighs, so that she was kneeling over his lap and wide open to him. He touched the vibrator to her again, this time pushing the tip inside. Her whole body shuddered with pleasure.

"You're so damn wet, I think you could take anything," he murmured, almost as if to himself. His quiet words were followed by a sharp plunge, and the thick, hard shaft sank into her waiting sex.

"Oh . . ." The sensation was excruciating. The shaft was enormous, filling her completely, painfully. Yet the vibration was exquisite, sending waves of near-orgasm quivering through her body.

"It's only halfway in. Can you take more? Do you want it? Tell me."

"Yes . . . yes, I want it." She was shaking all over, with need, with pain.

He slid it in another inch and she felt the walls of her sex stretching, trying to accommodate the solid girth of the object. Very slowly, he moved it inside her, then slid it back out, until only the tip rested in her hot, clenching sex.

"Just breathe, Magdalena. Hold onto that edge. Ride it out. I'll let you come soon."

She took in a deep breath, tried to concentrate. But all she knew was the shock of pleasure stabbing through her body. He twisted the vibrator and she gasped.

"Hold it, Magdalena. Hold it back."

"I can't," she panted.

"You can. You will do it for me."

He held the vibrator against the lips of her sex for several long, agonizing moments.

"Please . . . please . . ."

"Yes, now." He gave the instrument another twist, sending a shard of pleasure knifing into her body, then he shoved it deep inside her. Pain and pleasure fused, burst, and she screamed as she came. Sensation roared through her system like wildfire, searing her, branding her. She cried out again as she shattered in his arms.

Even after he slipped the phallus from her body she trembled and moaned, fell into his lap, tiny wisps of pleasure shivering deep inside her. His hands were all over her, stroking her everywhere.

He whispered, "I loved to hear you scream. I loved to see you come so hard for me."

He kissed her skin, between her shoulder blades, blazing a trail of hot kisses down her spine. More tears that she couldn't control. How could any man make her let go the way she just had with him? How could he make her feel these things?

The crying turned into a long, deep sob. He turned her over, gathered her in his arms and held her. "It's alright," he told her, his voice quiet, a little ragged.

And she felt that it was; that it was okay to cry in his arms, to let him hold her. To be weak in this way with him.

He untied her wrists and let her cry herself out. He didn't let go of her for a moment. When it was over she was limp all over, exhausted. She wiped at her face.

"I don't know what happened to me . . ."

"People often have an emotional release with this kind of play."

"I wasn't playing."

He paused for what seemed like a very long time. Then he said quietly, "No. Neither was I."

She looked up at him. His hazel eyes were burning. With what emotion she didn't know, but that intensity of expression drew her in. She couldn't look away. He swept her hair from her face, then moved his thumb down to trace the line of her jaw. The motion was so tender, so gentle, her throat seemed to close up completely. How could he be doing this? How could this man, this detached sexual sophisticate, be looking at her like this?

How could he make her feel like her heart was about to come apart in her chest?

He leaned in and brushed her lips with his. And before she had a chance to think about it her arms went around his neck, pulling him closer. He kissed her harder, as though he really meant it. She parted her lips, letting him in.

He tasted just as she remembered, but sweeter, somehow. His tongue delved into her mouth, the kiss crushing, bruising her lips. She didn't care. She needed this. Needed him.

When the hell had that happened?

She pulled back, turned her head away from him, into his chest.

"Don't, please." She was panting so hard she could barely speak.

"Maggie . . ."

"I can't, Damien. I can't do this if it . . . if it means something."

"Fuck." His breath was as ragged as her own. "Damn it, Maggie, it does mean something to me. I don't know why. But it does."

"Oh, God, don't tell me that. Don't tell me what I want to hear."

"I'm only telling you the truth."

She was quiet while a flurry of emotions moved through her body like physical sensations: fear, longing. She shook her head and insisted, "I can't do this."

He didn't say a word, just held her tighter than ever, as though he knew she needed that. Needed to feel safe while her heart hammered away, while fear flooded her veins.

He held on for a long time. Until, for the first time in her life, she did feel safe, felt as though she could give herself into someone else's hands. *His* hands.

But it was this very sense of safety that scared her to death. She knew better than to count on something that could be taken away from her on a whim.

CHAPTER EIGHT

HE COULD SEE HER FEAR. IN HER FACE, IN HER tightly strung muscles. He understood it. What he felt for this woman was the first thing that had frightened him in years.

God, she was too much of everything. Her gorgeous, pale skin, her sweet mouth, her fine mind, even her need for control. It all got right under his skin. And to know she was feeling the same things he was feeling . . . that made it even harder, even better. Torture.

He had decided a long time ago never again to become emotionally involved with a woman. Now that Maggie was breaking that wall down, he understood what he'd sacrificed in the name of protecting himself. It had seemed like a reasonable price to pay at the time. But finally, he had to stop and question the way he'd lived most of his adult life.

How could she have caused all of this change in only two days?

She was still trembling. He had to clear his mind, to care for her as was his responsibility.

"What do you need? Something to drink?"

She shook her head.

He pulled a white, cashmere throw blanket from the arm of the sofa, and laid it over her naked and shivering body. "You're cold."

"No. I don't know."

"Do you want to get dressed, to go back to your hotel now?"

"No!" This followed by a muffled sob that went right to his gut like a hammer blow.

He pulled her closer. "Okay. Okay. You'll stay here with me.

With me.

If only she could. But she would be with him tonight. And, if he was lucky enough, for the remaining days before she had to return to her life. That would have to suffice.

Why did that idea make his whole chest squeeze as though a heavy weight had been placed there, crushing the breath out of him?

He shook his head to clear it. Then, gathering her in his arms, he stood and carried her down the hallway, up the wide staircase to the second floor. Down another hall and into his bedroom, where he laid her on the soft, brown suede duvet on his bed. He could barely stand to leave her, but he had to get the wax off her.

He went quickly to his bathroom, returned with two cloths: one warm and damp, the other dry, as well as a bottle of almond oil. She was exactly as he'd left her, lying still on his big bed, the throw blanket from the living room wrapped around her, her still-hard nipples making alluring peaks against the cashmere. He leaned over her and pulled the blanket back, trying not to focus on the luscious mounds of her bare breasts. So tempting, this woman.

Gently, he peeled the hardening wax from her skin, then poured a few drops of the oil onto her. She was quiet as he smoothed it in, rubbed away the last remnants of the wax. She let out a soft sigh when he followed with the warm cloth, closed her eyes as he dried her.

Finished, he set everything on the nightstand. He turned back to her, saw that she'd curled on her side, looking like a small and frightened child. Innocent, somehow. Lovely.

He watched her for a moment, but it was pure torture not touching her, not being able to feel the heat of her body. He undressed except for his black boxers, climbed in beside her, pulled her close to him, and heard her quiet moan. She fit perfectly within the hollow of his chest. Even more so when she moved back into him.

He didn't mean for it to happen, but he went hard the moment her buttocks pressed into his lap. As tender as he felt toward her right now, the desire for her was simmering beneath the surface, ready to be awakened at any moment. Desire was easier to deal with. And more pressing, as his cock filled and throbbed.

He smoothed a hand over her skin, loving every inch of her. Stroking the curves and valleys of her body, shoulder, waist, hip, he listened to the increasing cadence of her breath. And his cock grew, hardened even more.

"Maggie . . ."

"Yes?"

"I want you. It's not right for me to ask you now. Not after what you've just been through." God, what was wrong with him? He'd never been tentative with a woman—or anyone—in his life.

"Please, Damien . . . please. I need you now." She surged back, her smooth flesh right up against him, every surface connecting. His cock gave a hard pulse.

"Christ, what you do to me," he muttered before pulling her over on her back so he could kiss her.

He kissed her hard, forced her lips apart, found the wet heat of her tongue. She kissed him back, eagerly, wantonly, threw her arms around his neck.

He filled his hands with the lovely mounds of her breasts, her nipples hard against his palms. He had to taste her.

He lowered his head and looked at the beautifully rising flesh before him. Such perfect breasts. The nipples were a dark pink against her pale skin. He bent and took one into his mouth.

She groaned and buried her fingers in his hair. He flicked his tongue at the stiff peak, pushed her breasts together with his hands and suckled first one, then the other. She was panting, her ragged breath making him crazy with need. Making his cock throb until it almost hurt. He'd never wanted a woman like this in his life.

When she reached down and slipped her hand into the opening of his boxers, wrapped her fingers around his cock, he had to fight not to go off like a rocket.

Control.

He wanted to make her come again before he did anything else, before he satisfied his own aching desires.

He slid down her body, moved her legs apart, and breathed in the honeyed scent of her arousal. Just that scent made him impossibly harder. He bent and tasted her.

Her hands tightened on his hair, then slid down over his cheeks. "Yes . . ."

He feathered his lips across her mound, paused to blow gently on it, loving her tiny gasps. Then he dove in, licking and sucking, pushing his tongue inside her while she squirmed and panted beneath him.

It was only moments before he felt the first pulse against his tongue. Then she was coming into his mouth, her hips bucking as she called out his name.

She was still trembling with her orgasm when he lifted himself over her body and slipped out of his boxers. Torture, to have to pause even long enough to find a condom in the night table and sheath himself. He paused at the entrance to her lovely body for one aching, exquisite moment before he slid inside.

She was so damn wet, her inner walls like heated velvet. He had to pause, to take a deep breath and command himself to calm down.

Her long legs wrapped around his back, pulling him in deep. She licked and sucked at his neck, sending shivers racing over his skin. When he felt he had himself under control, he began to move. Long sliding motions, in and out of her tight little sheath. He could hardly stand it; fucking her and trying not to come like some teenager.

But it wasn't just fucking, and he damn well knew it.

Later.

Right now he just wanted to push into her, pull out, plunge again, simply to hear her gasps and moans of delight. He wanted to give this to her, to make her come again.

He moved faster, every thrust bringing powerful waves of sensation, making his cock harder than it had ever been in his life. Making his balls and his stomach tighten up. He loved to hear her pant, loved when she raked her nails down his back, reveled in the pain. And loved it even more when he felt the first pulse of her climax deep inside her body.

"Please, Damien. I need you. I need everything."

He pumped harder, faster, pounding into her in a white blur of pleasure. She cried out, her sex clenched around his cock, sending him over the edge with her. And as he came, pleasure stabbing into his cock, his entire body, he looked into her eyes. And what he saw there was more powerful than the orgasm crashing over him.

He was coming so hard it hurt; it was better than anything he'd ever felt before. But beneath it all was her beautiful face, and his heart beating a million miles an hour.

His climax left him shaking. She was quivering beneath him, her arms wrapped around his neck. He was still trying to catch his breath.

What the hell had just happened? He had never had sex with a woman with whom he'd agreed not to. And sex itself had never meant anything to him beyond the momentary pleasure, not since Julia.

Don't think about her now.

No, all he wanted to think about was Maggie. For the first time in almost twenty years, a woman was foremost in his mind, even before his responsibilities as a Dom. Christ, he didn't care about any of that right now. All he cared about was the woman lying in his arms.

After two days, how was this even possible?

But it was the impossible, shattering truth. He was falling for her. And when he landed, he had a feeling it was going to hurt one of them like hell.

❧

Maggie was still dizzy with the aftermath of pleasure, pleasure so intense she wasn't sure she would ever recover. And above and beyond that physical ecstasy was the deep and certain knowledge that what had just happened between them was more than sex.

She'd had plenty of sex and didn't regret any of it. But she'd never had sex like this. Like truly making love.

Was she a fool to think that's what it was? No: Despite the fact that the act itself had been so primal, she could see it in the way he touched her, looked at her. Had any man ever looked at her like that? Had she ever allowed it?

The idea frankly scared the hell out of her. But she felt too good right now to take it apart, to figure out what it might mean for her. She pushed the thought away and looked up at him, losing herself in the pure, male beauty of him.

He was holding himself up on one arm, exploring her face with his eyes, stroking her cheek, her jaw. He traced her lips with a fingertip and she kissed it, not really know-ing why she needed to do such a thing.

"Maggie, we need to talk."

"Now? Do we really have to?"

"I went against the conventions of our agreement. I knew I was doing it, knew it was wrong, and I did it anyway."

"I wanted you to. I asked for it."

"Yes, but your judgment was compromised."

"Never enough to do something I didn't really want to do. Please, don't talk any more like this. It just . . . dirties it, somehow."

"Alright."

He bent and laid a soft kiss on her lips, and immedi-ately, her body was on fire again. She pulled his head close, kissed him hard, until she felt the tension in him melt away. His cock hardened against her thigh, making her smile, letting her know that despite being the sexual submissive, she had just as much power over him as he did over her.

"I want to do it again," she told him. "But this time I want a little more. I want some pain while you're inside me. Will you do that for me?"

"You know, you're getting a little bossy. But somehow I think I can learn to live with it."

He slid his hand down and found her cleft, his fingers sliding easily into the wet, wanting heat. He pushed in-side.

"You're ready," he said, his voice shaking and guttural.

"Just do it. Please. I want it rough, merciless."

"Ah, you are too perfect."

He rolled her over onto her stomach, wrapped an arm

around her waist and pulled her ass into the air. With the other hand he pushed her thighs apart. He slid right in with a groan, all the way to the hilt. He was so big, so hard, she felt as though she could barely take it. But she did, and it felt damn good.

He started to pump into her right away. With each strong thrust of his hips he smacked her ass, a hard volley of slaps against her skin that she loved as much as his cock moving inside her.

She arched back into him, into his cock impaling her as mercilessly as she had asked for, into his hard and wicked hand. Pain and an almost unendurable pleasure flooded her completely, until she was weak and helpless beneath him.

But still she begged him, "Harder . . . please . . ."

He slammed his hips into the soft curve of her ass, his cock pummeling her. The first waves of climax came crashing down around her, over her, drowning her like the vast ocean. Deep inside, where the pleasure radiated, multiplied, she felt him throb and pulse. They cried out together, fell in a tumble of sated and panting desire, and held each other all night.

She woke to the rich, acrid aroma of coffee brewing. She knew immediately where she was, why she was there. And her body flooded with the heat of desire immediately just being in his bed, surrounded by his scent, by the heady fragrance of sex.

She wanted him again. But she knew they'd have some things to figure out before she let it go any further. This was no mindless, emotionless fuck just for fun. Some things simply could not go unsaid.

She sat up and looked for her clothes, then realized they were probably still in the living room. She glanced around, taking in the room while she looked for a robe or maybe his discarded shirt. But the room was spotlessly organized, other than the rumpled white sheets on the king-sized bed. She ran her fingers over the smooth fabric. Probably Egyptian cotton. Nice.

The rest of the room was just as elegant and expensive-looking. The furniture was all made of a very dark wood, simple, almost spare lines, with some unusual architectural details, like the curved front of the dressers and nightstands. The walls were painted a pale grayish blue. Everything had an air of cool calm, just like him. Interesting.

There was not even a throw blanket to cover herself with among all this spare luxury. But what the hell, he'd already seen her naked and she was never one to be shy about her body. She got up and wandered downstairs to find him.

His back was turned to her in the gray and white kitchen, one hand braced on the granite counter where a newspaper was spread out. He was wearing a pair of blue striped pajama bottoms slung low on his hips. His bare back was leanly muscled and tapered to a narrow waist, just the kind of physique she loved. Her sex pulsed in response and she found herself wanting to draw a finger over the ridges and planes of his body. Her tongue would be even better.

He turned around, coffee cup in hand, and smiled when he saw her. God, he was even more beautifully put together from the front. She'd been too frenzied to really take him in visually before. His shoulders were broad, his chest smooth and muscular with just a nice sprinkling of dark hair. Another sharp clench of her sex when she followed the narrow line of hair leading down his abdomen, into the waistband of his pajama bottoms.

His smile faded as he took in her naked figure. He tried to joke. "I should have you visit my kitchen every morning." But his voice was graveled with lust.

He set his cup down and moved toward her.

She put one hand up. "Wait. We need to talk."

"You cannot show up in my kitchen perfectly naked and expect me to talk to you." He advanced on her.

"Well . . ."

But as he stepped closer she caught the masculine scent that was purely *him*. Her body went liquid and suddenly she couldn't find the energy to argue.

"Come here." He wrapped an arm around her waist and pulled her in close to him.

His mouth came down hard on hers, his hands sliding down to cup her ass. Lord, the man could kiss! He was inside her mouth, tasting, teasing, his tongue hot and sweet with the flavor of coffee.

She smoothed her hands over his back, lower, beneath the cotton waistband. His buttocks were taut with muscle. She pulled him in closer until his erection pressed into her belly. Not close enough. She needed him inside. *Now*.

As though reading her mind his arms tightened

around her and he turned, lifting her onto the counter. The granite was cold beneath her thighs, but the heat growing inside her kept her warm.

He spread her legs, took one hand off her body long enough to pull the drawstring at his waist and the cotton fabric fell away. He pulled her closer, she wrapped her legs around his back, and he entered her in one long, smooth thrust.

She gasped at the size of him while pleasure rippled over her skin, moved deeper inside. He fastened his mouth on her neck, his hands held her ass, and he stabbed deeper into her body.

She held onto his shoulders and let her head fall back while he plunged into her, pulled out, plunged again. Each strong thrust sent a thrilling pleasure into her, singing through her veins. She was panting, he was panting. He moved too fast, too furiously, for there to be any words between them. This was all hot, animal sex, an expression of the intensity of their need for each other. No words were needed.

Her climax came down on her fast and hard; the sharp, pulsing spasms started deep in her sex, in her clit, then moved outward, until she was nothing more than a being made purely of pleasure.

Only a moment later she heard his guttural groan, felt his body stiffen all over, then his hot, hard cock was ramming into her, carrying the last surges of her own climax away with his.

He pulled her off the counter, and she wrapped her legs more tightly around his waist while he held her. He kissed her neck, her lips, her forehead. She shivered at each tiny kiss, her heart pounding with exertion and emotion. And the only thought running through her mind was, *I cannot leave him. Ever.*

☙

They had been together for one week—the longest relationship Damien had had with a woman in years. Hell, he never had a woman at his house for more than a night or two. But everything with Maggie was different.

He leaned into the kitchen counter, a coffee mug in his hand. She was in the shower upstairs. Too tempting, to go up there and slip beneath the hot water with her. To run his hands over that smooth, wet skin, to take her up against the cool tiles, push into her hot, eager body . . .

A lovely image. Even better to know he really could do it. The idea was luxurious, somehow.

Don't get too used to it.

He shook his head, took a long sip of the steaming, black coffee. For the first time in his life, he found himself intimidated by another human being. He didn't care for the feeling. He frankly hated it. But every time he began to think about how damn much he wanted her, how vulnerable he was with this woman, she was right there, and he fell for her all over again.

He knew that's what it was. And he spent most of his days denying it. Easy enough to get lost in her, in the things they did together. It was only when he found himself alone like this, when she was showering, when he tore himself away to work at his desk for a few hours, that his mind latched onto these thoughts.

He did not want to think about it. But sooner or later

he'd have to. Their time was coming to an end. He had another week to figure out how to shut himself down again. He would have to do it, no question about it. When the time came, he would find a way. Because the truth was, he couldn't handle the alternative.

CHAPTER NINE

SHE MOVED LANGUIDLY BENEATH THE WEIGHT of the heavy down comforter, his unique scent the first thing she breathed in. Her eyes opened to another new day, their twelfth day together. During that time he had tied her up, spanked her, flogged her, paddled her, made love to her. They'd talked about art, films, international politics, all of the interests they shared. He'd taken her to the best restaurants the city had to offer. They'd even spent an evening at the theater together. And every day he kissed her like no other man ever had. But they did not once talk about the fact that at the end of the week she was due to return to New York.

She was afraid if they talked about the situation it would ruin the moments they had left together. She had no idea what his excuse was, but she was grateful for it.

Her body had never been so sated. She'd never felt so cared for, so treasured. But was this reality? Could a relationship ever be this wonderful, this utterly satisfying and exciting at the same time? Or was this only dream time because they both knew it would soon end? She didn't know, couldn't even guess.

She'd spent most of her life understanding the impermanence of things. Of everything. She'd never believed in forever. Why did she want to now, despite everything she knew? Foolish of her.

She didn't want to think about the fact that they had only two days left.

Maybe it would be better to end things now, to get it over with? But she couldn't stand to have one less moment with him than was possible. The idea of it made her heart twist in her chest until she could barely breathe. But sometimes, so did the idea of staying. Of giving their connection a chance to strengthen, to pull her in even deeper.

She sat up and pushed her hair away from her face. The early morning light shone through the sheer curtains. The air was dense with fog outside. She could see the floating wisps of gray and white through the paned glass, the way it mixed with the pale sunlight to cast a shadowy stillness in the room.

She often woke before he did, and watched him as he slept. In sleep his strong face looked so peaceful, almost innocent. It was only when he opened his eyes that he took command. But she loved these quiet moments when she could simply study him, appreciate the translucent lids of his eyes, the way his dark hair swept back from the smooth skin of his forehead. And it was during these moments she realized she didn't really know anything about him, nothing beyond the surface. Even though when they were together, in bed, while scening, it felt as though she knew everything she needed to know.

In the dim light of a new day, she understood that finally, it was time to face reality about who he was, who she was. Who they might be together. But no, what she really needed was to deepen her understanding of why, at the end of these two weeks, she should go back to New York and leave him behind forever.

His eyes fluttered open and she was greeted with a smile. His strong, white teeth always dazzled her. But this morning she ignored the surge of lust between her thighs.

"Damien, I want to talk. Need to talk."

"Mmm . . . okay. What about?" He sat up, pulled his pillows up behind him. The sheet fell away from his bare chest and she had to steel herself against the sight of all that beautiful skin.

"I want to know about you. Who you are, where you come from. Everything."

He was quiet a moment. "I don't talk much about my past. That mention of my mother last week was unusual for me."

"Aren't D/s relationships, however brief, supposed to be based on mutual trust?"

"Yes. Of course."

"Do you trust me?"

"More than I've trusted anyone in a very long time."

"Then tell me."

"Is this more of your unfinished interview?"

She felt a quick stab of guilt at having sacrificed doing her job to her own needs. But she'd have plenty of material to write her article on the plane on the way back to New York.

Too awful to think about leaving here, leaving him.

Don't think about it now.

"The interview is over. This is about you and me."

He nodded, his face serious.

"I want to know why you haven't trusted anyone in so long, as you said. And there are other things . . . What are you not telling me?"

"You are too perceptive for your own good."

"Maybe. Are you going to tell me?"

He ran a hand over his dark hair, closed his eyes, leaned his head back into the pillows. If she hadn't known they were having a serious discussion, she'd have almost thought he'd fallen asleep. Finally he lifted his head and opened his eyes.

"I was married once."

He paused, as though waiting for her reaction. But she didn't know yet what to think of that bit of information. She waited for him to continue.

"I met her in college. Julia. We got very serious very quickly. We married after only three months. I was twenty-one. I'd already experimented with domination and sadomasochism. She knew about it, knew I was into it. She went along with it. Even derived some pleasure from it. But she never quite got it. I was too young to understand how that works."

"So you had a marriage that wasn't entirely built on truth?"

"Yes. But I didn't know to what extent until we'd been married for a year, when I found her in bed with a friend of ours."

"Oh, God."

"It was as traumatic as these things always are. She told me it was because of my 'perversions,' as she called it. She said she couldn't take it, didn't want to do it. But she hadn't felt able to tell me that. She was afraid I wouldn't hear her, that I loved it too much, loved it more than her. Well, she was probably right about that."

"But you did love her?" Why did it seem so important that she know that? That he was capable of love?

He was quiet a long time. She watched his face harden, his mouth tighten into a thin line. "Yes. In the way I was able to at that age. But the thing is, at that moment I came to understand I could not indulge my desires and have a relationship, as well."

"But aren't there people in this lifestyle who have successful, long-term relationships?" A stab of panic made her stomach knot up.

"Yes, of course."

"Then why should you be any different?"

"I failed miserably, didn't I?"

"You were young. Practically a kid. How could you possibly expect to make intelligent decisions at that age?"

"I always had before. I've always been hyperresponsible, I suppose you'd call it. Nothing less was expected in my family. My father was in the military, a colonel. I'm sure you know the type. And I've already mentioned my mother to you."

"Yes." She was quiet, absorbing everything he'd told her. In the end, it sounded like a bunch of excuses to her, frankly. Or was that just because she didn't want to hear these things from him?

She looked down at the suede comforter and rolled the edge between her fingers. "Are you trying to tell me something?"

She glanced up again to see him shrug. "I suppose I am."

"That you're not relationship material?"

He paused. His eyes were absolutely blank, all life gone from them as though an opaque curtain had been drawn down. His voice held a flat tone that made her feel as though she'd been tied to a rock, then thrown in a river. All emotion gone. All warmth. This was a different person sitting here and talking to her.

"This conversation has reminded me of why I don't get serious with any woman. Why in two days you will go back to New York and we will both get on with our lives."

The knot that had formed earlier in her stomach twisted painfully. "Haven't things changed for you at all this last week? Because I could swear I saw . . . I saw something in your eyes. Felt it from you."

He didn't say a word, just sat there and stared at the bed as though he were carved from stone.

Her eyes stung with tears. "Don't try to tell me you haven't felt something for me, Damien. That's bullshit. That's just you making excuses."

God, she hated that she sounded so weak, so needy. She would not beg this man to love her.

Love? When had that happened?

She wiped at her face as the tears spilled onto her cheeks. God, she was pathetic.

"I do feel something for you. But I shouldn't. I'm not

constructed that way. My apologies if I made you hope for something more—"

"Don't you dare apologize for this, for what we've had!"

"We both knew you'd be returning to New York at the end of this week. Had you really thought to change those plans? To stay here?"

"I hadn't thought anything through. I haven't had time to think." She hadn't wanted to think. But it all amounted to the same thing.

"Neither have I. Perhaps that's the problem. I should have thought about this." He paused, ran one hand through his hair. "I should have been more realistic, more honest with you about what you could expect from me."

"You were honest enough in that the subject didn't need to be discussed initially. And it's been as much my fault the last few days. I was putting it off. Maybe on some level I knew that when I did bring it up, this is exactly what would happen."

He was quiet again. His eyes were so shadowed, so guarded, she couldn't tell what was going on in his head. But she couldn't stand that he could sit there and give her nothing. His indifference made her furious, all the more because she knew it was a lie. She'd expected more from him.

She threw back the covers and stood up.

"Where are you going?"

"If that's an invitation to stay, it's not terribly effective. Perhaps you need to work on your technique, Damien."

She spent a few moments gathering her clothes, dressed as quickly as she could, picked up her purse, and left. He didn't bother to follow. She didn't look back.

The cab ride back to her hotel was one of the most depressing rides of her life. The city still slept under the early morning blanket of fog, silent as any city ever could be. It was absolutely gray, dull, lifeless.

She remembered now why she could never bear to return to San Francisco. Beneath the colorful Victorian houses, the view of the bay, the busy life of its inhabitants, there was this almost constant gray. Not a great place in which to be depressed. But then, was there such a place?

New York was bound to be even worse. As angry and disappointed as she was, she didn't know how she was going to stand being so far away from him.

God, this was really happening! This was it. It was over. Her heart twisted, tightened in her chest, and she swore she could feel it crumbling, breaking apart. She bit her lip, hard.

She would not cry.

The cab pulled up in front of her hotel. She paid the driver and took the elevator upstairs. Inserting the plastic key card into the lock, she remembered him doing it that first night, remembered his kiss. A shiver ran over her skin. If only she'd known then how complicated this relationship would become, would she have done what she had with him anyway?

Yes. Impossible to deny it. The attraction between them was too cerebral, too basic, too intense.

And ultimately, as painful as a stab through the heart.

How had she fallen for this man in less than two weeks? She did her best not to think about her feelings for him, her pain, while she packed her bags, and called the airline to book a flight out that afternoon. When she hung up the phone she had to fight a wave of panic. She was really leaving.

Tears stung her eyes, held her throat in a choke hold. But she would not cry.

Finally, she went downstairs to have coffee and make the necessary notes for her column. She would have to fight the constriction in her chest, the constantly threatening tears, and do her job. She found a table in the spare luxury of the hotel lounge, all sleek, modern lines and gray and dark blue suede. She pulled out her laptop and began.

I have just had the adventure of a lifetime. The sensual world of BDSM is far different from what most of us would imagine. It is not only about the ropes and chains, the whips and paddles. Of course, these things are often elements. But what it really is about is power. Energy. Trust.

You must be capable of striking a delicate balance to play this rather serious game. You must be willing to give a piece of yourself. And this piece can sometimes be larger, more crucial, than you imagined.

I met a man. A most intriguing man. He is elegant, sophisticated. A man of wealth and privilege. A true sensualist, a true sadist. But he is also a man who takes his role as a sensual dominant very seriously. Perhaps too seriously, but then, that's only my opinion. For him, the responsibility involved in his role is acutely important. I believe it is a large part of why he does this.

My time with him has been absolutely overwhelming, in every single way. This is not something you can go into without involving every cell of your being. Body, mind, and soul.

"And heart," she whispered, a tear sliding down her

cheek, her heart aching so hard she had to hold one hand over it, as though to keep it from breaking apart, shattering into her hands.

Too late.

A small sob escaped her lips.

"Maggie."

She closed her eyes, took in a deep breath. She bit down on her lip, hard. She would *not* cry. God, not in front of him.

Why was he doing this to her? She looked up at him. His eyes were dark, clouded, but she could see the emotion there. No matter how hard he tried to hide it. And he was here, wasn't he? But she knew better now than to allow herself to melt into him, even though that's what she wanted to do more than anything at this moment. To drown in his embrace, breathe in the scent of him, feel the safety of his arms around her. But they were still on dangerous ground.

Don't even think about it.

"What do you want?" So damn hard to speak to him, to make her throat open, to make the words come out.

"So cold. All my fault though, isn't it? May I sit down?"

"Only if you intend to talk to me. Really talk to me."

He sat in the chair opposite her and was quiet, as though gathering his thoughts. She hated that he looked so good, even with that haunted look in his eyes, his dark hair tousled. Her heart hammered in her chest. With fear, with an almost unbearable longing. Her eyes stung so badly, it was hard to see.

He shook his head. Then, "I have a lot to say to you. Things that would be better said in private."

"You can talk to me right here."

If she were alone with him she knew she'd do something completely foolish, like get down on her knees and beg him to be with her. Here, in public, she could keep herself and her emotions under control. Just barely, but it would have to be enough.

He sighed, ran a hand back over his hair. Other than when he first woke in the morning, this was the first time she had ever seen him in need of a shave.

"I behaved like an ass."

He paused, but she remained silent, waiting to see what else he had to say. His hands twisted together on the table.

"Look, I'm long out of practice at this sort of thing."

"This is not the kind of thing where you practice, Damien. This is not about perfection."

"Yes. You're right. But I understand if I don't say the right things to you now, I'll never see you again."

"You're right about that." So damn hard to say this to him, but she had to. Had to stand her ground with him. Had to be strong.

"This is my one fear. And fear is unacceptable to me."

"Refusing to feel it doesn't make it go away."

"No. I've just figured that out."

"And—I'm sorry to say this, especially to a man like you—but in my opinion, running away from what frightens you seems . . . cowardly."

He looked at her, his hazel eyes blazing, and she knew

she'd just challenged him in a way he wasn't used to. She wanted to apologize. To throw herself into his lap and beg him to be with her. But she didn't. After a moment the fire in his gaze burned itself out.

"You're right. And I don't like that about myself. Are you sure we can't go up to your room to finish this conversation?"

"Yes, I'm sure."

He stood up suddenly, paced the floor for a moment. Then he sat down again, pulling his chair a few inches closer to hers. He was close enough that she could smell him, all clean male, yet dark and smoky at the same time. Her insides quivered. She wanted to draw back, to save herself. But she couldn't do it when every nerve in her body was reaching out to him. The tears that stung her eyes and fought for release were simply because he was so near, yet she couldn't reach him. Not in the way that counted, and that hurt too much.

He put a hand on her arm, his fingers meeting the naked skin below the cuff of her blouse. The touch went through her like an electric current. She tried to shake him off, but he held on, his touch burning into her skin.

"Maggie, I cannot allow you to leave like this! I have too much to say. If you force me to, I'll say it all right here."

He met her eyes, challenged her. She didn't back down, even though she was trembling with emotion and pure need for him on the inside—trembling so hard she was afraid she might come apart.

"Alright, damn it. Right here then." He took her chin firmly in his hand and she almost lost it. His voice was low and sure. "I am in love with you."

She shook her head, but that only served to let the tears that had filled her eyes spill over onto her burning cheeks. Her heart surged with hope, with absolute terror. Had he really just said that to her?

He went on. "I know it seems impossible to you—hell, it seems impossible to me, but that's what it is. That's what I feel. That's what I wanted to run from this morning. But I knew the moment you left that I couldn't run from this. I couldn't run from you."

Her throat seemed to close up on her. Her eyes burned, and the tears slid down her face. But there wasn't a damn thing she could do about it.

"Maggie, say something."

"Are you sure? Because I really couldn't stand it if you changed your mind."

"I've never been so sure of anything in my life. Do you love me, Maggie? Tell me."

She nodded. "I love you. I do. I don't care how improbable this all is."

He moved in then, crushed his mouth to hers, and nothing had ever tasted sweeter to her. Her arms went around his neck as he pulled her in close. He kissed her long and hard, broke for breath, then kissed her again. She couldn't stop crying.

Finally, he pulled away to look at her. He kissed her cheek where her tears had left a damp trail, let her go long enough to pull a handkerchief from his pocket, then wiped the tears from her face.

She watched him in amazement. No one had ever cared for her in this way. Not any of the men she'd ever been with, not even her own mother. This was the first time she knew what it was to feel cherished. How could she ever give that up? How could she ever give him up?

"Damien, what now?"

"Now you let me take you back to my house so I can show you how I love you."

She shook her head. "I mean that you live here, and I live in New York. I have a home there, my career."

"We'll figure it out. That's not the important part. We can see each other on weekends until we do. I'm very good at solving problems."

She smiled at him. "I can see that."

He gathered her close again and pressed his lips to hers. The kiss was more tender this time, more sure.

She was sure for the first time in her life. Sure of him. She'd never expected this to happen, but wasn't that the way life usually worked? When you least expected it, life took a totally unpredictable turn.

She'd never expected to be drawn into the subject of her research, but he had drawn her in like a fly into a spider's web. Yes, he was predatory in that way, clever. But she didn't mind that about him. She needed a man with a good mind. The wicked twist to his would only make life more interesting, wherever it took them from this point on.

He pulled back again, stroking her hair from her face with careful fingers.

She said, "Do you remember in our first conversation when you said it takes many of us a number of years to truly know what we want?"

"I remember every word we've ever exchanged."

"I thought I knew what I wanted, but I was wrong. I was hiding. From myself, I suppose. From things I didn't even know I wanted because going there made me too vulnerable. I couldn't stand to lose control, even for one moment. Even in bed. I couldn't let go."

"I think the same could be said of me."

"Yes, that's it exactly. That ultimately we had the same lesson to learn."

He cupped her face with his hand. "I wouldn't have wanted to learn this with anyone but you."

"I couldn't have learned this with anyone but you. The BDSM play is what opened me up to you."

"It does that."

"But you remained closed off for years, despite the fact that you'd been practicing this lifestyle the whole time."

"I'm a stubborn man. It took more for me. It took you." He glanced at his watch. "And it took me almost four hours to realize this today, to stop arguing with myself and come after you."

"Oh, no! What time is it?"

"A quarter to eleven."

Her heart fluttered in panic. "My flight leaves in two hours."

"Cancel it. Stay with me." He slid a hand down her arm, lifted her hand, and brushed a kiss across her knuckles.

How could she refuse? For once, she was going to allow something to happen to her without having to be the one in the driver's seat. She was going to take a chance. On Damien, on love, on the uncertain messiness of it. She would allow him to love her, to let herself love him back, and to simply see what would happen, regardless of the unknown. Finally, she was letting go. It felt damn good.

About the Author

EDEN BRADLEY lives in southern California with a small menagerie and the love of her life. She can be contacted at www.edenbradley.com.

If you enjoyed
The Darker Side of Pleasure,
look for

Exotica

by EDEN BRADLEY

coming soon from Black Lace

PART ONE
SEVEN DAYS OF
KAMA SUTRA

CHAPTER ONE
LIVE THE FANTASY

EXOTICA. An exclusive fantasy resort set in the sultry warmth of Palm Springs. The place for a woman to experience her most secret desires in a safe, discreet environment, surrounded by sheer luxury. Choose your dream theme from among our five Ultimate Fantasy worlds:

*Casa Blanca: Live the glamorous and seductive era of the 1940s.

*Wild, Wild West: Guaranteed to be the wild experience of a lifetime.

*The Castle: The romance of medieval times brought to life.

*Pirates' Cove: A pirate adventure you'll never forget.

*Kama Sutra: The ultimate in exotic fantasy.

**And coming soon: Arabian Nights: The sensual luxury of a sultan's palace.

Relax in absolute privacy at one of the world's finest luxury resorts. Come to EXOTICA, and live the fantasy . . .

THE LIMOUSINE SPED through the desert, the sleek length of it gliding like a snake across the hot sand. Heat shimmered on the highway, the glare of the sun warming the darkened windows of the limo, even though the air-conditioning kept the car at a comfortable seventy-eight degrees inside. Still, Lilli's hands were damp as, for the tenth time that morning, she looked over the brochure her friend Caroline Winter had sent her.

She and Caroline were old friends from college. They'd hardly spoken over the years, but they'd found each other through the college alumni association last year, just as Lilli was going through her divorce. They'd talked a bit through e-mail, and then by phone. Lilli could hardly believe it when Caroline had admitted what it was she did for a living, managing Exotica. But the idea had become more and more intriguing, until finally, Lilli hadn't been able to resist Caroline's repeated invitations.

Was she really going to this place? Was she actually daring to do this?

She shifted on the leather seat, the smooth surface sticking to her bare legs beneath the linen skirt she wore. She felt naked, somehow, just reading about Exotica, imagining what might happen to her there. Gloriously yet shamefully naked. But then, her life was full of contradictions lately, wasn't it? Had been since she'd found out what a sham her marriage was all these years. But that was behind her now, and coming here was a step toward making her new beginning. From now on, her life would be of her own creation, her own choices.

Still, she had to stop and wonder if she'd been completely insane when she'd signed on for this adventure. Or was it simply old habit, one instilled by Evan, to question herself, to worry?

Staring out the window, Lilli took in a deep breath, and tried to calm her racing pulse. Long stretches of sand dunes swept past, punctuated by tall, stately date palms clustered around the entrances to beautifully landscaped homes. She'd always loved Palm Springs; she found the desert soothing, serene. Why did she have a feeling after this adventure, she'd never see the desert in quite the same way again?

The driver's voice came over the intercom. "We're here, madame."

A pair of enormous iron gates rolled back in front of the car. There was no sign here. The resort was far too exclusive, too discreet for that. Nothing more than those imposing gates closing it off from the rest of the world. Almost another world in itself, she thought, as they drove past sweeping lawns with peacocks wandering beneath the palm trees. Gorgeous hedges of blooming bougainvillea in shades of red and pink climbed the high stone walls on either side. Her heart beat faster as they pulled up in front of a long, low building, done in the same stone that seemed to blend naturally with the jagged mountain peaks in the distance.

The car came to a stop and the brochure fluttered from her hand as the driver opened the door and helped her out. She was breathless suddenly, standing in the heat and the brilliant sunlight. Dazed.

"Lillian DeForrest! You're here at last."

"Caroline." Lilli looked up to see a woman approaching her, an attractive woman with long brown hair pulled back into a sleek ponytail. She was dressed in a chic, simple summer dress of white linen. The same beautiful, striking blue eyes Lilli remembered. Caroline had hardly changed at all.

Her friend leaned in and gave her a hug, enveloping her in a warm, spicy scent. She stood back, and Caroline smiled at her. "Welcome to Exotica."

"It's so good to see you. You look wonderful."

"So do you. All that curly strawberry hair of yours; I've always loved it. You haven't aged at all, Lilli. But, come inside. It's too warm today to stand out here in the sun."

She followed Caroline up a wide, shallow staircase and into the cool interior of the building. Inside, it was all sparse, calm elegance. High ceilings made the space feel airy. Polished tile floors led to a high, curved reception desk made of some light-colored wood.

An attractive young woman greeted Lilli from behind it. "Welcome, Ms. DeForrest."

"Samantha, please see that Ms. DeForrest's luggage is sent to the Kama Sutra suite."

"Yes, Caroline. Right away."

"Would you like to see a little of the grounds before I take you to your suite?"

"I'd love to. This place is . . . intriguing."

Caroline smiled at her. "Come with me, then."

She led her across the cool expanse of tiled floor, beyond the reception desk, down a wide hallway, and through a pair of French doors at the back of the building.

Dazzled by sunlight, Lilli pulled her sunglasses from her purse and slid them on her face. In front of her was the brilliant green of a wide, sweeping lawn with meandering pathways twisting beneath the towering palms. In the center of the lawn was an enormous rectangular pool of calm, sparkling water. Bronze statues of male nudes done in classical Greek style stood sentry at each corner. They were graceful. Erotic.

Bordering the lawn were high walls, punctuated by gates in various styles.

"It's like an adult Disneyland, isn't it?" Caroline asked her. "Each of our fantasy suites are really tiny cities done in different themes, complete with servants' quarters, background players, the appropriate architectural details. See there? You can see the tower of the medieval castle over the wall."

Lilli followed Caroline's gesture and saw what appeared to be ancient stone parapets that could have belonged to King Arthur, with colorful flags flying in the slight breeze.

"It's beautiful."

"We do everything we can at Exotica to make the fantasy as real as possible for our guests, to make it all come alive. We want you to immerse yourself, to enjoy all that we offer here to the fullest. That's why our companions work on bimonthly rotations, with thorough medical checks in between. Condoms break the fantasy far too easily. All of the men here are clean, so our clients never have to worry."

Lilli shook her head, her pulse fluttering. "It's so . . . strange that you can talk about such things so matter-of-factly. And I can hardly believe I'm here. That a place like this exists." She laughed. "That you work here, run this place."

"Sometimes I can hardly believe it myself." Caroline shrugged. "But it's just my life now. And after your first night here, you'll hardly be able to remember your life anywhere else."

A small shiver went through her at Caroline's words. What was she so afraid of?

Caroline put a hand on her arm. "Don't be nervous. Our companions are highly trained. He won't do anything you don't want him to do. We guarantee it."

"Oh, God. That word: *him*. That makes it seem all the more real, for some reason."

"Would you like to come back inside and have some iced tea before you meet him?"

"Yes, I think I would like that. Do you have time to sit with me? Talk with me?"

"Of course. We can get caught up. And I'll answer any questions I can. Come."

Caroline led her back into the artificially chilled interior of the reception building, but this time she took her into what Lilli supposed was Caroline's private office. It was as open and airy as the reception area had been, with tall banks of tinted windows overlooking the lawns. Caroline gestured to a pair of beige leather couches, but too restless to sit, Lilli paced the floor, gazing out the window, as Caroline went to the intercom on her sleek glass-topped desk to ring for drinks.

"Lilli, come sit down with me on the sofa and tell me what I can do to make you more comfortable."

"I . . . I'm not sure. This sounded so wonderful when you first told me about it. Okay, a little . . . fantastical, maybe. But after you explained it to me, after I thought about it, I realized it was exactly what I've needed. But now that I'm here it's a bit intimidating. Just . . . letting go, you know?"

Caroline nodded and said quietly, "I think I do."

"Do you . . . have you ever become involved with any of the men here?"

"What? No, of course not."

"Why 'of course not'?"

Caroline shifted in her seat. "I have to maintain a certain professional distance. It helps me to do my job with a clear head."

"I guess that makes sense." Lilli paused. How could anyone work in such a place and remain so unaffected by what went on here? "Is it because . . . of what happened with Jeff? That ability to distance yourself?"

Caroline blinked, looked away.

"I'm sorry, Caroline. It's not my place to bring that up."

"No. It's fine. There's no one else anymore who even knows about that, other than you. It's been five years. It's long behind me. And I think I get that ability to detach from my mother. You know how cold she was."

Lilli could see the belying flush on her friend's cheeks. "I'm sorry," she said again. "Yes, I know how your mother was. It's just that, after that . . . episode with Jeff, you kind of shut down. And . . . I suppose it's none of my business, but it seems to me that maybe your detachment from what goes on here generates from that experience. Because I know I couldn't be so cool, so removed, working here. Surrounded by all of this. By the men, frankly."

Caroline gave her a wan smile. "Well, maybe that just makes me the perfect person for the job."

"Maybe." But Lilli wasn't so sure of that.

A soft knock at the door and a uniformed maid brought in a tray with two tall glasses of iced tea, a small bowl of sugar and another full of lemon slices.

"Thank you, Marcy." Caroline held a glass out to Lilli, then took one for herself, squeezed a lemon wedge into it.

Lilli sipped her iced tea. "I just wish I could calm down and relax."

"It's perfectly natural to be a little nervous. This isn't the sort of thing most people do every day." Caroline grinned at her, her cheeks dimpling.

Lilli couldn't help but grin back. "You can say that again. But how do I do this? How do I let go and just . . . experience whatever's offered?"

"Rajan will help you. He's one of our best."

"Rajan?" Her pulse sped up, her stomach clenched. She hadn't even seen this man, yet she was suddenly overwhelmed with anticipation. "Is that his name? The man who will be my . . . companion?"

Caroline nodded. "Your Kama Sutra lover."

Lilli took a long drink from her glass, trying to cool the blood racing fast and furious through her veins. "Oh, God. I'm really doing this, aren't I?"

Caroline nodded, smiling at her. "Are you ready to see your suite? To meet him?"

"I think so." She pulled in a long breath, blew it out. "Yes. I'm ready."

Caroline stood, offered Lilli a hand. "Good. I'll take you to the Kama Sutra suite. To your fantasy."

Back out in the bright sunlight, they climbed into a neat, white golf cart and followed one of the paths across the lawn. When they reached a pair of heavy iron-scrollwork gates, a guard nodded them through.

Instantly the air felt different. More moist, sultry. Dense, tropical foliage crowded the edges of the narrow, pebbled path and the scent of flowers was heavy in the air. From somewhere in the distance, Lilli heard birds call.

The cart rounded a turn in the path and Lilli caught her breath as a structure came into view. A long, narrow pool of pure, blue water led to what appeared to be a small reproduction of the Taj Majal, complete with graceful minarets and domes, and walls inlaid with graceful calligraphy and flowering patterns of colored stones.

"I've never seen such a beautiful place."

"It does take your breath away, doesn't it?"

Caroline stopped the golf cart at the front entrance. They got out and walked up a short, tiled pathway to the open archway leading inside. Lilli's heart was pounding, yet she was overwhelmed by the sheer beauty of her surroundings. She put her hand out to touch the carved stone of a pillar, then pulled back.

"It's all right. You can touch it. You can touch anything you like here."

Lilli turned to Caroline, saw her smile, then

turned back to the column and laid her fingers against the surface. She was surprised at how soft it was, almost like soapstone. And the jewels set into the carving looked like real jasper, rubies, sapphires.

"Incredible," she whispered.

"There's more inside."

Caroline parted the dark red silk curtains hanging like a sheer mist across the entrance and Lilli walked through.

Inside was a private garden courtyard, surrounded on all four sides by the walls of the building. Clusters of date palms stood here and there, glorious flowering vines climbed everywhere, and birdcages stood on pedestals amidst the lush vegetation. Greens in every shade, splashes of red, pink, gold, and the sweet perfume of exotic flowers surrounded her. The delicate strains of sitar music floated on the air.

Caroline guided her along the path, up a shallow flight of steps and into what appeared to be a bedroom. There were few solid walls, just the silk-curtained archways. The floors were made of gorgeous tiles interlocking in a complicated pattern. In the middle of the room stood a bed on a high, carved teak platform. The four intricately carved posts were draped with lengths of embroidered silk, the bed piled high with pillows in every shade of the sunset and sunrise: pinks, oranges, reds, ambers. On a low table inlaid with mother-of-pearl stood a silver burner full of incense, the smoke lending an exotic fragrance to the air that smelled like pure sex to her.

She turned to Caroline. "This is too lovely."

Caroline nodded. "Wait until you see Rajan. I should go now. He's waiting for you on the terrace. Will you be all right?"

Lilli nodded. She was nervous again. She felt like some shy schoolgirl. But she was an adult, nearly forty. She was being ridiculous.

"Thank you, Caroline."

Her friend gave her a quick hug. "Call me if you need anything."

Lilli nodded, then watched as Caroline left. Once she'd disappeared through the curtain, she turned to face the open archway leading to the outer terrace.

He was on the other side.

She set her purse down on a small table, smoothed out her linen skirt, which suddenly felt too heavy on her skin. She tucked a strand of her curling hair behind one ear. And went to meet her Kama Sutra lover.

Pulling the curtain aside, she stepped through, onto the tiled mosaic floor. The sun was softer here, filtered by the silk drapes fluttering at the edges of the terrace. The sun shone through the silk, casting shadows in red and gold everywhere.

At first all she could see was his silhouette against the sun, the shifting colors of the silk playing over his skin. He was long and lean, resting on the edge of a pool of water, a fountain making music from the center of the pool. He was shirtless, and she could make out the rounded curve of wide shoulders and strong, muscular arms.

"I am Rajan."

A deep voice, edged with a soft, husky tone, and an accent that was English and exotic all at the same time. She took another step forward, and the glare of the sun moved into shadow, revealing him to her.

Long, dark hair curling to just below his shoulder blades framed a face that was all chiseled planes, softened by the lush curve of his mouth as he smiled at her. Teeth so white and perfect. Dazzling. His eyes were dark, nearly black. His skin was the color of dark honey, and so smooth. Touchable. She unconsciously flexed her fingers.

When he stood, graceful as a cat, he towered over her five foot four frame. She felt small, delicate in his presence. He moved toward her, one hand outstretched, slowly, gracefully.

"You must be Lillian."

"Lilli, please." Why was her throat so dry? He was only a man.

But no, that was a lie. He was the most spectacularly beautiful man she had ever seen. Her skin was alive, tingling, simply looking at him.

In a moment he was in front of her, that smile making her lightheaded as her blood rushed through her veins. She had to look beyond him for a moment, to the view of the rugged, dusky gray mountains like paper cutouts against the backdrop of stark blue sky.

Her breath went right out of her when he touched her hand. Like fire. Like electricity on her skin.

"Come and sit by the water with me. It's cool out here."

His fingers folded around hers and her skin went hot beneath his touch as she followed him across the terrace silently. She couldn't speak, could barely think. She'd never been so stunned by the mere presence of another person in her life. She gave herself a mental shake.

Calm down.

He led her to the edge of the marble pool. The water was blue, sparkling. She watched the play of it in the fountain in the center. Someone had placed handfuls of flower petals there, and they danced as the water moved.

Then his hand was on her chin, lifting her face so that she was forced to look into those bottomless, black eyes.

"Don't look away, Lilli. I want to see you. And you need to see me, to know me. We're going to become very close during our time together. You mustn't be afraid."

She blinked up at him. "I'm not. I'm just . . . you're a little larger than life."

He laughed, a deep-throated tone that was a natural reaction. She felt her shoulders drop at the sound. His mouth was too beautiful when he smiled. And she was going to touch it. To kiss him.

God.

Too good to contemplate, really. But she needed to calm herself, to let go of her fear, her tension, if she was going to enjoy this. And he was far too good not to enjoy. She pushed away those lingering doubts about him not finding her pretty enough, sexy enough, with a good mental shove. This was for *her*.

"You're very thoughtful, aren't you, Lilli? I'm not speaking of being considerate, although I have a feeling you're that, too. But your mind is working. I can feel it."

"Yes." She felt heat creep into her cheeks.

"I believe I may have the perfect cure for that."

That smile again, practically knocking her to her knees.

She wouldn't mind being on her knees for this man. Oh no, not at all.

He moved around behind her, slid his hands over her shoulders. He was so close she could feel the heat of him against her back. When he leaned in she felt the warmth of his breath in her hair. His voice was low, soft. "Give yourself over to this, Lilli. To me. I will take care of your every need, I promise you. And if I don't anticipate something, all you have to do is ask. But I'll try not to make you ask. I'll do my best to read you, to know what it is you desire before you can put it into words."

A shiver ran through her, making goose flesh rise on her skin.

He went on. "But you must learn to relax. To let go all of those thoughts running through your mind, holding you back from the pleasure of the moment. I'll help you."

His hands slid down her bare arms. His soft palms were warm, reassuring, and lighting tiny fires of need on her skin that arrowed down, deep in her belly.

"Will you allow me to do this for you, Lilli?"

God, right now she'd allow him to do anything he wanted, this total stranger. This beautiful stranger. *Her* stranger.

The word came out in a whisper. "Yes."

Want more sexy fiction?

September 2012 saw the re-launch of the iconic erotic fiction series *Black Lace* with a brand new look and even steamier fiction. We're also re-visiting some of our most popular titles in our *Black Lace Classics* series.

First launched in 1993, *Black Lace* was the first erotic fiction imprint written by women for women and quickly became the most popular erotica imprint in the world.

To find out more, visit us at:
www.blacklace.co.uk

And join the *Black Lace* community:

🐦 @blacklacebooks

f BlackLaceBooks

BLACK LACE

The leading imprint of women's sexy fiction is back – and it's better than ever!